HER
BLEEDING
HEART

BOOKS BY D.K. HOOD

D.K. HOOD

HER BLEEDING HEART

bookouture

Published by Bookouture in 2022

An imprint of Storyfire Ltd.
Carmelite House
50 Victoria Embankment
London EC4Y 0DZ

www.bookouture.com

ISBN: 978-1-80314-325-5
eBook ISBN: 978-1-80314-324-8

To the specialists who repaired my sight and the nurses who cared for me. I am eternally grateful.

PROLOGUE

SUNDAY NIGHT

The realization that something was terribly wrong gripped Dianne Gilbert in a wave of terror. She hardly knew the man sitting opposite her and accepting his offer of dinner at a remote ranch had been an error of judgement. He didn't even look the same as his social media image, and his excuse of shaving his beard and wearing contact lenses instead of his thick-rimmed spectacles to impress her had achieved the complete opposite. Yet, he'd mentioned all their recent conversations. Was he telling the truth? Or was he a different person than Julian Darnley, the CEO of Darnley Financial?

The house smelled of stale air and mold, as if it had been shut up for months. She couldn't believe he actually lived here. Accepting a ride with him had been a mistake and she couldn't just get up and leave. She'd remained for the awful meal and tried to converse with him. He seemed nice enough and she'd relaxed a little after a while, but now her stomach clenched and her head hurt so bad. Lightheaded, the room shifted and moved in and out of focus. The table and the glass of wine set before her swam in a nauseating swirl. Why would he ask her to dinner to drug her? She shook her head, fighting the stupor. The next moment, her limbs grew heavy and fear had her by the throat. How could she have made such a stupid mistake? As a grown woman, she should have had more sense than to allow a stranger to drive her to an unknown location—but was he really a stranger?

They'd met online months ago and she'd liked the financial advisor. He'd been so nice to her and they'd got along so well, she'd figured they had a future together. At first, Dianne had taken Julian's advice and invested a small amount in cryptocurrency and it had doubled in value. She'd welcomed his offer to take over as her financial advisor. It had been an offer too good to be true. The dinner had gone really well and they'd chatted about a future together. Julian was allergic to nuts, but after discovering her favorite dessert was almond and coconut pie, he'd prepared one especially for her and insisted she eat a large slice. It was bitter, so she'd washed it down with liberal amounts of wine. Although full to bursting, she'd eaten more just to be nice. The moment she'd finished, he'd gone quiet, and after finishing his glass of wine he just sat staring at her with a strange expression on his face.

She blinked, trying to keep him in focus. It was becoming difficult to think straight, but she tried desperately to go over what had happened. During dinner they'd toasted her success after transferring her entire fortune into his cryptocurrency account. She'd make a profit and there'd be no taxes to pay. Before he'd served dessert, he'd set up his laptop and after a convincing chat had suggested he manage her entire estate. She'd jumped at the chance and given him access to her accounts. He'd promised to make them both rich and she'd believed him, especially after enjoying the success of his previous investments. She'd trusted him, but as soon as she'd consumed the pie he'd changed. His expression concerned her, and the way he drummed his fingers on the table as if waiting for something to happen had set off alarm bells in her head.

Could he be waiting for the drug to take effect? She glanced around from beneath her eyelashes. Maybe she could make an excuse to use the bathroom and slip out the back door and call for help. Fighting to keep conscious she reached for a glass of water and swallowed as much as possible. "I need to use the bathroom. Where is it?"

Before he could reply his phone chimed, and when he stood and walked into another room to take the call Dianne struggled to her feet. She gripped the table as the room moved in and out of focus. Convinced he was planning to harm her, she staggered along the hallway to the front door. She had to get away from him and find help. Fumbling with the lock, she managed to open the door and stepped into the rainswept night. As she stumbled down the three steps leading to the driveway, she realized she'd left her purse behind. All hope of calling someone for help was dashed in that second.

Dragging in deep breaths of damp air, she headed along the driveway. The rain lashed at her cheeks and soaked through her clothes. The night air chilled her damp flesh but did nothing to improve the nausea. Pain shot through her head and she fell against a tree and bent over to vomit, but only bile coated her tongue. The gagging only made the headache worse, but she needed to keep moving before he missed her. Straightening, she dragged heavy legs along the driveway and onto the road. She splashed through deep puddles and stepped into a pothole up to her knees. The fall jarred her teeth and pain shot from a turned ankle. Sobbing in agony, she tried to ignore the stinging grazes on her hands and knees and dragged up her aching body. She must keep going.

Moving as fast as possible, she limped along the blacktop in the pitch dark. Her shoes were not designed for hiking. The heels caught in vegetation alongside the road and, frustrated, she kicked them off. Mud squished between her toes with each step as she peered ahead in the darkness, searching for any signs of life. Pushing rain-soaked hair from her eyes, Dianne let out a sob. A wall of rain was all she could see. Ahead was nothing apart from the yellow line down an old deserted road.

The roar of a car engine came from behind her, and she turned to see lights coming down the driveway. Terrified, she searched madly for a place to hide. He wouldn't know which way she'd gone. The road seemed to stretch for miles in either direction. She hobbled across the blacktop and stumbled blindly into a clump of trees. Dizzy and uncoordinated, she pushed her way through bushes, grabbing hold of the trunks of rough pines to steady herself. Underfoot rocks cut deep into her feet, and with no light to guide her, she tripped and stumbled over exposed roots. As the headlights from the vehicle swept across the woods she fell flat on her face and just lay there too scared to move. Footsteps heading in her direction splashed in the puddles and the beam of a flashlight moved through the trees. Her heart was beating strangely, thumping in her chest so fast and missing beats. She didn't have the strength to lift her head as the light hit her full in the face.

"How much longer will it take you to die?" Julian grabbed her by one leg and dragged her over the soaked ground.

Teeth chattering and horrified that the man she'd trusted had suddenly turned on her, Dianne wanted kick out at him, but she couldn't move. She tried to ask him why he was doing this to her, but her mouth wouldn't form words. Pine needles, branches and gravel cut into her flesh as he dragged her deeper into the forest. In the distance she could hear water running. The recent storms and heavy rainfall had swollen the small rivers throughout Black Rock Falls. Some part of her confused mind told her she was somewhere in Stanton Forest, but no one would be around to help her in the middle of the night in a storm. Dropping in and out of consciousness as Julian dragged her closer to the edge of the river, she stared up at him, blinking as rain splattered her face, filling her eye sockets. Agony shook her as he arranged her body and took her purse from under his slicker and tucked it under her arm. She tried to bat away his hand as he opened the buttons on her blouse and pushed something deep down inside her bra. Pain wracked her body in waves of torture, and she stared up at him, trying to force her mouth to form words of protest. Fighting for each breath as her heart jumped and staggered, she could no longer feel the rain on her face. *I'm dying.*

When Julian bent to stare into her eyes, his face blurred. It was as if he peered at her through a rain-soaked window. In the dark, all she could make out was the flash of a white hideous grin.

"How do you like your dream lover now?"

ONE

MONDAY

Thunder rolled across the lowlands and the sky opened again. Lightning flashed so close to the house that Sheriff Jenna Alton could see trails of smoke from where it had taken out trees. Torrential rain hammered the rooftop and pelted the tin roof over the porch like an automatic weapon firing at the house. Duke, Deputy David Kane's bloodhound, gave a whine of sheer terror and Jenna heard scratching of claws on wood as he careered down the hallway and into the bedroom to squeeze himself under the bed. Jenna stared out of the front window and frowned. Somewhere out in the torrential rain her husband, Dave Kane, was out on horseback, checking the fences after the alarm system signaled a break. Knowing the storm was on its way, he had insisted Jenna stay inside and had ventured out alone to inspect the perimeter of their secured area. Jenna chewed on her bottom lip. Her ranch spread out over many acres, but the secured area encompassed the house and enough land necessary to graze their three horses. In another life Kane, a special forces sniper and Secret Service agent, had worked close to POTUS. After being targeted in a car bombing that killed his wife and left him with a metal plate in his head, the government had changed his appearance using cosmetic surgery and given him a new name. They'd hidden him in plain sight as her deputy sheriff in the backwoods town of Black Rock Falls. With a bounty on his head, he was officially off the grid but could be called into active duty at any time. As a highly trained professional who could cope with most situations, it was unusual for him to not answer his phone. It had been over an hour and concern for his safety was mounting as the minutes ticked by.

Jenna had realized over the last few years that fate hadn't placed them in the same small town. It had been planned. When her life as DEA Special Agent Avril Parker went to hell after bringing down a drug cartel, she'd being threatened and consequently had gone through much the same as Kane. She'd had to reinvent herself as Jenna Alton. The blonde FBI agent was gone forever and now with a new face and occupation she'd become the leader of a specialized team of serial killer investigators. She figured the romance with Kane had always been there, bubbling under the surface, but it took some time for him to mourn his wife. Now four years or so on they looked forward to a life together fighting crime. Black Rock Falls had become known as Serial Killer Central and now boasted a series of true crime books depicting the cases of some of the most notorious serial killers in the history of the state.

Unfortunately, the series might be good for tourism, but the last thing Jenna or Kane needed was being in the spotlight. Past threats hovered over them and they believed it would only be a matter of time before their identities were discovered and someone would show up to collect the bounty on their heads. Jenna checked her watch again. It was unusual for Kane to not pick up when she called him. It was fall and bears were spending their time filling their bellies for winter. If one had broken through the perimeter fence or, worse still, a mother and her cubs, Kane could be in danger. She glanced over one shoulder toward the bedroom door. Duke never left Kane's side unless there was a storm. The dog was an early warning system for trouble and had become an important member of their team. Making up her mind, Jenna went into the bedroom and collected her shoulder holster and M18 pistol. She grabbed a slicker from the mudroom and, grabbing a pair of thin leather gloves, and her rifle, headed through the front door and over to the barn, her rifle in one hand.

It didn't take her long to saddle her horse and thumb a quick message to good friend and Kane's handler, Dr. Shane Wolfe, explaining the situation just in case anything was amiss. She ducked her head against the sheets of rain and rode out following the perimeter fence in the same direction Kane had taken a couple of hours earlier. With the hood of the slicker pulled over her Stetson, she ducked under spiky boughs of pine trees along the fence line. Thunder rumbled all around her and her mare, Seagull, danced sideways, her ears flat against her head. "Steady girl." Jenna ran her hand down the horse's soaked neck.

Scanning the forest in all directions for any sign of bears or other wildlife, she urged the horse forward, weaving along the narrow pathway they'd created when constructing the elaborate security fence. Apart from being twelve feet high and topped with razor wire, the fence contained a sophisticated wireless network of sensors and CCTV cameras. One of the sensors had triggered the alarm in the early hours of the morning. They'd watched the screen array in the office until daylight and then Kane had taken off to check the boundaries. His instructions to her had been to lock down the house and remain inside until he'd determined the threat. He'd checked in after the first hour, saying a bison had pushed its way through the back gate. It had snapped the locks clean through. He intended to move it back outside the fence line and back to the herd on the other side of the forest, but then the storm had hit in earnest. Jenna had expected him to deal with the bison and then return home, but after not hearing from him for almost two hours, and not sighting him on any of the camera feeds, she had no choice but to go and look for him.

Jenna spoke to her phone. "Call Dave."

Again the call went to voicemail. Jenna screwed up her eyes against the pouring rain and urged Seagull along the track. The storm clouds had leeched every bit of light from the edge of the woods surrounding the ranch, turning everything to various shades of gray and dark blue. The wind gusts increased, making the pine boughs bend and lash against her and spooking Seagull. It was all Jenna could do to keep the mare under control and away from the fence. The last thing she needed was for her horse to be injured. Concerned, she edged into the forest, moving slowly along the tree line. After searching for almost half an hour, worry gnawed at her gut. The smell of smoke lingered in the air, but with the amount of rain, there would be no chance of a wildfire. Frequently calling Kane, she pushed through the trees.

Seagull suddenly went ballistic, dancing sideways, rearing and refusing to move forward. Her horse was terrified of fire after being caught in a wildfire on the mountains previously. Any smell of smoke sent her into a panic. Turning her horse around in circles to calm her, Jenna stared all around her, searching through the pouring rain and dense forest for the source of the fire. Standing up in her stirrups, she noticed a small plume of smoke some way in the distance. She urged her horse forward, but Seagull wouldn't move and turned around, trying to bolt in the opposite direction. Jenna dismounted, and after securing Seagull to a pine tree, grabbed her rifle and headed out on foot. She heard a whinny and Kane's black stallion, Warrior, came hurtling toward her through the forest. The horse was agitated but came to her. Kane's mount was as solid as a rock and not afraid of anything. The thought that he might have thrown Kane was unimaginable, so why was he running loose through the forest? Jenna swung herself into Warrior's saddle and headed in the direction the horse had come from.

The stench of burning flesh and hair reached her before she made out the broken smoking tree and a mound of something brown and very large. She stared in disbelief at a bison lying on its back, legs stuck up in the air. Most of the fur on one side was smoldering. The bison had been struck by lightning, the hit taking out a tall pine and splitting it in two. She edged Warrior closer, and the horse snickered. Screwing up her eyes to see through the pouring rain, she made out another lump close by and her heart raced with fear. "Dave. Oh my God!"

TWO

Jenna jumped down from Warrior's back and ran through the smoking bushes, falling on her knees beside Kane. His slicker was singed, as was one leg of his jeans. His Stetson had fallen off and rain soaked his face and hair. "Dave." She dragged off her gloves and pushed cold fingers down the neck of his shirt to feel for a pulse.

A beat, slow but steady, thumped against her fingertips. She checked him over, looking for any signs of damage. Finding only a scrape on his cheek, she rolled him onto his back and tapped his face. "Dave, wake up. Come on now. You can't just lie here in the rain." She gave him a shake and lifted his eyelids.

Panic gripped her when she couldn't rouse him. Concerned she'd missed something, she pushed her hands under his clothes and checked his torso for injuries. Finding nothing, she shook him again. "Dave, wake up."

"Can you stop shouting at me? I have the headache from hell." Kane opened his eyes and blinked away the rain. He tried to sit up and then flopped back down in the mud again. "What happened?"

Troubled by his confusion, Jenna took his hand and rubbed it. "I think you've been close to a lightning strike. You must have been riding nearby when the bison over there was hit."

"I feel as if I've been run over by a truck." Kane pulled his hand away and held his head.

Fighting back tears of relief, Jenna sat down in the wet beside him. "What can you remember?"

"I remember you yelling at me. Everything else is kind of a blur." He inhaled a deep breath and grimaced. "Was I on horseback?" He blinked as if trying to focus and scanned the area.

Grabbing his arm and helping him to sit up, Jenna pointed to Warrior, calmly eating tufts of grass. "Yeah, and Warrior is fine, but the bison is toast—literally. The lightning struck a tree, splitting it in half and taking out the bison as well."

"Are you sure the horse is okay? Did you check him for burns?" Kane struggled to stand and clung to a nearby trunk, unsteady on his feet.

Not surprised by his confusion after being on the tail end of a lightning strike, Jenna nodded. "He looks okay and came straight to me, and I wasn't on the trail. I figure he heard Seagull making a fuss and came to find us. I left her over yonder and rode him here. He led me straight to you. Do you remember riding out to check a perimeter breach?"

"Nope. I guess the force of the blast must have thrown me. I don't make a habit of falling from horses." He ran a hand through his soaking hair and spent a few seconds examining his scalp. "I don't think I'm injured, but my head hurts and my eyesight's a little fuzzy."

"I'm not surprised. Let me help you." Jenna pushed her shoulder under his arm and encouraged him to take a few steps. "It's too dangerous to stay out in this storm. We must get back to the house. Do you think you can ride?"

"Yeah, just give me a few minutes to get my balance back."

He leaned one hand against a tree and stared at the body of the bison. "You'll have to call someone to field-dress that bison and haul it away. That's good meat going to waste. I'm sure a local shelter would love to have it." He turned and looked at her. "What made you come and look for me?"

Frowning, Jenna stared at her bedraggled husband and sighed. "I hadn't heard from you in over an hour, so I figured I'd better come and look for you. It's been two hours since you last checked in."

"Two hours?" Kane pulled up his sleeve and stared at his watch. His eyebrows rose and he blinked and looked again. "I've been out for over two hours?"

Jenna's phone chimed in her pocket and she pulled it out and stared at the caller ID. It was Deputy Jake Rowley. "Can I call you back Jake? I'm out in a storm and Kane was struck by lightning."

"Is he okay?" The sound of an engine hummed through her earpiece.

Jenna swallowed her concern and stared at Kane's ashen face. "Yeah, I think so. We're heading back to the ranch now."

"Shane was concerned about you. We're heading your way now. Don't worry. Rio and Anderson are manning the office." Rowley disconnected.

She turned to look at Kane, who seemed confused. With a metal plate in his head, the strike could have done untold damage. She bent to pick up his Stetson, shook off the water, and pushed it on his head. "Hang on to that tree for a few more minutes. I'm going to bring Warrior to you. Wolfe and Rowley are on their way. Can you ride? I'll need to get you back to the house."

"Yeah, I'll be fine. Don't worry." Kane gave her a thin smile and rubbed his forehead. "Thanks for searching for me."

Shaking her head, Jenna stared at him. "Did you honestly think I'd leave you out here in a storm? It would be an irresponsible thing to do." She gave an exasperated sigh and went to collect Warrior.

After boosting Kane into the saddle, Jenna climbed on behind him and they headed back to the ranch, collecting Seagull along the way. At the house, she left the horses and assisted Kane inside. "Let's get you out of those wet clothes." She led him, dripping water all over the floor, to the bathroom.

"Don't worry about me. You go and tend the horses." Kane leaned against the wall for support. "Once I've had a hot shower I'll be as good as new."

Jenna snorted and shook her head. "If you don't fall flat on your face taking your pants off."

"I really don't need your help." Kane eyed her dubiously and tried without much success to pull the slicker over his head. "I just need a few more minutes to get my head straight."

Glaring at him, Jenna grabbed hold of the slicker and pulled it over his head. "Well, the sooner you let me help you, the quicker I can go and tend the horses."

After helping him undress and seeing his unyielding combat face set into place, she turned on the water, checked the temperature, and with some reluctance left him alone. She'd seen that expression many times before. Kane had dropped into the zone where he could practically deal with any situation, and it was best to leave him be. Hurrying to the front door, she spotted Wolfe's white SUV heading toward the house. She stopped on the porch to greet Wolfe and Rowley as they climbed out of the truck. "Dave's in the shower but he's very unsteady on his feet. I'm going to tend the horses, so make yourself at home."

"I'll go and tend the horses." Rowley, dressed in a black slicker, squinted at her in the rain. "I'm sure Dave doesn't need me to help him in the shower."

Heaving a sigh of relief, Jenna smiled at him. "Thank you.

Could you check Warrior over for injuries? Dave was riding him when they came close to being hit by lightning."

"Yes, ma'am." Rowley touched his hat and collected the horses.

"What does he remember?" Wolfe followed her into the mudroom and shook the rain from his hat and slicker before hanging them on a peg. "Does he have any unusual symptoms?"

"He's said nothing about the lightning strike." Jenna pulled off her slicker and hat. "Actually, he hasn't said too much, apart from having the headache from hell. He couldn't stand up and seems uncoordinated, dizzy, and complained his eyes are out of focus. He's a stubborn man and refused to allow me to help him. He practically ordered me out of the bathroom to go tend the horses. Problem is, he always says he's fine. He sure doesn't look fine." She turned to look at him as she toed off her boots. "I lost contact with him for about an hour and a half, almost two hours. I saw the smoke from the house at least an hour before I went looking for him. He could have been unconscious for an hour or more." She led the way into the kitchen. "He gave me his combat face when I insisted on undressing him for the shower. He said he could manage, so I thought it best to let him be."

"We shouldn't leave him alone." Wolfe's eyes narrowed. "With the plate in his head, being hit by lightning would be equivalent to having electric shock treatment. All the symptoms are the same, apart from nausea. Maybe he just didn't tell you about that one." He frowned. "Temporal amnesia... ah... temporary loss of memory is possible. The symptoms are usually loss of recent memory. Did he know you?"

Jenna laughed. "Well, he did get annoyed when I tried to pull off his jeans, but then he hates being treated like he's sick."

"Hmm." Wolfe rubbed his chin. "I'll need to take a look at him." He frowned at her as if seeing her for the first time. "You're wet through. You need to get changed. I'll go and see to him."

Shaking her head, Jenna led him toward the bedroom. "Are you sure? He's not in a good mood." She caught Wolfe's eyeroll and shrugged. "Okay then, I'll grab some dry clothes and take a shower in one of the other bathrooms. You go talk to Dave. Oh, and Duke is hiding under the bed."

THREE

Hot water poured over Kane's head as he pressed both hands against the shower's white tiles, trying to recall what had happened. He remembered zip, and where the hell was he? Who was the woman who'd tried to remove his pants as if she'd known him all her life? His gaze rested on his left hand. Astonishment hit him like a sledgehammer at the sight of a wedding band. It wasn't his wedding band because it was in a safety deposit box in DC and this one was wider and a different style. He gave his head a little shake and pain pierced through his temples, making him nauseous and blurring his vision. He ignored a rapping on the door, but when a familiar Texan drawl came from the other side, he stepped from the shower and grabbed a towel. The voice was as familiar as breathing, but how could his handler be here in person? He'd never met the man, but Terabyte had assisted him on many missions and he trusted him with his life. "Yeah, come in. I'm decent."

Kane stared at the tall broad blond-haired man with interest. He'd imagined him to look like a Viking marauder and couldn't stop the smile curling his lips. This man looked as if he'd stepped out of a longboat, and he glanced at his hands to make sure he wasn't carrying an ax. He remained silent, waiting for his handler to introduce himself using his code name. He needed answers fast, and if Terabyte was here, something had gone to hell.

"Is something wrong, Dave?" Terabyte looked at him with narrowed gray eyes. "Jenna said you had a bad headache and were a bit unsteady on your feet after the lightning strike. Any other problems? Memory loss, for instance."

After being trained to the highest level in special forces Kane understood the different ploys the enemy used to discover information. He wouldn't be surprised if they'd drugged him and then tried to make him believe he'd suffered memory loss and was in a safe US town just to get information out of him. He stared at the man who sounded like Terabyte, his handler, and waited.

"Oh, this is worse than I had imagined." The man shook his head slowly. "Okay, let's see how far back I need to go. You're Ninety-eight H and I'm Terabyte. Does that make sense? My name is Dr. Shane Wolfe. We're close friends and no one here knows your real identity. Here, you're Dave Kane. We discussed your choice of name while you were in rehab after the car bombing. Only you and I know that, Dave, and the fact that Annie gave you that name before she died."

Allowing the tension to drain out of him, Kane grabbed another towel from the rail and dried his hair. "Okay, I know that much about my identity, but not yours. I've never seen you before in my life but recognize your voice. Just to clarify, what are the names of your daughters and where was Annie kidnapped?"

"Emily, Julie, and Anna. Outside the US Embassy in Israel." Wolfe dropped his bag on the vanity. "Do you know today's date?"

Pushing his hands through his hair, Kane raised an eyebrow and gave him the date. "This is where things become a little confused because the last thing I remember is seeing snow on the ground, and this sure don't look like Helena."

"Let me check your eyes." Wolfe took out a flashlight. "Look straight ahead." He moved the flashlight over Kane's eyes. "No concussion and I can't see any electrical contact burns. I'll give you something for the headache." He went into his bag and pulled out a bottle of pills. "You'll remember these? You've taken them for your headaches since the accident. Now, what's the last thing you remember?"

After examining the bottle and the contents closely, Kane swallowed a couple of pills. Glad his sight had returned along with is equilibrium, he searched his memory. "I recall taking delivery of my truck in Helena, which I've affectionately called the Beast." He glanced around. "Do I have any dry clothes here?"

"Through there—in the bedroom." Wolfe opened a door and ushered him inside.

Kane rubbed his aching head. "How come I've lost my memory? I'd be dead if I were actually hit by the strike."

"It seems to me you had some fallout from the lightning strike that hit the bison." Wolfe gave him an appraising stare. "The metal plate in your head acted as a conductor and you've suffered something similar to electric shock therapy. I have no idea to what extent, and it would be a good idea to do an MRI. I figure the result is temporary amnesia. It might last a few hours, worst case a week, but that would be unusual. It's more than likely it will be fully restored by morning. You've had memory loss before, so it's not unusual to suffer it again after such a traumatic injury."

Kane searched through the nightstand and found drawers filled with women's underwear and the like. In other drawers he found his own distinctive brands. Confused, he went to the closet and peered at the row of black shirts, jeans, and highly polished boots on one side, more casual wear on the other. The other closet was packed with female attire. A belt and holster, carrying a M18 pistol, hung from the back of a chair, and on the bedside table, a set of keys and a sheriff's department badge. He dressed and stared at the ring on his finger and then back to Wolfe. "I figure you have a few things to tell me. Am I undercover and what does this mean?" He wiggled his fingers at Wolfe to display the wedding band.

"It's probably not a good thing to tell you too much. You need to allow the memories to return on their own, but I'll give you the basics." Wolfe sighed.

Annoyed, Kane lifted his chin. "I want more than the basics. If this is temporary, I'll need to function at my normal level and I can't if I don't have any intel. If I don't know who the good guys are, someone is going to get hurt."

"Okay, fine, but you're not undercover. This is your new life, the one we discussed, and you've settled in really well. The downside is, this town has come to be known as Serial Killer Central, but I figure you enjoy chasing down serial killers." Wolfe cleared his throat. "I guess as it's a security issue you should know how much time you've lost."

Astonished when Wolfe told him the date, Kane sat down hard on the bed and stared into space. "Over four years? I remember everything fine before arriving at Helena. Annie, the missions. I was heading to Black Rock Falls to meet up with Sheriff Jenna Alton. Was that her before?"

"Yeah, that was Jenna. She undressed you and wondered why you were acting so strange." Wolfe rubbed the back of his neck. "She's your wife."

Staring at him in disbelief, Kane swallowed hard. "My *wife*?" He looked up at Wolfe and then ran both hands down his face. "I don't recognize her at all." He shook his head slowly. "The poor woman—I'm broken and damaged. Why would she consider risking her life with me? Do we have kids?"

"Not yet, but it's only been a few months. Jenna loves you

and waited a long time for you to mourn Annie. She's a very strong woman and nursed you through something similar after you were shot in the head a couple of years back. She'll understand about the amnesia. So it's up to you to make it easy on her." Wolfe stared at him. "It won't be for long. Everything will be back to normal in no time. Try not to worry too much. It will only make things worse."

Swallowing hard, Kane lifted his chin. "I'm not going to fake being in love with a stranger or lie to her—it's not fair—but I will be gentle with her. We'll tell her the truth from the get-go. What does she know about me?"

"She doesn't know your real name but does know what you are and who you work for. She also knows who I am. Of course, any missions you performed are still classified and she won't ask for details. She's in witness protection and was once an FBI DEA agent who took down a cartel and is in constant danger of being discovered. Like you, she had her appearance changed." Wolfe smiled. "POTUS sent me to keep an eye on both of you and at present I'm the medical examiner for here and the surrounding counties. You've been working side by side taking down notorious serial killers since you arrived. You haven't lost a case yet. Jenna has a solid team: Jake Rowley and Zac Rio in the office, and she can call on FBI agents Ty Carter, an ex-Seal, and Jo Wells."

"I know the last two." Kane frowned. "Jo Wells is the behavioral analyst who lectured at the conference you sent me to in Helena. Carter was working on the bombings in DC when I was there."

"Do you remember Poppy Anderson?" Wolfe rubbed his chin and his eyes became troubled. "You two weren't involved, were you?"

Smiling at the memory, Kane sighed. The pain of losing Annie had been a physical ache in his heart but strangely it was no longer there. Had Jenna erased the pain? He recalled the vivacious Poppy and shook his head. "No, not so soon after losing Annie, but maybe if I'd stayed in town a little longer, it could have been a possibility. Why? Do we have history?"

"Not that I'm aware but she's one of the deputies now. Jenna has her on desk duty. She's not on the team for a reason I won't go into right now. It's a long story and can wait." Wolfe whistled through his teeth. "I sure hope you regain your memory soon. I could insist you stay home until you get your head straight."

"No way. I feel fine, apart from not remembering the last four years." Kane shook his head. "I'm deputy sheriff, and I'll work my way through the problem. It won't affect my ability to perform well in law enforcement. Solving crime is second nature to me even with a headache." He pushed a hand through his damp hair. "The familiarity of the surroundings will probably help me regain my memory. Sitting here doing nothing, in a place I don't know, will send me stir-crazy."

"This is your home. You'll remember it soon enough, I'm sure." Wolfe's eyebrows rose. "It's a large ranch Jenna purchased when she arrived here. It's safe. We've turned it into a fortress."

What Wolfe had said about Jenna confused him. He had a bankroll, but it was old money, from investments in an offshore bank account set up way before he "died." Kane frowned. "How come someone in WITSEC had the cash to splash on a ranch?"

"Oh, that." Wolfe rubbed the end of his nose. "I know she's told you everything and it's no secret she took the money back from the cartel."

Appalled, Kane rubbed a hand down his face. "So, you really want me to believe I married a woman living off the proceeds of crime?" He barked a laugh. "That would never happen. I don't roll that way and you darn well know it."

"She's never held back anything from you. Well, not once she discovered your clearance status." Wolfe shrugged. "I can only guess she gave you the abridged version of what happened." He sighed. "When her parents died, there was a massive insurance payout, over ten million. Before she went deep undercover, she moved her entire fortune into an offshore account as a get-out-of-jail-free card. It was just as well she did because she'd be dead if that cash hadn't been available to her in an instant. To get closer to Michael Carlos, the son of the cartel boss, she used the persona of an heiress. When she married him, he insisted on setting up a joint bank account. It happened too fast for the DEA to act—Carlos wanted his hands on her fortune and she needed the cash in a hurry, so used her own money. She'd be dead if she'd waited for the red tape, so she made an agreement with the DEA to use ten million of her own money and have it refunded after the bust. The day she escaped, she transferred ten million and not a cent more into her untraceable offshore account. All the details are included in her debriefing. The powers that be commended her for her quick thinking. What she did saved the mission. It was her money, Dave. You should know that she refused to accept Michael Carlos' life insurance when he died in jail, although it was written up as he 'accidentally fell and cut his throat in the shower.' She was his only beneficiary and as his legal wife was entitled to it, but she wouldn't touch a cent. It didn't go to waste. Carlos' insurance money was donated on her behalf to an organization that helps abused women, men, and kids return to normal life."

Relieved, Kane nodded. "I'm glad she's honest."

"Not only that, Dave." Wolfe's expression was serious. "She'd take a bullet for you, and I'd trust her with my life and my family's. You've married a very special lady."

A roll of thunder crashed overhead and a whine came from under the bed. Kane stood as scratching noises announce the arrival of a large bloodhound. The dog leaned against his legs, trembling. "I'm guessing he's mine. What's his name?" He rubbed the dog's ears and looked over at Wolfe.

"That's Duke." Wolfe smiled. "He hates storms and is never far from you since you rescued him a few years ago. He's a tracker dog and part of the team. He saved your life recently, so you're square."

Rubbing Duke all over and watching the thick tail wag in doggy happiness, Kane smiled. "I've always wanted a dog and we have horses as well. I'm liking what I see so far."

"Hey." Jenna opened the door and smiled at them. "The coffee is ready and I've made sandwiches." She looked at Kane and frowned. "You look like hell. Bad headache?"

Hearing a familiar voice, Kane swallowed hard as he took in the small beautiful young woman with the bluest eyes he'd ever seen. She looked so different from the mud-splattered soaked stranger dragging off his clothes earlier. He could see how she'd stolen his heart and the honeysuckle scent that came into the room with her was so darn familiar that a warm glow went straight through him at the sight of her. One thing for darn sure, his heart knew her very well and picked up pace. Images stirred in his mind and he concentrated on pulling them to the surface. A flashback of her wrapped around him crying and caked with mud filtered into his mind for a second, then vanished. That had to be a positive step. He met her eyes and nodded. "I've had some meds. I'll be fine, Jenna." Her name rolled off his tongue and the sound of it was familiar.

"I think you need to sit down." Wolfe placed a hand on her arm. "We have a small problem."

FOUR

After listening to Wolfe's rundown on Kane's condition, Jenna stared at him in disbelief and then turned her attention to Kane. "You don't *know* me? Not at all? Isn't there anything familiar about me?" Her throat closed as she fought down a sob of distress. "I can't believe it. It's like living a nightmare. We take two steps forward and ten back."

"Hey, don't worry too much. Shane figures it will only last a few hours." Kane went to her and took her hands, his thumb running over her wedding band and engagement ring. "I know we're married, and my gut instinct tells me being with you is right." He searched her face as if familiarizing himself with her. "The moment you walked in I recognized your honeysuckle scent and I recalled sitting on the side of a mountain covered in mud with you crying on my shoulder." He leaned back a little and looked at her, his head tilted to one side. "That has to be a positive start, right?"

Unable to control the tears filling her eyes, Jenna leaned into him. "Yes, you're starting to remember me, thank God. It's not all gone though, is it? You obviously remember Shane. Who else do you remember? Do you recall Rowley?"

"Nope. The last thing I remember is being in Helena before I came to Black Rock Falls and everything up to that time. What's missing is the last four years I've been here." Kane met her eyes and shrugged. "Being with you feels right and I don't have the pain of losing Annie anymore. I guess I have you to thank for that, Jenna. I figure we work through this one day at a time like we always do." He took a step back and sighed.

Blinking, Jenna looked at him. "How do you know we do that?"

"I have no idea." Kane smiled at her. "I figure my memory is just hovering under the surface. Something in here"—he tapped his chest—"tells me I should be here with you."

"That's a good sign, as is having a memory about you and Jenna in the mudslide." Wolfe nodded and slapped Kane on the back. "That was only a few months ago. If you get any other flashbacks, talk to Jenna about them and try to expand them."

Swallowing the emotion, Jenna smiled at him. "That was the day you asked me to marry you. I was crying with happiness."

"Hmm." Kane rubbed his chin. "I must have changed some over the years to be proposing in a mudslide."

Laughing, Jenna shook her head. "It was very romantic. It couldn't have been any better." She led the way out into the hallway. "You'll feel better when you've eaten. You usually do."

"Sure." Kane turned to Wolfe. "Can the MRI wait? I'm feeling okay now. My head is fine and I'm a little tired. Nothing a strong cup of coffee won't fix."

"I think so." Wolfe followed them to the kitchen. "You've suffered way worse than this, as you know, and can function at a higher level than anyone else I've ever known—and that's sayin' something." He pulled him to one side. "This isn't a mission, and if you need time, it's okay. So if the headache gets worse, don't drive, get Jenna to bring you to the morgue."

"The what?" Kane snorted with laughter.

Jenna turned to look at him. "That's where you receive all medical treatment." She wiggled her eyebrows at him. "We don't want anyone to discover you're a cyborg, now do we?"

"A what?" Deputy Rowley filled cups on the table from a large coffee pot. "Is there something I should know?"

Grinning at him, Jenna shook her head. "No, I was joking. The lightning strike caused Dave to lose some of his memory. He doesn't recall anything over the last four years."

"Oh, well then, I'm Jake Rowley." He offered his hand. "You're my twins' godfather. We're close friends."

"Am I? Well, that's wonderful and your name is very familiar, so that's a good sign." Kane shook his hand. "Don't worry, this memory loss is only temporary. It won't interfere with my work." He reached for a sandwich from a plate on the table. "It hasn't affected my appetite, that's for sure."

As they ate, Jenna answered all of Kane's questions about the running of the sheriff's department. She found it very strange that he didn't ask when they'd married or how long they'd been together. It was as if he'd just arrived in town and his first priority was the hierarchy in the office. She'd encountered Secret Service agents once or twice in her career and now here was one, on the job, professional, and hiding in her husband's body. It scared the heck out of her.

Rowley's phone chimed and he left the room to answer it, returning almost immediately.

"Jenna." Rowley paused at the door, holding up his phone. "It's Rio. Someone found a body in Spring Falls Lake. They figured it washed down in the storm." He looked at Wolfe. "Rio is on scene and wants to know if he should call Webber to retrieve the body?"

"No, tell him to ask Webber to take the van there." Wolfe stood. "I'm on my way."

Jenna held out her hand. "Let me speak to him." She took

the phone from Rowley and put it on speaker. "It's Jenna. What have we got?"

"Caucasian female, fully dressed apart from her shoes. She looks in her late twenties. I figure she hasn't been in the water long by the look of her, maybe overnight." He sighed. *"I can't see any injuries on her at all apart from a few scrapes. She doesn't look like she fell and hit her head. She wasn't floating in the water. She'd washed up on the riverbank faceup."*

Jenna grabbed the notepad and pen from beside the phone and made a few notes. "Who called it in, and why didn't you inform me?"

"One of the forest wardens, Joe Spike." Rio cleared his throat. *"He was conducting a routine check of the flooded areas and found her about twenty minutes ago. I've just arrived on scene. It doesn't look like a homicide and I didn't want to disturb you on your downtime."*

Frowning, Jenna glanced at Kane. "I'm on my way." She handed the phone back to Rowley.

"We're on our way." Kane swallowed his coffee and stood. "Don't look at me like that, Jenna. My memory might be offline but I'm okay. All I needed was a cup of strong coffee and something to eat. I do recall how to work a case." He met her gaze. "Although it would help if you could tell me where I keep my wet-weather gear?"

Knowing how stubborn Kane could be, Jenna looked straight at Wolfe. "Is he okay to come with me? It's only been a couple of hours since I found him unconscious."

"I'm fine, Jenna. This is nothing to worry about. I was functioning fine after I woke up from a coma." Kane's eyebrows rose. "Although I hadn't lost my memory and my body was a mess, my brain was firing on all cylinders. I've been shocked before, half drowned, frozen to near death, buried alive, and I could still carry on. I'm different than most men and you know it." He met her gaze. "If I'm not okay, I'll tell you. You have my word. I wouldn't risk driving the Beast without my full faculties. It would be like riding on the back of a guided missile."

Jenna nodded at Wolfe's shrug. "Okay. I guess it's good you remember the Beast. Our gear is in the mudroom. Everything else we need is in the truck." She turned to Wolfe and Rowley. "We'll meet up on scene."

She went into the bedroom to strap on her weapon and waited for Kane to do the same. "As I'm a stranger to you, I'm sure you won't be happy sharing this room. We have plenty of spare bedrooms, if having your things in here makes you uncomfortable."

"I don't get uncomfortable, Jenna—and you're not a stranger. I do remember fragments of being with you and more memories will return. We'll see how things go today. Right now, if I'm being honest with you, I'd be happier sleeping in the spare room, but I won't move my things." Kane attached his badge on his belt same as always and pulled on his Black Rock Falls Sheriff's Department jacket.

Jenna swallowed hard and forced out the words she didn't want to say. "If being here with me is a problem, you could move back to the cottage. You spent a few years there before we became involved."

"We're married and unless you ask me to leave I'm staying and hoping my memory will return." He gave her a long, considering look. "If it doesn't, we'll worry about the next steps then, okay?"

Swallowing emotion, Jenna stared at him. "Next steps? What exactly does that mean? Divorce?"

"I don't do divorce, Jenna. When I give my word, it's forever. I'll talk to Shane about electric shock treatment." Kane shrugged. "Maybe it will jolt back my memory."

Concerned but keeping her expression neutral, Jenna slid her weapon into the holster at her waist and lifted her chin. "Before we married, we were best friends. We've been through

hell and back so many times. This"—she waved a hand at him—
"is a hiccup, is all. You've lost your memory before and it came
back. Don't overthink it. Just let it happen." She grabbed
surgical gloves and masks from a drawer and filled her pockets.
"Bring your boots. You'll need them at the office. Your rubber
boots are in the mudroom, and if we get wet, we have a change
of clothes at the office."

She led the way to the mudroom and handed Kane a dry
slicker. "I guess you don't know but it's been raining for days.
We have local flooding. Black Rock Falls has rivers and lakes all
over. A river runs alongside part of our ranch, but it's not
causing any problems at the moment because nobody lives past
the snowplow guy next door."

As she pulled on her rubber boots and slicker, Duke came in
behind them and looked up at Kane. She rubbed the dog's ears
and handed Duke's coat to Kane. "Duke is dependent on you.
He frets when you're away and we have to spell things like b-a-
t-h and v-e-t or he becomes neurotic and hides under the bed."

"Oh. I'm glad you told me. So, he's neurotic. Does he
bite?" Kane bent to slip the coat on the dog and then stood,
slowly blinking his eyes. "I just had an image of him really
skinny and filthy. I was angry but it wasn't about the dog." He
rubbed both hands down his face and stared at her, his mouth
turned down. "Oh Lord, someone was abusing kids. I wanted
to kill the person responsible. It's all kind of crazy and mixed
up in my head. I recall the dog's condition made me sick to
my stomach. I carried him to the Beast and cared for him
myself."

This is going to be harder than I imagined. Worried if the
sudden memory flashbacks would make him a liability on the
job, Jenna blew out a breath. "No, Duke doesn't bite and you
had a flashback about a case we handled years ago. Wolfe said
your memory might come back in bits and pieces, so don't worry
about it. We've handled some very violent cases over the last

four years. I hope you don't react like this every time you remember one of them."

"I've never suffered from PTSD and I've witnessed more horror than you could imagine." Kane pulled his slicker over his head and reached for his hat. "I figure these sudden bursts of memory are similar to a PTSD episode. It's like my memory is short-circuiting, but I can deal with it." He slid on his hat and looked at her, eyebrows raised. "Have we talked about the zone before?"

Jenna nodded. Kane's ability to drop into the zone to function under extreme circumstances was part of his special ops training. "Yeah, I'm used to your combat face and remote mood. Do what's necessary to function, but right now my priority is getting to the crime scene. We can discuss anything else later."

"Yes, ma'am." Kane waved a hand toward the front door. "After you."

FIVE

To make things easier for Kane, Jenna put the coordinates for Spring Falls Lake into the GPS. Rain was falling in sheets, but the storm had moved on. There was water everywhere, changing the lowlands to a muddy swamp. As they drove along the wet roads, Jenna's attention centered on the brown water gushing through the ditch alongside the blacktop. It carried fall leaves, grass, and twigs at high speed and was destined to cause a blockage in the draining system. It would only be a matter of time before her ranch would be isolated. They headed through town and out on Stanton. The flooding had extended nearly to the highway, spilling across intersections and leaving a muddy gravel-filled slurry behind. As they drove, the smell of damp leaves and wet pine trees seeped into the vehicle. The forest certainly had his own unique smell during a rainy spell.

Kane had said little to her during the trip and the silence between them was broken only by the swish of wiper blades on the windshield and the directions from the GPS. Jenna turned to look at him. "You're quiet. I'm used to you singing along to the tunes on the radio."

Kane frowned and flicked her a glance. "I didn't think that

was appropriate, seeing as we're heading out to a possible homicide."

The robotic Kane was sitting beside her—the in-the-zone person wearing his combat face and emotionless. She shrugged. "I guess it was your way to break the tension. You have a very wicked sense of humor. It was a special part of you I loved."

"Uh-huh." Kane's attention moved back to the road. "It doesn't sound like me. I prefer to block out emotion. It's unnecessary and gets in the way of doing my job."

Jenna sighed. Kane might be distant, but to her relief he handled the Beast with his usual skill and twenty minutes later they pulled up behind the medical examiner's van in a parking area close to the lake. She patted Duke's head. "Stay here, boy. It's too wet out there for you today."

Pulling the hood of her slicker over her hat, she squelched through the sodden grass to the knot of people standing on the riverbank. The lake was moving at a rapid pace, spilling into the small river that ran through the outskirts of Black Rock Falls and all the way to the next town, Blackwater. The lake had broken its banks and brown muddy water was up to her ankles as she made her way toward the body.

A terrible smell of death hit her, and she reached for a mask with a grimace and handed one to Kane along with gloves. The first thing that Jenna noticed was the body didn't look like a typical murder victim. The woman was lying on her back fully dressed, with her arms spread out as if floating in the water. Her hair spilled out around her, moving with the current and making her appear almost alive. Her brown eyes had become slightly cloudy and fishlike. Wide open, the woman's eyes stared into the stormy sky, the sockets filling with rain and spilling down her cheeks like tears. She was fashionably dressed, as if she'd been out to dinner or on a date. She could clearly see rings on the woman's fingers, a bracelet, earrings, and a gold chain around her neck. Moving carefully through the slippery mud, Jenna went to Wolfe's side. "What do you make of this?"

"I'm not sure." Wolfe beckoned for Webber to bring the gurney. "I'll need to take a look at her back at the morgue. I can't see any visual signs of trauma."

"Just a minute." Kane bent and unbuttoned the front of the woman's blouse. "I thought I could see something through the wet material. Take a look at this." He indicated toward a playing card pushed deep inside the woman's bra, with just one corner peeking out. "The jack of hearts. If that's not a killer's calling card, my name's not Dave Kane."

Moving closer, Jenna blew out a long breath. "I think you're right. I thought for once we had just a plain old accident." She turned to Rio. "Capture everything here and take photographs of the scene before Wolfe moves her."

"Yes, ma'am." Rio moved his camera around. "I've recorded just about everything already. All I need is a few photographs of the playing card's position and we're good to go."

Jenna scanned the area in a full circle and noticed the forest warden sheltering under a tree with his horse. She turned to Kane. "We'll go speak to the forest warden. I know that Rio took a statement but that was before we had a possible homicide."

"That would be following procedure, ma'am." Kane looked down at her, spilling water from his black Stetson.

Jenna touched his arm. "I'd prefer it if you didn't call me ma'am, Dave." She removed her mask as they walked away and gave him a tight smile. "I'm Sheriff on the job and Jenna in the office. You're my deputy sheriff and my husband. Calling me ma'am is freaking me out. You wear what clothes you want, carry your weapon the way you want. Maybe if you'll come out of the zone and start acting human again, we'll be able to solve this case together like we always do."

"That's not a good idea." Kane looked into the distance. "Right now, I'm recalling all of the bad things. Who the heck is

James Stone? His name is like an earwig. Is it someone we hunted down? Why do I want to draw my weapon every time I see this man's face in my head?"

Swallowing hard, Jenna moved him some way away from the others. "We encountered him twice on the job. He used to be a lawyer, and we dated a couple of times, but I broke it off and he became a pest. You stepped in and he backed off. I had no idea he was a psychopath and very violent. He was responsible for your last memory loss. He shot you in the head and you tumbled down a ravine. You were in Walter Reed for some time. The doctors replaced the metal plate in your head. You'd smashed up your knee as well. You stayed with me until you recovered." She examined his expression. "Sometime later, Stone escaped from jail and tried to kill us. I took him down—he's dead."

"You took him down, not me?" Kane searched her face.

Jenna looked at his troubled expression. "We were in the middle of a wildfire. You were on one side of a ravine and I was on the other. I took down a psychopath intent on killing us both. I did my job, Dave, without hesitation."

The rain was coming in sideways and soaking Jenna, but she remained with her hand on his arm watching his reaction. She could tell by his expression that some disturbing memories had resurfaced. "It's been a tough four years, Dave, but we move on one day at a time. It's not been all bad. We've had some fun times too."

"Did we kill all of them?" Water dripped from the end of Kane's nose. "Let me rephrase that—did I take all the others out?"

Flinching from the clenched muscle under her palm, Jenna shook her head. "No, I prefer to take them alive if possible. I want to hear their story. We have taken down a few and, yes, you have as well as me. I don't have you along just as a sniper. Your skill in profiling alone is incredible. We work very well as a team." She sighed. "If being my partner is a problem, you can team up with Rio."

"As he's not aware of who and what I am, it would be counterproductive to change partners." Kane met her gaze. "The team would figure something was up, especially as we're married." He ran a hand down his face and flicked away the rain. "You and Wolfe are the only people I can talk to, so if I become a problem, I'll go work with Wolfe."

Not sure if she wanted to laugh or be angry, Jenna snorted. "If you could recall what you've put me through in the last four years, you wouldn't say that. Trust me, you can never become a problem for me. Just don't shut down on me. Wolfe said you need to expand on your memories, and I don't care how long it takes. I'll be here for you." She smiled at him and headed toward the forest warden, hoping that he would follow her.

The warden lifted his hand in a wave as she approached. Jenna moved under the tree and stood beside him. "Mr. Spike?"

"That's me, Sheriff." He indicated toward the body with his chin. "I guess you want the rundown of how I discovered the body? I was conducting a routine examination of the local flooding. We have mudslides in this type of weather and a ton of animals get washed out of their habitats. I came from the south side of the forest, noticed what I believed was a bundle of clothes or something similar and went to investigate. I left my horse here and went on foot the moment I realized it was a body. I checked for vital signs and then called 911 and spoke to Deputy Rio. He asked me to remain on scene until he arrived. I'm afraid that's all the information I have to give you. I haven't seen anyone apart from your team this morning."

"Have you given your details and the time this occurred in your statement?" Kane moved to Jenna's side. "Did you move the body at all? Did you take precautions not to contaminate the scene?"

"Yes, I did take precautions and, no, I didn't move the

body." Spike's eyes narrowed as he looked at Kane. "We're trained in various types of investigation. This wouldn't be the first time a warden has discovered human remains."

The forest warden appeared to be cold and tired. Jenna smiled at him. "Thank you for remaining on scene. If there's anything else we need to know, I'll call." She turned and headed back to the group around the body. The creepy feeling that someone was watching her crawled up her spine. She stopped walking and turned a full circle slowly, scanning the trees alongside the lake and riverbank. The rain-diffused light made it difficult to see and she reluctantly turned back toward her team.

Behind her, Kane managed to walk without making a sound, even through the muddy water. She wondered if this remote stranger was becoming a reality. The easy casualness she'd enjoyed with Kane had vanished and he was all business on the job. She hoped that he'd act more like his normal self at home.

"I'm done here Jenna. I have no idea how this woman died. We need to get an ID, ASAP. We can't list this as a homicide just from finding a playing card on the body. Its source is undetermined at this time, so I'll need next of kin's permission to do an autopsy." Wolfe rested his forensics kit on top of the body bag on the gurney. "We'll need help getting the gurney through the mud and back to the van. He looked at Kane. "Do you mind?"

"If you're planning on pushing it, I do mind." Kane scanned the area back to the van. "Give Webber your bag and we'll carry it." He smiled at Wolfe. "Unless you want Rio to do it for you?"

Jenna smiled. It was the first time she'd seen a glimpse of Kane's old self coming through the serious exterior. Since Wolfe had arrived in Black Rock Falls, Kane had joked about Wolfe keeping in shape, even to the extent of helping him build a gym in his cellar. She doubted Wolfe needed to be reminded to work out. He never gained an ounce of fat and always seemed to be in top shape. As she followed the team back to their vehicles, Rio fell into step beside her.

"Rowley mentioned that Kane was struck by lightning earlier today." Rio turned to look at her. "He's acting real strange. Is he going to be okay?"

Jenna pushed wet hair out of her eyes. "I sure hope so."

SIX

The office smelled of damp clothes, and her team still looked a bit bedraggled as they filtered into her office. Jenna waited patiently for Kane to arrive and finally gave up. He'd been waylaid by Poppy the moment he'd entered the office and had stopped to speak to her. Jenna understood how confused he must be. It would be like living a nightmare. It was no wonder he gravitated toward Poppy. She was the only person on the team he remembered apart from Wolfe. No matter how much seeing Kane so relaxed with Poppy hurt her, she'd suck it up. Right now she had a case to concentrate on and her personal life would wait.

She looked at Rio and Rowley. "We need to ID the corpse ASAP. Wolfe's hands are tied until we have permission for an autopsy. If she'd been drugged, for instance, the evidence could be negligible over time." She pushed her hands through her hair. "We have to assume she's a local, so run her through the usual checks. I'll start with the DMV and see if I get a match on a driver's license. Rowley, you run her prints, and Rio, I'll leave it to you to write a short media release. We'll set up the hotline. I'm afraid we'll need to divulge the fact we found a body, so give a brief description and ask for information on anyone who might be absent from work or whatever." She pushed to her feet as the deputies left her office.

Intending to bring Maggie, the receptionist, up to date and to give Deputy Poppy Anderson the hotline to monitor, she headed downstairs. She frowned as Poppy's girlish giggles came from the office below. Poppy had arrived in Black Rock Falls with the intent of beginning a relationship with Kane and her attentions toward him had become a problem. Before Jenna had the chance to deal with her, Poppy had been kidnapped by a psychopath. On her return, and after a long and serious talk about sexual harassment in the workplace, she'd sent Poppy to receive counseling to control her behavior and to determine if she'd suffered any long-term effects from the kidnapping. After receiving a good report and ensuring the sexual harassment counseling would continue for a time, she'd offered her a temporary position for three months. It had been against Jenna's better judgement as it seemed, even with counseling, a leopard couldn't change its spots. Although, Poppy had been instrumental in apprehending a killer, so they'd all decided to give her a second chance. Her probationary time as a deputy was coming to an end and although she'd tempered her ways to a degree, Poppy hadn't made a good impression with any of her team and lacked work ethic. Not being able to trust her, Jenna kept her out of the loop and in the front office on desk duties.

She went to the front counter to ask Maggie to set up the hotline and turned around to look for Kane. She found him at his old desk, drinking a cup of coffee and chatting with Poppy. She walked up to them and cleared her throat. "You've missed the meeting."

"I thought this was my desk, so I was trying to get into the computer to bring my files up to date." Kane smiled at Poppy. "Then Poppy tells me that I share the office with you now. We were just reminiscing about old times. It was nice to be able to speak to someone I can remember. Time got away from me. I'm sorry. What did I miss?"

More like Poppy held you up to annoy me. "I'll give you a rundown upstairs." Jenna looked at him. "Deputy Anderson will be manning the hotline for information on the identity of the body we found today. Rio is sending out a media release as we speak." She swung her attention to Poppy. "Do you need instructions on how to take down the information from the callers when they come in?"

"I figure I'll manage just fine." Poppy stood and headed for the front counter.

"Just call me if you get into trouble." Kane pushed to his feet, smiling at her.

"I sure will, Dave." Poppy flashed him a too-white smile. "It's great having the real you back again. The lightning strike did you a favor."

"Thanks. I'm here to stay." Kane's smile froze on his face when he looked at Jenna.

Jenna held up a hand. "Just one second." She followed Poppy back to the front counter, looked around to make sure they weren't overheard, and leaned closer. "Do you recall our little chat?"

"Vividly." Poppy lifted her chin. "You can't fire me for talking to Dave."

Keeping her voice low and controlled, Jenna smiled. "No, I can't, but I can for suggestive remarks. I've told you before that I won't tolerate sexual harassment in the workplace. It makes the deputies and me uncomfortable. It's unprofessional and not what I want in a deputy. I'll be writing a report and sending it over to Mayor Petersham. I offered you a chance to redeem yourself, but you just keep ignoring the rules."

"I won't chase after your husband if that's what's worrying you, okay?" Poppy rolled her eyes. "He has a mind of his own, you know. You can't stop him liking me. You're acting like a control freak."

Refusing to allow her to get under her skin, Jenna shook her head. "Get back to work before I change my mind and fire you." She turned and walked back to Kane.

"I can't believe she's here." Kane shook his head. "It seems like yesterday we were having lunch at the conference. She mentioned being kidnapped and I saved her. How did that come about?"

Pushing down the need to roll her eyes, Jenna shrugged. "If you really want to know, she came here to make a claim on you. She arrived in town assuming you were interested in her. She made inappropriate advances toward you in the office and in public. When you ignored her, she stormed off and vanished into thin air. The next thing, we get an email from her resigning and saying she was moving to Colorado. About three months later, we discovered she'd been kidnapped and held prisoner in an underground mine. You were there when we found her. You're her knight in shining armor." She shook her head. "She hasn't found a chink in your armor yet though."

"Why is she working in the office if she harasses people?" Kane raised an eyebrow and looked at her. "She's a very attractive woman and it would be easy for a guy to fall for her, so why would she need to act like that? Considering what you've told me, I'm surprised she had the guts to ask me to her place for dinner tonight to talk about our time in Helena to jog my memory."

Keeping her face neutral, Jenna shrugged. "And what did you say?"

"I said I was a married man and she needed to stand down." Kane raised one eyebrow. "I'm surprised you don't fire her."

Sucking in a deep breath, Jenna shrugged. "I've had a talk to her about sexual harassment and she promised to change. She only focuses on you and has been okay for a time. I'm not threatened by her, Dave. Poppy was around before you asked me to marry you. As far as I recall she was annoying the heck out of you, so if that continues, I'll fire her for sexual harassment—not because we're married or I'm jealous."

"I know we're married Jenna, and if we're as good together as I've been told, why isn't she hiding her attraction toward me? She confuses the heck out of me." Kane frowned. "I hope she didn't think I was encouraging her before. I was just happy to see someone I recognized, is all."

Jenna snorted. "Yeah, I noticed." She folded her arms across her chest. "So I couldn't just fire her for talking to you, could I? I gave her a lecture, but if she comes on to you again in the office, I'm firing her. She's had enough chances."

"I wish I could remember more about our time together, but my head is scrambled right now." Kane rubbed the scar under his hair. "Don't worry, my memory will return soon, I'm getting bits and pieces back, but they all blend together. Nothing is clear." He lifted his chin toward Poppy. "I do remember her, and Wolfe mentioned a problem with her. Does she hit on men everywhere she goes... or is it just me?"

Jenna forced her tone to be casual. "I've spoken to Poppy's counselor, mainly to see if she has problems that go back to childhood, you know, to find some excuse for her behavior, but she doesn't have any. It seems that Poppy believes that every man is available." She shrugged. "She doesn't want *you*. She just doesn't want *me* to have you. If you left me for her, she'd drop you and try to break up another couple. It's what she does. It's a game to her. With your profiling expertise, surely you can see through her? Or can't you?"

Seeing his confusion, she stepped closer and hugged him. His entire body stiffened. It was like hugging a stranger. She pushed down the wave of uncertainty and stared straight into his eyes. "It will be okay." She straightened and stepped away. "I've had enough of talking about her, and as her superior, you should refer to her as Deputy Anderson. I'll send another sexual harassment update to the mayor's office, as he hired her. She has a good friend in Mayor Petersham, and if I don't push this issue, she'll be putting her name forward for sheriff in the next election with his full support."

"Okay, I understand." Kane's brow creased into a frown. "I'm sorry, Jenna. To me, none of that happened and I was just speaking to an old friend. I had no idea it would cause a problem between us." He glanced at his watch and sighed. "I figure we need to get back to work."

Annoyed, Jenna stood her ground. He'd told her it was only lunch at the conference and they hadn't been involved. Suddenly it seemed like they were more than just friends. She shook her head slowly. "You've got it all wrong, Dave. I'd never suggest who you can talk to. For heaven's sake, talk to her all you want. Go to her place for dinner if you must. You do owe me one thing, Dave. If you discover you have feelings for her, tell me, because as sure as hell, I don't want a husband who doesn't love me." She picked up her iPad and headed for the stairs.

Inside her office she leaned against the counter of the small kitchenette at the back of the room. Taking her cup from a rack beside the sink, she poured a cup of freshly brewed coffee, added the fixings and an extra spoonful of sugar. The problems with Kane would just have to wait. She pushed Poppy to the back of her mind and went to the whiteboard to make a list of everything they'd discovered about the body in the river. She wrote down the woman's description from the files Rio had uploaded to her iPad. Before long she'd receive an email from Wolfe containing the woman's personal effects and images of her jewelry. She sat at her desk and watched the footage Rio had taken of the scene. She zoomed in, checking all around for anyone hiding in the forest and found no one.

"Jenna." Kane walked into the office waving a piece of paper with Duke close at his heels. The dog went to his basket, turned around, and dropped down with a sigh. "The local bank manager called. He watched the report on the TV that Rio called in. The body we found sounds very much like one of his bank tellers. She had mentioned to his wife about going on a blind date last night. He gave her a call just before and it went to voicemail. Her name is Dianne Gilbert, a divorcée bank teller out of 7 Fairview, Bison Ridge. Do you want me to drop by the house and see if she's home?"

Jenna stood and stared out of the window to the mountains shrouded under a blanket of thick rain-filled clouds. "Bison Ridge is past Bear Peak. The road up there is good but might be subject to flooding as part of the falls feeds a river close by. It's on the other side of the ravine and water streams down that side of the mountain in a storm." She turned to look at him. "There could be a ton of reasons why she's not answering her phone. With the heavy cloud cover she might be having trouble getting bars. Most of the mountain is the same and we need our satellite phones most times." She sighed. "We'll head out now. I'll get Rowley to run a background check on her. He'll get details of next of kin. It will save time if it is her in the morgue."

"Don't worry, the Beast will be able to make it over most terrain." Kane went to the coffee pot and filled two to-go cups. "Do we have any cookies?"

At the mention of cookies, Duke went from dozing in his basket to fully alert in a split second. The dog sat in front of Kane and barked. Jenna laughed. "You said the magic word and, yes, we do. Above your head to the right is a glass jar of chocolate chip cookies. I make them for you because you're always hungry. We have a ton of energy bars too if you need them." She grabbed her jacket and a dry slicker from a peg behind the door. "I'll meet you at the front counter." She picked up one of the to-go cups and headed downstairs to instruct Rowley.

Jenna checked her watch and walked to Rowley's desk. "We'll be some time. You can order from Aunt Betty's for lunch, put it on the department tab." She glanced behind her. "Order for us too. Just ask Susie to do up our usual order." She had faith the manager of the diner knew what they liked after years of knowing them. "I'll call in when we arrive."

"The list of personal possessions just dropped into my inbox." Rio looked at her from his desk. "I'll print the images and add them to the whiteboard in your office."

Glad of his efficiency, Jenna nodded. "Great, and keep an eye on Anderson on the hotline. Her attention wanders, and we might be missing important information."

"Copy that." Rio grinned at her. "Last time Carter dropped by, he said her lights were on but no one was home." He snorted. "Kinda fits her, doesn't it? Are you planning on keeping her around? She's getting close to the end of her trial period. It would be better to hire another clerk if we can't find another deputy to take her place."

Jenna shrugged. "I'm in a very difficult position when it comes to her. As you know, Mayor Petersham gave her the job against my better judgement. He is actually paying her out of the council budget. I'm not sure why he wants to keep her around unless it's to appease his old friend who used to be Anderson's boss."

"It sounds more like he was just trying to get rid of her." Rio's eyebrows rose. "He must have jumped at the chance when she asked him to transfer here."

"I've tried to help her, but she ignores me." Rowley, who rarely said anything about Poppy, looked up from the computer screen. "She seems to know about forensics. Maybe she shouldn't be here at all. Do you think you can convince Wolfe to employ her?"

"Wolfe would never allow her near his delicate apparatus." Kane had walked up behind Jenna without a sound. "If he needs help, he's got Emily. He knows Poppy, and I don't think he'd want to be working with her on a daily basis." He shrugged.

"She wouldn't cope with his frozen stares. Trust me, when I was out with him on my bachelor night, any woman that approached him left in a hurry."

Turning around to stare at him, Jenna's heart picked up pace. "You remember your bachelor party, the morgue, and Emily?"

"It seems that I do." Kane smiled at her and pushed on his black Stetson. "Ready?" He turned and headed for the door.

The tension in Jenna's shoulders seemed to slide away and she looked at her deputies. "Feed me information as it comes in. If this isn't our Jane Doe, then we'll need to keep looking. We know that Dianne Gilbert is a bank clerk and friends with the manager's wife. Follow up on that as well. The bank manager's wife might be able to give you more details of Gilbert's social life, friends, and immediate family."

"Yes, ma'am." Rowley nodded toward the door. "I hope by the time you get back Kane has recovered his memory. It's weird working beside someone who should know you and doesn't. I say something to him and he gives me a blank stare in response."

Looking over her shoulder at Kane waiting at the counter talking to Maggie with Duke leaning against his leg, Jenna nodded. "Can you imagine how lost he feels, and yet he's here working the case. He's getting his memory back in pieces, but it's only been a few hours. Give it time. I'm sure he'll be okay." She hurried after Kane.

SEVEN

It could keep raining forever as far as Shelby O'Connor cared. Although only in her mid-thirties, she'd believed the chances of finding romance again were impossible. She'd taken her friend's advice and joined a dating app and found the man of her dreams: Julian Darnley, a forensic accountant who was the CEO and owner of Darnley Financial. She'd checked him out and found his company online, which was a huge relief because the attraction between them had been instant. She'd always loved a man with a full beard, and the spectacles added to his professional persona. As she ran a cattle ranch, she'd been overjoyed to find a man interested in fine dining and books. Her late husband had been thirty years her senior and an old-style cowboy who was only interested in the next cattle sale. She'd loved him dearly and had been heartbroken when he died of a heart attack, leaving her the ranch and a sizable fortune. She'd been surprised to discover just how much money she had, but with the income from the ranch it just sat in the bank and she had no kids to leave it to. Her friends all invested in one thing or another, but the idea intimidated her and she didn't trust strangers.

Now she had Julian. They'd communicated over four months. So keen to be close to her, Julian had recently purchased a house in Black Rock Falls with plans to open another branch of his company in town. Perhaps the new man in her life would be able to guide her in the right financial direction. Although she hadn't asked him, not wanting him to believe her interest in him was entirely due to his profession. As his phone calls were coming almost nightly now, she thought long and hard of a way around it. Her phone buzzed right on time. After exchanging pleasantries, she drew a deep breath and dived right in. "How's your day been? You must work very long hours."

"It depends on the client." Julian sighed. "My interest is investing, not searching through people's books to find out if their accountant has been cheating them or the IRS." He laughed. "I've been diversifying lately into cryptocurrency, and between you and me, I've made a fortune. All my friends and family are involved and now everyone is living the high life. Best of all, the IRS can't touch it. I can buy and sell things using the currency just the same, but I'm saving thousands on taxation." He sighed. "Oh, I'm sorry. I'm boring you. How was your day?"

Grinning, Shelby wanted to punch the air. "Oh, the usual. It's much the same day to day on a cattle ranch. The manager does everything for me and I spend most days reading. I'm very interested in what you do and wish I had the courage to invest. You already know I'm widowed and own a cattle ranch. My friends all say I should invest some of my inheritance, but I don't know where to start. I don't trust anyone. A woman alone is a target for unscrupulous people."

"I understand completely." Julian sighed. "Many of my clients we're in the same position as you. It is difficult to trust people with your money. I'm glad my company has a good reputation and can alleviate any fears. It's not just me. It's a whole

*network of people working together to get the best outcome for
our clients."*

Trying to contain her excitement, Shelby sat at the kitchen
table. "What are the safeguards in place that make your
company better than a single financial advisor?"

"My company guarantees you'll make money with us."
Julian cleared his throat. *"Clients' funds are placed in a
company account and investors receive a share of the profits
minus a small commission for the company. At the moment
cryptocurrency is the biggest money spinner on the planet. I'm
not sure how long it will last, but I'm sinking a great deal of my
personal fortune into it as well."* He paused a beat. *"I'm reluctant to ask you to join us, as we are on the edge of a beautiful
relationship. I wouldn't want you to believe I was interested in
you for the sole reason of asking you to invest in my company.
The truth is we're overwhelmed with prospective clients."*

Bursting with enthusiasm, Shelby grinned. "Could you
make room for me?"

*"Well, I wouldn't want to be seen offering you an advantage
over the others on the waiting list."* She heard Julian tapping
away on a keyboard. *"I guess, I could add you to my personal
investment."* He sighed. *"Are you sure, Shelby? I wouldn't want
you to think I was encouraging you in any way. The decision
must be yours and not influenced by anything I say."*

Shelby trembled with excitement. "What do I have to do?"

"That would depend on how much you wanted to invest."
Julian brightened. *"You should start with a small amount first,
like five thousand. To see how it goes and then make up your
mind what you want to do."*

Shaking her head, Shelby gripped the phone so tightly her
fingers ached. "The ranch brings in money every week, so I
don't need the money in the bank for day-to-day expenses. I
want to invest it all—the complete inheritance, which at the last
count was approximately twenty million." She chewed on her

bottom lip, concerned he wouldn't accept her as a client. "What do I need to do to get the money transferred to your account?"

"It's simple enough if you have access to your accounts online." Julian hummed in amusement. *"I've just arrived in town and was calling you to ask if you would like to meet me for dinner at my new house. I thought you might be able to help me select new furnishings and here we are discussing finances."*

Worried she might have given the wrong impression, she changed tactics. "Oh, I love interior design. It would be fun shopping for everything, but I don't even know your taste in furnishings. Sorry to be pushing my money on you. I'm really not that shallow."

"I figure I know you well enough by now, Shelby. This is the first time we've discussed finances." Julian's voice became almost singsong. *"Oh, okay. You've twisted my arm. You're in and if you'll come to dinner tonight, we can make it happen. Just bring your account numbers and passwords and I'll walk you through the process—but then no more shoptalk. I want some time to get to know you better."*

Trying to calm her excitement, Shelby giggled. "I'd like to get to know you better too."

"Good." Julian's footsteps echoed through the phone. *"My new place is a little hard to find in the dark, so maybe it would be safer if I came by and gave you a ride? Or perhaps it would be better to meet me somewhere? I recall you mentioned the ranch manager is a little attached to you. I wouldn't want to make life uncomfortable for you."*

Nodding, Shelby glanced out of the window at the manager of the cattle ranch. He had showed interest in her after her husband died, but now she wanted to cement the relationship with Julian. "I'll drive. I have a GPS."

"I can't let you do that. The roads in this area are narrow and dangerous. There are too many flooded areas." Julian sounded serious. *"I'll meet you in the Triple Z Bar's parking lot at eight,*

close to the entrance. It's on the high part of town and safer for you to get to. I'll be driving a rental. It's a white Yukon. I've been using it today to collect the odd pieces of furniture to make the place more like home, but I'm hopeless at this kind of thing. I can't wait to get your opinion."

Shelby's face grew hot. "Okay, apart from my bank details, what else would you like me to bring? A bottle of wine or dessert?"

"Oh... well, I'm in town for the entire week." Julian chuckled. *"If you're not needed on the ranch, I'd love your company. Maybe pack a few things and we can sample the delights of fine dining and fly to Helena to visit the stores. I hear the Cattleman's Hotel restaurant is highly regarded. I'll take you anywhere you want to go."*

Wanting to pinch herself to make sure she wasn't dreaming, Shelby blew out a long sigh. "That sounds wonderful." She glanced out of the window. "I'll let the manager know I'll be gone for a time. I'll see you at eight."

EIGHT

Mist covered the forest as Kane pushed the Beast up the mountain. The rain was increasing in intensity and water ran like rivers alongside the blacktop. The muddy water snaked its way toward them in all directions, spilling sand, gravel, and pine needles across the road. The wipers were working overtime. The *swish, swish, swish* as they swung back and forth only gave a second or two of the way ahead before a sheet of rain distorted the view. The conditions didn't worry him. He'd driven through much worse in his lifetime, but then he had some idea of where he was going. As they drove past the signpost to Bear Peak, flashes of memory surged through his brain. He recognized the dirt road heading into the mountains and turned to Jenna. "I've been here before. I recall driving up that road."

"That's good in one way but bad in another. It's a place I'd rather forget." Jenna's attention was fixed on the way ahead. "Bear Peak is a murderer's playground. There are secrets there. Blackhawk has told me many stories about this part of the mountain. I figure because it's so isolated it's become the perfect place to commit murder and, unfortunately, we've had to attend many crime scenes in this area, so I'm not surprised you remember it." She glanced at him. "Bear Peak lies on one side of the ravine and Bison Ridge on the other. Just ahead we take a fork in the road. It goes over a natural bridge, formed when the ravine cut its way through the mountain. It's known locally as Bison Hump." She sighed. "Do you recall the ravine? You spent some time in the freezing water down there recently."

As memories came flooding back, he smiled at Jenna. "Atohi Blackhawk? He's a Native American tracker who works with us, isn't he? I remember him. He's a good friend of ours."

It didn't take a genius to know that Jenna had withdrawn into herself. He wanted to reassure her that they would be okay, but he'd messed up big-time by giving Poppy his full attention. He wished that Wolfe had given him the intel on Jenna's feelings toward the woman. All he could do now was to concentrate on the case and support her.

As he took the fork in the road, the ravine opened up in front of him, a one-lane bridge disappearing into heavy cloud cover. He slowed the Beast and crawled forward, peering into the misty expanse dropping away on each side of them. "I can't see two feet in front of me. Just how safe is this bridge?"

"Blackhawk believes it's been here since the beginning of time, so I'm sure it will last another day." Jenna grinned at him. "Don't tell me Mr. 'I've Got No Fear Gene' Kane is concerned about driving off the bridge?"

Shaking his head, Kane grinned back at her. "Nope, I'm not scared, but I didn't know if you could swim."

"Oh, so you figure we'd survive the fall, do you?" Jenna chuckled. "Oh, yes, I remember *optimistic* is your middle name."

Happy to see her smiling again, he shrugged. "Well, I know the Beast is bombproof, so there's always a possibility." As they reached the other side of the ravine, he listened to the GPS giving him instructions. "I figure Mrs. Gilbert's house is about five minutes away. If she's not answering the door, how do you want to play this? Do we assume she might be in trouble and break in to check on her?"

"I don't want to do any unnecessary damage, but I'm sure you'll be able to pick the lock." Jenna sipped from her to-go cup of coffee. "I know you're pretty good at kicking in doors, but maybe we take a gentle approach this time."

Kane turned onto Fairview and peered through the rain, looking for any sign of a house number. He could make out an open gate and crawled along the road. "There's number one, and her house is number three, so I would imagine it's on the other side of the road. Or do the properties in this area run consecutively?"

"Your guess is as good as mine." Jenna buzzed down her window. "There it is. There's a sign saying Gilbert out front."

Kane drove into the short driveway and up to the stoop. There were no vehicles in the garage and the doors sat wide open. He glanced at Jenna. "It looks to me like she's not at home. Wait here and I'll go check." He caught a flash of annoyance in her eyes and cleared his throat. "It's pointless us both getting wet. If she doesn't answer the door, I still figure we should go in and check out the house. There might be a clue inside to tell us where she's gone."

"Then I'm coming with you." Jenna pulled up her hood. "Let's go."

Kane could almost sense that the house was empty. On days like this most people who lived in the mountains had a fire going and there was no smoke coming out of the chimney. He rapped on the door and they waited, dripping on the stoop. He tried a few more times and then used his lock picks to open the door. "Mrs. Gilbert. Sheriff's department."

Nothing.

They stepped inside. The paved area led to a mudroom and, rather than mess up the polished wooden floors throughout the house, he stripped off his slicker and wiped his feet. "There's nobody here. The house is cold."

"See if we can hunt down any information." Jenna looked around. "Look for a phone or an office. She may have left a note or written down details of where she was going. I'll go left, you go right."

Kane moved out. "Copy."

He stepped into the family room. The furnishings were older style, but the room was clean and tidy with a slight lavender smell. The mantel held an array of photographs in frames. He walked over to them and let his gaze slide over the images of a man wearing military uniform. "Maybe this is why you are so off the grid. Did your father leave you this place?" He shook his head. So many soldiers had returned from a tour of duty unable to cope in the towns or cities, preferring the quiet of the forest.

He bent and examined the logs in the fireplace. A warm swell of thin smoke still rose from the ashes of the wooden logs, which would indicate Mrs. Gilbert had only been missing for a short time. He straightened and scanned the room for a telephone, without luck. He moved around the room, checking every nook and cranny for any information on the woman's blind date. Finding nothing of interest, he moved to the next room. It was a small study lined with books. In the center sat a polished antique mahogany desk with a leather top. A mahogany captain's chair was tucked in on one side. The study was masculine in content, from the array of pens set in a neat row to the leather-bound journal. He flicked open the cover to discover the name of the owner and shook his head. He had assumed the diary journal belonged to Mrs. Gilbert's ex-husband, but the name inside wasn't Gilbert. Perhaps these things once belonged to her father?

The phone on the desk was the old-style type with a spinning dial. He lifted the receiver and dialed his phone number. The ringtone coming from his inside pocket, told him the phone was working just fine. He hunted through the drawers for a notepad and found one. Under the heading Financial Advisors was a list of names. Using his phone, he made a copy. He heard Duke bark and the hairs on the back of his neck stood to attention as the boards on the front stoop creaked. Someone was coming and entering in stealth. At the familiar metallic sound as the intruder cocked a pump-action shotgun, Kane slid along with his back to the wall. Had Jenna heard him? He turkey-peeked around the door. The man was tall and broad and carried the shotgun high with the butt tucked into his shoulder. At that moment, Jenna walked out of the kitchen and froze like a deer in the headlights. The man moved slowly, with the shotgun aimed at Jenna.

There could be no way out for her unless the man dropped his weapon. Kane moved silently into the hallway, sliding his weapon from the holster and estimating the danger of taking the problem out without killing Jenna. Spook the intruder and the finger resting on the trigger would blast a hole in Jenna as big as Texas. The man moved closer, and Jenna's eyes fixed on him and she raised her hands.

"I'm Sheriff Jenna Alton. Drop your weapon."

An angry male voice boomed out as the stranger abused Jenna in German and held the shotgun with a steady hand. He meant business. It was act now or he'd fire, and Jenna didn't stand one chance in hell. The situation was escalating along with the tirade of foul language.

"I don't understand you." Jenna kept her gaze on the man. "Dave, please tell me you still speak six languages?"

Kane slipped into German easily, but he kept his voice low and unthreatening. "Sheriff's department. Lower your weapon and let's talk."

The man, who he assumed was in his fifties, spun around, aiming the shotgun at him. "You want to talk. You thieving dogs.

I saw you breaking into Dianne's house. You don't look like cops to me."

Although staring down the twin muzzles of a pump-action shotgun wasn't his idea of fun, it had turned the odds in Kane's favor. Skilled in negotiation and fluent in German, he figured he could talk this lunatic down. He flicked a glance at Jenna, tipping his head slightly. Relieved when she got the message and took cover behind the refrigerator, he kept his weapon trained on the man. "Why we are here is none of your concern. Drawing down on two law enforcement officers is an offence. Lower your weapon—now!"

He had the man's full attention and noticed a flicker of doubt in his eyes. When the man's finger moved from the trigger, Jenna moved silently from behind the refrigerator, weapon drawn. Kane kept the intruder's attention. "This is a simple misunderstanding. Lower your weapon. If you shoot me, the sheriff will kill you. Lower your weapon and you walk out of here a free man. No harm, no foul."

From the expression on the man's face, Jenna had pressed the muzzle of her weapon into the man's back. The shotgun in the man's hand lowered to his side and Kane stepped forward and grabbed it. He unloaded the cartridges and dropped them into his pocket. "What's your name?"

"Luca Schneider." Schneider shrugged. "I live next door and saw you arrive. Your truck doesn't resemble any police cruiser I have seen before. I believed you to be intent on robbery. I was only doing my civic duty by protecting the property."

Figuring if the man kept a close eye on the goings on in this road, he could have noticed when Mrs. Gilbert had left the premises, he offered him a break. "Okay, I'm sure the sheriff will accept your apology."

"I am sorry." Schneider turned to Jenna and removed his hat. "I don't want to go to jail."

"What did he say?" Jenna hadn't lowered her weapon.

Kane explained. "He might know something. I'll ask him some questions."

"Okay." Jenna holstered her weapon. "I guess it wasn't our day to die, huh?"

Kane smiled at her. "It's not over yet."

"Right." Jenna snorted. "I forgot. I've got to stop tempting fate." She waved a hand at Schneider. "Get on with it. He's getting restless."

Straightening, Kane turned to Schneider. "Did you happen to notice what time Mrs. Gilbert left yesterday? Her friends are concerned about her."

"Yes, she left at about seven-thirty. She mentioned something about a blind date last time we spoke, so I figured that's where she was heading. Last night, she just gave me a wave as usual and continued on her way." Schneider's face reddened. "You're not going to arrest me for just being neighborly, are you?"

Kane shook his head. "Not this time. Did she mentioned the name of the man or where she was meeting him?"

"No." Schneider opened his arms in an exasperated way. "I only spoke to her in passing."

Kane looked at Jenna and dropped back into English. "He said he was just being neighborly and keeping an eye on the place. He believed we'd broken in to commit a robbery." He turned back to the man. "What vehicle was she driving?"

"A silver Buick Encore. It's almost new. It has a Black Rock Falls shooters club sticker on the front bumper."

Kane nodded and looked at Jenna. "Do you want me to just let him go? He gave me the time he saw Mrs. Gilbert leave yesterday and a description of her vehicle. He said, she went on a blind date but he didn't have any details."

"Sure, let him go but take down his details in case we need to speak with him again." Jenna ran a hand through her hair and shrugged. "We have enough to do without worrying about him at the moment."

Kane relayed Jenna's message, and Schneider nodded to her briefly and then headed for the door. He turned back to Jenna. "I couldn't find zip apart from a list of financial advisors in the top drawer of the desk. The problem is there's no way of telling how old the list is. The desk is antique and the decor very masculine. I couldn't imagine her ex-husband leaving it behind after they divorced, so I'm assuming it belongs to a male member of her family."

"We'll give them a call and see if any of them have heard from Mrs. Gilbert lately." Jenna's gaze narrowed. "Mrs. Gilbert was in her mid-thirties, wasn't she? So where is her computer or laptop? I honestly don't know anyone at that age without one thing or the other."

Kane smiled. "I figure most people do things on their smartphones these days. Although, I do agree most people have laptops or some form of connection to the internet."

"Smartphones, yeah maybe, but she worked in the bank." Jenna pushed hair behind her ear and frowned. "People who work on computers usually have them at home as well." She sighed. "Never mind. Her clothes are here, the kitchen is stocked. If she is alive, she left here by her own volition. I figure we search social media. She must have discussed this blind date with at least one of her friends." She headed for the mudroom. "Oh, good. It's stopped raining for a spell. You'll be able to give Duke a run before we head back to the office."

Suddenly finding the situation amusing, Kane smothered a grin. "I hope we haven't jumped to the wrong conclusion and Mrs. Gilbert shows up as we're leaving and does the walk of shame." He wiggled his eyebrows at Jenna. "Maybe the blind date went better than she expected?"

"Can you imagine arriving home and finding the sheriff on your doorstep, your house broken into just because you decided to go for coffee with a new boyfriend?" Jenna snickered. "If this is a possibility, we'd better make sure we've left the place as it was before. Did you move anything?"

Kane shook his head. "Nope." He met her gaze with a shrug. "I'm starting to feel my age, I think."

"Why is that?" Jenna led the way out of the house and waited as Kane closed the door behind them.

"Well, going for coffee was just drinking a cup of coffee when I was dating." Kane gave her a long look. "Hmm. I figure you're a good ten years younger than me. What made you marry such an old man?" He chuckled. "Not that I'm complaining. I'm just asking, is all."

"Just how old are you? You don't look old." Jenna squinted at him. "I know you have a new identity and face like me. Your file said you were thirty-five when you arrived here. Did they add a few years or take them off? I figured your birthday is incorrect. They wouldn't risk leaving that the same. They didn't on my paperwork either."

At that moment, Kane realized, he could say anything and Jenna would believe him. Their relationship must be as solid as a rock for her to trust him implicitly. He owed her the truth. "My real birthday is May twenty-eighth. I'm thirty-five now, so they added a few years. You?"

"How old do I look?" Jenna went to the back of the Beast and unclipped Duke from his harness.

Kane shrugged. "You look maybe twenty-five but you're what I call an old soul. You don't trust people, which is deep-set, but you trust me. When I look at you, my gut tells me you're in constant danger and I need to protect you."

"I'm thirty-three, Dave, and my birthday is January fifteenth. I didn't trust anyone when I arrived here but it's getting better. The team is like family and we've all got each other's backs." Jenna tossed her slicker in the back of the truck and held out a hand for his. "You've always protected me, smothered me sometimes, but we're working through it." She bit her bottom lip. "I married you because I loved you. I think I always have."

Memories came flooding back and he was standing in a pergola marrying her. The rush of love that engulfed him made his knees weak. He pulled her close and hugged her. When he pulled back, tears streamed down Jenna's cheeks. He cupped her face and wiped them away with his thumbs. "Please don't cry, Jenna. I do remember marrying you." He pressed a kiss on her forehead. "The rest will come back in time. Let's get out of here. I'm starving and it will be dark soon." He whistled to Duke and hauled him into the back seat. "Let's just hope no one else has gone missing while we've been away."

NINE

Confused didn't come close to describing Jenna's mixed emotions. After a man had stuck a gun in her face, Kane had acted just like normal and made jokes to break the tension. She dragged her mind away from worrying about his memory loss and concentrated on the evidence, or lack of it, they'd found at the house. After attaching the satellite sleeve to her phone, she called Rio and gave him the list of names Kane had discovered. "Explain the situation to them and ask if Mrs. Gilbert has contacted them recently. Ask Rowley to hunt down all the usual social media platforms and see if he can find her. She might have discussed going on a blind date or she might have mentioned who introduced her to the man. Check the dating apps most used by people in her age bracket. You might be lucky and find her. If necessary, we can always contact Bobby Kalo."

"Copy that." Rio tapped away on his keyboard. *"Are you heading back now?"*

Jenna's phone signaled an incoming call. "Yeah, I think so. I have another call. If I'm delayed, I'll call you." She disconnected and accepted the call, putting it on speaker. "What do you have for me, Shane?"

"It's a homicide and we have a match on the fingerprints. It's Dianne Gilbert." Wolfe blew out a long breath. *"Due to the possibility of missing an administered drug by waiting, I took some blood samples. It's conclusive Mrs. Gilbert was poisoned with hydrogen cyanide. I opened her up straight away and discovered she was dead when she hit the water. I believe she ingested the poison, so I'm running tests on her stomach contents. Time of death is inconclusive."*

Jenna tapped her bottom lip. "I have a witness that says he saw her leaving her house at seven-thirty last night."

"That's good to know." Wolfe cleared his throat. *"The time of death was compromised by the temperature of the water. It slows decomposition and the body had cooled to the outside temperature. So we can easily now say the time of death was between seven-thirty last night and when the forest warden reported finding her body this morning. It's a small window and surely somebody saw her around town last night. If she went on a blind date, we'll need to check the local eateries and ask if anyone has seen her. There could be a possible link to the poisoning. What about her ex-husband? We need to know their history. He might be involved."*

Jenna made notes and nodded. "Yeah, hunting him down had been my next move. Good idea about the eateries. I'm on it. I'll get a BOLO out on her vehicle as well. We're heading down the mountain now. I'll call you later, and thanks." She disconnected.

"Who is Bobby Kalo?" Kane frowned at her. "His name sounds familiar, but I don't know why."

Jenna turned to him. "He works with Carter and Jo. He's an IT whiz kid and chases down things for us at warp speed."

"Carter and Jo work together?" Kane turned onto the road heading down the mountain and onto the bridge. "I'd love to know the story of how they got together. Last I heard, Carter was off the grid after a PTSD episode."

Jenna smiled. "Yeah, they're out of Snakeskin Gully and our local FBI field office. Jo is divorced and Carter was a pain in the butt for a time but he's good now."

As they reached the center of the bridge, an ominous rumbling echoed through the ravine. A shudder rippled through the mountain and all around the trees shook. Birds sheltering from the rain took flight in great clouds, moving in opposite directions as if terrified. There had been so many extreme disasters around the world of late anything was possible. Fearing an earthquake, Jenna expected the ground to open up and send the bridge tumbling into the ravine. Heart thundering in her chest, she buzzed down her window and searched the mountainside. Trees quivered and a river of mud was inching its way through the forest and pouring over the rock face in a brown waterfall. "Mudslide." She turned to Kane. "I don't know how far away it is. The sound is echoing through the ravine. Cloud cover is blocking my view of the mountain."

"Hold on tight." Kane accelerated and the Beast's engine roared into life. "It's only just started. We'll try and beat it down the mountain or we'll be stuck here indefinitely." He hadn't taken his gaze off the narrow bridge. "Look for falling debris and animals running toward us. They'll give us the direction the landslide is heading."

Swallowing the rising panic as they hit a patch of water sending a spray over the railing on each side of the bridge, Jenna nodded. "Copy."

The noise grew louder and a herd of bison thundered down the mountainside and skidded onto the soaked blacktop, turning just in time to prevent a catastrophic fall into the ravine. The mass of steaming bodies and rolling eyes hurtled onward, flattening the bushes alongside the road. Jenna gaped in horror as the cloud of mist turned a dirty brown on the mountainside above them. The breaking and cracking of branches as trees were torn from the earth roared across the forest. "It's coming too fast. We'll never get past the herd. We'll be trapped."

"They'll be trapped too if they stay on the road." Kane peered out of the windshield. "We'll have to encourage them to go across the forest. They'll be safe if they can make it to the other side of the mountain. The mudslide is heading for the ravine going on the direction of the water."

Staring at him in disbelief, Jenna gripped the center console as Kane accelerated over the bridge and headed toward the spooked herd. "Just how do you intend to do that?"

"Lights and sirens." Kane flicked them on and the sound boomed through the ravine. "They'll want to get away from us and won't run into the ravine, so they should cut back into the forest away from the landslide."

Heart pounding, Jenna swallowed hard. "Are you sure?"

"Nope." Kane flicked her a glance. "I haven't had much to do with bison, but it's all I've got right now."

As the Beast closed in on the herd, Jenna held her breath, but just as Kane had predicted, after about two hundred yards the bison turned away from them and swept back into the forest, clearing a path on their way. They were moving fast and would be out of danger but unable to follow them in the Beast, they wouldn't be so lucky. Keeping one eye on the mountain, Jenna gasped in horror as trees tumbled and a wall of mud could be seen heading their way. Digging her fingers into the seat, she let out her breath. "We'll never outrun it. It's coming too fast."

"There's no such word as *never* in my vocabulary, Jenna." Kane slid the truck around the next bend. "Hang on, this is going to be a bumpy ride."

Ahead rocks and boulders the size of small dogs littered the blacktop. Gravel and dirt rained down on them, pinging on the roof and bouncing off the hood of the truck. All around, trees cracked and screamed as the force of the mud snapped them like twigs. Terrified by the breakneck speed Kane was pushing his truck alongside a drop to certain death, Jenna bit down hard on her bottom lip to avoid screaming. If they were going to survive, there would be no slowing down. She had to trust in Kane's skill as he swerved around the debris. As the back wheels spun, she remembered Kane's memory only went back to the day he'd taken possession of the Beast. Panic gripped her and her attention shot to him. "Please tell me you remember how to drive this truck."

"It's a bit late to ask me that now." The nerve in Kane's cheek twitched as he spun the wheel. "Unless we meet someone coming in the other direction, we'll outrun it. The road ahead looks clear, and the mudslide is heading for the ravine. I hope it hasn't taken any cabins along with it."

It would be too late for any cabins caught in its path, but the realization of what it would mean for the town hit Jenna in the pit of her stomach. "Oh my God, a torrent of water will flood the town."

Trying hard to ignore how close the wheels of the Beast came to the edge of the ravine, she grabbed her phone and, with trembling fingers, called the mayor on his direct line. "Mayor Petersham, this is Jenna Alton. We have an emergency. You'll need to clear everyone from the south end of Spring Falls Lake. A mudslide is heading down from Bear Peak and into the ravine. It will send a wall of water toward that part of town."

"I'll activate emergency protocol." Petersham was calm and in control. "Where are you, Sheriff?"

As Kane swerved, skidding the back tires around another bolder, Jenna took a deep breath to steady her nerves. "I'm on the mountain with the mudslide on my tail. I'll call it in and get my people out to help evacuate the townsfolk."

"God be with you." He disconnected.

After Jenna called it in, the blacktop ahead looked normal

apart from the deluge rushing across the road. She turned in her seat to stare behind them and then turned back to look at Kane. "You're right as usual. The mudslide is heading into the ravine. I hope it won't cause too much of a problem downstream."

"The ravine is very deep and wide. I figure we're looking at an initial surge as the mudslide hits the river but the pressure from the falls will soon open up a path for the water." Kane flicked her a glance. "Do many people live in the vicinity of Spring Falls Lake?"

Relaxing her grip on the seat a little, she shook her head. "Not a great many homes, but there are cabins all through the forest and there'll be increased local flooding." She wet her dry lips, suddenly able to breathe again. "The mayor sounds an alarm when people need to evacuate the forest in a hurry. It's usually for fires. Mayor Petersham will get the word out. Messages are sent to all the residents' phones and a warning is issued on the TV and radio stations." The noise behind them continued and she turned around and looked behind them again. "I hope no one was injured in the forest, but I doubt anyone would be out in this weather. There are cabins up there all over, but not many people live there permanently. Most live out of Bison Ridge. I guess they believe serial killers won't cross the bridge." She smiled at him. "Search and rescue will be activated and they'll have choppers up as soon as it's safe. It's all part of the evacuation plan."

"That's good to know." Kane gave her a sideways glance. "I had another jolt of memory when the mud wall came through the trees. Like déjà vu. Like before when you were there but different, I had my back up against a boulder. I figured it was from my time in service, on account of my sniper rifle."

Not wanting to relive that particular nightmare again, Jenna paused a beat to keep her voice neutral. "Yeah, that happened just up there a ways. Duke was digging your sorry ass out of a rockslide. He saved you, and without him, I'd never have found you. Duke is one special dog and tore up his paws getting you out. He never left your side, even when you took a shower. I guess he figures you shouldn't be trusted out alone."

"I have a wife, a dog, and a handler watching my back. How sweet is that?" Kane smiled at her. "Are you always so calm in an emergency?" They'd reached the end of the road and he turned onto Stanton. "Beautiful, smart, and calm in a crisis. You're one in a million, that's for darn sure."

Nerves shattered and trembling, Jenna laughed off the compliment. It seemed so out of character. Kane rarely verbalized his feelings toward her and the old Kane would never have mentioned the fact he considered Poppy Anderson attractive. He usually played his cards close to the vest. Was this a part of his old life emerging, the part he'd kept hidden?

His memory of her must still be fuzzy because she'd never been hysterical—not ever—and he should know that about her. Although, the past few minutes had shaken her more than she'd like to admit. *If only he knew.* "Seems to me, you're the one watching everyone's backs, Dave. I put my trust in you to keep us safe and you've never let me down yet."

TEN

Excited and a little nervous that evening, Shelby O'Connor drove into the entrance of the Triple Z Roadhouse to meet Julian and made a big loop of the massive parking lot searching for his vehicle. Trucks of every description were parked in rows, and she drove past each line until she caught sight of a white Yukon. She pulled in behind it and peered up at the massive trucks on each side of her like steel walls. Not sure if she should climb out of her vehicle or just wait for him to come to her, she sat for a few seconds staring out of the window. It was still raining and her wiper blades moved back and forth, blurring the image as a man climbed out of the truck wearing a slicker and cowboy hat. He gave her a wave and walked toward her. She buzzed down her window, eager to see him in person. "Hi, Julian. It's good weather for ducks, isn't it?"

Just at that second her manager's ringtone played on her phone. She gave Julian an apologetic shrug. "I'm sorry. I have to take this. It's the ranch manager."

She listened to some excuse he'd given her about an order for hay and sighed. "That's why I pay you the big bucks. Just deal with it. I've no idea why you're asking me. I've never ordered hay in my life." She disconnected and looked out of the window at Julian. "I'm sorry. I have no idea why he's bothering me at this time of night."

"I'll take your bag." Julian flashed her a white smile. "Why don't you leave the phone behind. I'm sure he can manage without you for a day or so. I wouldn't like him to spoil our time together." He opened her door and offered his hand. "I parked here to shelter us from the rain."

Nodding, Shelby turned off her phone and tossed it onto the passenger seat. She grabbed her overnight bag and took his hand. "It's so great to meet you in person at last."

"Your social media image doesn't do you justice." Julian took the bag and led her to his truck.

As she got into his vehicle, she gave him a sideways glance. The bushy beard and dark-rimmed spectacles made him look super smart. In a nerdy handsome type of way. "I feel like I'm sixteen again and on my first date." She giggled. "Although I don't recall taking an overnight bag on my first date."

They arrived at the ranch-style home twenty minutes later. She'd been flattered by his questions about her life. He was very attentive and acted like the perfect gentleman. She had expected a bare-bones interior but found the home fully furnished. After shucking her raincoat, she looked around the spacious family room and then turned to him. "This is a beautiful house. The furnishings are nice. Why would you want to go to the expense of changing them?"

"These are other people's memories." Julian shrugged and took her hand. "I want fresh ones. I want this place to be somewhere I can call home." He led her into the kitchen. "Before our dinner arrives, do you want a glass of wine and then we can get the business out of the way? When we spoke earlier, I could hear by your voice that you're anxious to finalize matters and I want you to have a relaxing time with me. Once everything is in place, we can spend the rest of the time enjoying ourselves. I don't want finances to be the elephant in the room while I'm with you."

"Me neither." Shelby pulled a small notebook out of her purse and sat down at the kitchen table. "I have all of my account numbers and passwords in this book. When my husband died my lawyer suggested I keep everything in one place so I could keep track. I have an accountant that overseas our books for the ranch, but I keep that separate from my personal finances."

"Well after tonight you won't have to keep track of anything." Julian held out his hand for the notebook. "You'll have my personal attention. You'll be surprised at just how much money you make in a very short time. By this time next week, I'll be able to show you our profits. It's up to you if you want these filtered into one of your accounts or, to avoid taxation, I can set you up with a separate cryptocurrency account, which you can use to buy anything you need. More and more companies are accepting cryptocurrency now. If you need an amount transferred back into cash, I can do that for you in the blink of an eye. When banking is done online, it's instant." He winked at her. "One of my clients is a bank clerk and she had no idea how much money she could make until I explained." He chuckled. "She nearly choked on the amount when I told her."

Eyes wide with amazement, Shelby stared at him. She couldn't believe he was offering to manage her fortune without asking a fee. It was so generous of him she couldn't believe her luck. "I have all the money I need from the ranch. Is it possible to leave everything in your account to just grow bigger? You'll know when to pull the pin when the time is right."

"I will indeed." Julian smiled at her and opened his laptop. "This won't take too long at all." He tapped away on the keypad, flicking his gaze to the notebook every so often. "I've closed all your accounts because they just attract fees. I'll open new ones for you the moment you want to withdraw your funds from my account." He took a pen from his inside pocket and put a line through the account numbers. "There you go. The only account remaining is the one fed by the income from the ranch. Now you are my silent partner. Welcome to the world of the rich and incognito." He laughed. "You should do a ceremonial cutting up of your credit cards. It's goodbye to high taxes and the start of enjoying life without being overseen by Big Brother." He poured two glasses of wine and handed one to her. "Let's drink to our future together." He raised his glass and took a tiny sip.

After finishing three glasses of superb wine, Shelby had relaxed maybe a little too much. She could hardly keep her eyes open. "I hope dinner won't be too much longer. Any more of this delicious wine and I'll be asleep. I'll go and wash my face. Where's the bathroom?"

"We have only one right now but I'm planning on adding another to the master bedroom. It's down the end of the hallway to the right." Julian stood. "Do you want me to show you?"

Shelby smiled at him. "No, I'll be fine. Do you think the caterer has gotten lost?"

"I hope not but the weather is causing havoc in town right now. The news mentioned a mudslide and it pushed a wall of water downtown." Julian took the glasses to the sink, washed them, and meticulously dried them on a paper towel. "It's white wine with dinner."

Lightheaded and feeling happy, Shelby made her way down the long hallway. The house was spread out over one level. The footprint large and sprawling. She used the spacious bathroom with twin basins. It seemed untidy for a newly purchased home. Most she'd visited were pristine and every surface polished or cleaned. Surprise followed quickly by suspicion raised its ugly head at the array of hurriedly discarded women's toiletries on the vanity, and a cup holding four toothbrushes. She opened the cabinet above the sink to find every shelf filled to capacity.

People wouldn't leave behind medication and other assorted items when they sold a house—unless they'd died. Her inquisitive side got the best of her and she moved silently down the hallway and opened one of the doors. Inside was a typical teenager's room. The dressing table mirror held photographs of teenagers at a football game, all grinning at the camera. Posters of bands covered the walls. The bed was unmade and a teenage girl's clothes littered every surface. A backpack spilling school books stuck out from under the bed. Julian hadn't mentioned having children and seeing what was obviously a girl's bedroom concerned her.

Heart pounding but determined to discover what the heck was going on she backed out of the room and closed the door silently behind her. Without hesitation, she crept along the hallway, testing doors and peering inside. Sure, this was the ultimate in snooping, but Julian had given her the impression they had a future together, so what was with the family he'd neglected to mention? The linen closet was full, and taking a deep breath, she reached the next room and turned the handle. The door opened silently and she peeked inside. This room belonged to a school-age boy. A TV sat opposite the end of the bed, beside it a stack of games piled up beside a games console. Stuck on the mirror of a closet was a calendar with the word *vacation* spelled out in capital letters across two weeks—starting the previous weekend. It was obvious the kids were away. She turned to look at the photographs on the shelves beside the window. Images of a young boy with his dirt bike, another dressed in football gear, a shot with his sister and a couple. She moved closer and stared at the couple. The man in the picture, with a remarkable resemblance to the young boy, was not Julian Darnley.

The egg of uncertainty emerged into a full-grown maggot and Shelby's stomach cramped with uncertainty. Had Julian purchased a house from a family recently killed or—worse—

murdered? Or was he playing her for a fool? She slipped out of the room and headed farther down the passageway. It didn't take long to find the master bedroom. She froze in the doorway, sure she'd seen a face at the window. It had been a fleeting glance of someone with their head covered. Staring at the window, heart pounding, she waited but no movement came from outside and only rain spilled down the windowpane. Stepping inside the perfume-scented room, she scanned the photographs on the nightstand. Pictures of a pretty woman holding a baby, family portraits—and Julian was missing from all of them. Panic gripped her. Had she just transferred her entire fortune to a scammer? Leaning her back to the wall, she listened for footfalls in the hallway. Terrified of being discovered snooping, she peeked out of the door. The way was clear but what was she going to do now? She couldn't just tell him she changed her mind and ask him to take her home. He already had her money. Trying to steady her nerves, and make her brain work through the haze of alcohol, she straightened and headed back along the hallway. Her only choice was to go to the authorities and make a complaint against him. First, she needed to get as far away from him as possible. She touched the pocket of her jeans where she usually kept her phone and came up empty. Fear gripped her stomach. He'd driven her and with no phone she had no means of escape. She allowed her mind to drift back to the master bedroom. No, there hadn't been a phone beside the bed. In fact, she hadn't noticed a landline anywhere inside the house. She wet her dry lips and walked slowly back to the kitchen. For now, she'd have to bluff her way through, perhaps pretend to be sick—anything to get away from him. Her only hope would be to ask the delivery driver for a lift back to town.

"Shelby." Julian's voice drifted from out of the kitchen. "Are you okay?"

Pressing a hand to her head, Shelby stood at the kitchen door. "I have the most dreadful headache. It's probably drinking on an empty stomach. I really need some fresh air. I'll just step out on the porch for a while."

"It's raining." Darnley gave her a quizzical stare. "I don't have an umbrella."

The certainty that this wasn't his home hit Shelby like a sledgehammer. She had noticed more than one umbrella stuck into a tall ceramic pot in the mudroom when they'd arrived. Had Julian broken into this house just to make her believe he owned a home in Black Rock Falls or had he brought her here for some other reason? It wasn't to seduce her, that was for sure. He'd kept a good distance away from her the entire time. His only interest had been transferring her funds into his account. "I'll just stand under the eaves. I'll be fine. It's only for a few minutes. It is so stuffy in here and I'm allergic to something in the potpourri you have on the table in the hallway."

"Okay." Julian smiled at her. "Don't get cold. Maybe you should wear a jacket your arms are bare." He hurried out of the kitchen and returned moments later and opened the front door for her. "The delivery driver should be here soon. Perhaps when you've had something to eat, you'll feel better."

Shelby wanted to leave right now but nodded. "Yes, I hope so. It would be a shame to spoil our weekend together."

As Julian moved with her toward the door, she turned and looked at him. She forced herself to relax and take a nonchalant pose. "I'll be fine. Why don't you set the table? I'll be right here, just outside the door."

"Sure." Julian gave her a stiff smile. His eyes flashed with something that could only be described as anger.

The look he gave her sent chills up her spine. Suddenly afraid, she waited for him to turn away, slipped out of the front door, and headed to a pathway on the side of the house closest to the driveway. Rain soaked through her clothes in seconds and she stopped to shelter under the eaves. Pressing her back against the red brick wall, she stared around, searching for another house. In the distance she made out the sound of a vehicle heading toward her. After a few moments, headlights lit up the driveway. A man wearing a slicker and rubber boots climbed out carrying a few bags. He went to the door and Shelby listened as Julian greeted him and ushered him inside.

"Shelby, where are you?" Julian stood on the front porch looking in both directions. He cussed almost silently but she heard him. "Stupid woman. Why did you have to make it so complicated? Now I'm going to get wet searching for you." He raised his voice into a singsong tone. "Shelby, where are you? Dinner is getting cold. Come out, come out, wherever you are."

Footsteps sounded on the driveway as Julian headed in her direction. Gripped by panic, Shelby ran along the side of the house but her heels dug deep into the rain-soaked gravel, slowing her down. She rounded the first corner but Julian was gaining on her. She stumbled over flowerpots alongside the backdoor and dashed around the next corner, making it just as his footsteps increased to a run. He'd seen her. As she ran back toward the front of the house, the delivery man stepped out of the front door. Sobbing with relief, Shelby ran to him. "Can you give me a ride back to town?"

"You must be Shelby." The man had her by the arms. His fingernails dug into her flesh and his mouth stretched into a grin. He glanced over her shoulder as Julian's footsteps came up behind them. "I have her. She ran straight to me."

"You've made it so easy for me, Shelby." Julian's breath was warm on her soaked cheek. "You had everything, but it was never enough, was it? Now you have nothing—not even a life to look forward to. I don't need a partner. I already have one. Now all I have to do is kill you."

Furious, Shelby tried to twist away to give Julian a piece of her mind. "I'll go to the cops. You won't get away with this."

"Won't I?" Julian chuckled. "Now, let me see."

Something fell over her head and tightened around her

neck. So tight, she couldn't take a breath. Struggling, she fought like a wild woman, but the delivery man's steel-like grip held her tight. As the cord bit deep into her flesh, she opened her mouth wide, trying to suck in air. Darkness crept into her vision and her knees buckled. She stared at the deliveryman's face, willing him to help her. She opened her eyes wide, but her sight had faded. Black spots filled her vision. Why was this man refusing to help her? She stared into his eyes, wanting the answer to her question, but he just stared into her face and smiled.

ELEVEN

The storm was relentless, and Jenna filled the last bag from the pile of sand dumped buy a truck earlier. Back aching and fingers stiff, she passed the bag to Kane and leaned back, stretching her muscles, ignoring the rain soaking her face. It was a little after nine and they had worked nonstop since arriving back in town. Alongside the townsfolk and emergency services personnel, they'd built a retaining wall to divert the floodwater threatening the town into the lowlands. The area was so vast the water would dissipate quickly. Working by streetlight, every able man and woman worked side by side until the job was completed. When Kane returned to her side, soaked through to the skin and as pale as a ghost, she grabbed his arm and led him along Main and into Aunt Betty's Café. She gave the manager, Susie Hartwig, a wave as they went to their reserved table at the back. She grabbed a pot of coffee and headed their way. Shucking her wet slicker, Jenna sat down with a sigh and looked at Kane. "Do you recall this place?"

"Aunt Betty's Café." Kane smiled at her. "Best apple pie in the West." He took the paper towel Susie handed him with a smile and dried his face. "Thanks." She glanced around. "No Duke tonight?"

"He's out in the truck." Kane chuckled. "Water is enemy number one." He placed a massive order and leaned back in his chair. "I read about this place before I arrived. The reviews are all five stars. I figure it has to be good." He piled sugar and cream into the cup of coffee Susie had poured him, sipped, and sighed with contentment. "The coffee is great."

Disappointed, Jenna nodded and added the fixings to her cup. "You practically live here. Although, at home you do most of the cooking. I'm pretty good at burning toast, although I can make an omelet if push comes to shove."

"Uh-huh." Kane studied her face for a long time as if trying to remember and then gave his head a little shake. "I know about the toast, Jenna. There are bits and pieces coming back. Considering it's only been ten hours or so, I think I'm recovering pretty well." He covered her hand and gave it a little squeeze. "Don't worry. I'm going to be okay. I am a little fuzzy about what happened the last time I lost my memory. It wasn't after the car bombing. I recall everything just fine after that. Wolfe mentioned being shot in the head in the line of duty. How long did it take for me to recover?"

"I can't really remember. A couple of weeks maybe." Jenna didn't really want to remember that time. She'd believed Kane had left Black Rock Falls and returned to his life in the military. She didn't know where he was or what was happening to him. Somehow, she'd managed to get to see him and he'd asked her to bring him home. "Nothing I can tell you about that time will help you now. I think it's best we just keep moving forward. Wolfe believes everything will come back as soon as the morning. How does your head feel? You're sheet white. Have you been taking the meds for your headache?"

"Yeah, I took some pills, but just like you, I'm cold and hungry." Kane took another long drink of his coffee. "It's been a very long time since breakfast. You're pale as well, and you have shadows under your eyes, but I'm not surprised. You've worked so hard. I can't believe you filled sandbags nonstop without a break for the last three hours straight."

Jenna snorted. "I'm expected to lead by example. Now that I'm sure everyone is safe, I can worry about us. In case it slipped your mind, we haven't finished yet. If we make it home through the floodwater, we have the horses to tend. They must be wondering what's happened to us." She leaned back as Susie arrived with their meals. "Then I guess we'll be up half the night chasing down information in the current homicide case. I'll need to be up to date by the morning's briefing. We have suspects to hunt down and people to interview. I hope the team made some headway while we were avoiding a mudslide."

"Whoa." Kane lifted a forkful of prime rib to his mouth, sighed, chewed, and swallowed. "If I recall, you sent the team out to evacuate the townsfolk caught up in the floods. Since then, they've been working nonstop to save the town. I don't figure they've made much of a headway in the case this afternoon." He took another bite and then looked at her again. "We do only what's necessary. Tend the horses, feed the animals, have a long hot shower, and get some sleep. Everything else can wait for the morning when we're clearheaded and rested." He shrugged. "If you keep pushing yourself at this rate, Jenna, you'll suffer from burnout and then thinking straight and reasoning suffers. This makes solving a case difficult. You have a highly trained team around you. I'm sure over the time we've been together, you've delegated various parts of the investigation to different members of your team." He shook his head slowly. "You can't continue to carry the entire burden yourself."

Rolling her eyes, Jenna took in the part stranger beside her. Yeah, he was Dave, her husband, but the man she'd first met out on a highway in the middle of winter—the Secret Service straight-down-the-line pain in the ass—was hovering just under the surface. At the time, it was obvious that Kane wanted to be anywhere but in Black Rock Falls. He'd been used to being in charge. Coming to a backwoods town and finding who he believed to be a twenty-five-year-old inexperienced sheriff as his boss must have taken a lot of getting used to. "Let it go, Dave. I'm exhausted."

"You know I'm right." Kane shrugged. "Or are you too darn stubborn to admit it?"

Bristling, Jenna lowered her voice so only he could hear. "We'll be just fine as long as you stop telling me what to do. We've solved many crimes as a team—a team, Dave, and I do delegate." She met his gaze. "You had the same attitude when you arrived. You didn't have confidence in my leadership and it showed. To you, I was a woman who needed protection." She stabbed her finger into the table. "Since I arrived, I've been to hell and back so many times I've been given a free pass. Trust me, I'm the sheriff because I earned it."

"I admire that about you, Jenna." Kane smiled around his cup as he eyed her over the rim. "You say what you think. Now, if you'll allow me to take my foot out of my mouth, ma'am, I figure I'll try some of the apple pie."

TWELVE
TUESDAY

Hail pelted the windows as Kane stretched and opened his eyes. He stared into the dim light, one hand moving across the bed in search of Jenna. The sheets beside him were cold. Rolling over, he blinked. It was after six and he'd never slept past five in years. He scanned the room and scratched his chin. Why was he sleeping in one of the spare bedrooms? He sat up and pain shot through his head like an ax. Something had happened and he'd blanked it out. *This can't be good.*

Concerned he done something to upset Jenna to be banned from her bed, he turned on the bedside lamp and, seeing his meds, took a couple and then headed out of the door. Making his way straight to the master bedroom, he took a deep breath and knocked on the door. "Jenna. Can I come in?"

"Yeah." Jenna sounded sleepy. "I'm awake. I've been up for hours checking the weather alerts. There's local flooding but no one is in immediate danger."

Kane had no idea what she was talking about. He walked inside and stood beside the bed looking down at her tousled hair and drawn expression. She always had a smile for him even when she was cranky. His gut tightened and he stared at his hands before meeting her gaze. "Okay, what did I do? Did I have a flashback or something? Why am I sleeping in the spare room and why is my head aching? Did someone hit me and I lost it? Please don't tell me I hurt you? I don't remember a thing about last night. If I've suddenly turned violent, handcuff me to the porch and call Shane." He looked around. His bloodhound was missing. "Holy cow, even Duke has deserted me."

"Okay. Calm down. You haven't hurt anyone and nobody hit you, Dave. Duke went out the doggy door about five minutes ago. He hasn't left you. He won't be long. I hear thunder in the distance." Jenna sat up pushing the hair from her face and yawned. "Do you recall when we got Pumpkin?"

Confused Kane frowned. What did their cat have to do with his headache and banishment to the spare room? "I feel as if I've walked into another dimension. That question is irrelevant, Jenna. What the heck is going on?"

"Everything is okay now, so stop worrying." Jenna patted the bed beside her. "Sit down. I'm testing your memory, is all. Now answer the question."

He sat down and stared at her. She was looking at him warily. Had he done something to frighten her? Something was wrong, that was for darn sure. Too worried to touch her, he swallowed his concern and nodded. "Of course, I remember Pumpkin. It was Halloween, and she arrived here covered in blood. After we found a bloodbath at the Old Mitcham Ranch."

"Okay and what day is it?" Jenna took both his hands. "Date and year too, if you don't mind."

Fearing the worse, Kane studied her face. She didn't appear to be worried, more elated than anything. "It's Monday." He gave her the date. "Oh, now I'm getting déjà vu. Did I dream the perimeter alarm sounded and I went out in a storm to check the boundary fences?"

"It's Tuesday and, yes, you did go and check the fences yesterday. A bison broke through the gate and then was hit by lightning, but Wolfe called someone reliable to fix it for us because we were busy with a case. He had the bison taken away as well. It's all fixed and nothing to worry about." Jenna squeezed his hands. "Think now, can you remember everything back to when you came here?"

Still trying to fathom how he'd lost a day, he nodded. "Yeah, every gruesome detail and our honeymoon disaster in Florida. Now what happened on Monday?"

"I'll tell you over breakfast." Jenna flashed him a brilliant smile, leaned forward, and kissed him. "I put the coffee on before, but I thought I'd leave you to sleep. It was an exhausting day yesterday."

Kane made breakfast and listened to his missing day. Pumpkin rubbed around his legs, waiting for a tidbit of bacon. "It sounds as if I acted like a real jerk." He slid stacked plates onto the table and sat down opposite her. "Is that why you sent me to the spare room?"

"That was your idea." Jenna's mouth twitched up at the corners. "You being you, and not quite recalling our wedding day... well, it wasn't appropriate in your mind, I guess." She chuckled. "You confused the heck out of Duke."

As if on cue, the doggy flap in the back door slapped shut and Duke bounded into the utility room and shook, sending water flying in all directions, his long ears windmilling. When he'd finished, he stared at Kane with a wide doggy grin. Kane stood and grabbed a towel from a hook by the door. "You must have been desperate to go out in rain like this." He rubbed him all over and smiled when Duke licked his cheek. "It's all good. I'm back now. You've been such a good boy." When Duke whined, he glanced at Jenna. "Did you remember to feed him?" He went to the sink and washed his hands to remove the eau de dog.

"No, I let him starve to death." Jenna snorted. "Can't you see how skinny he is?" She nibbled on a strip of bacon. "Those rolls of fat are just hiding his ribs." She grinned at him. "As if I'd forget Duke. His kibble feeder is full to the brim. That's just an act to get more snacks, is all." She sighed. "I'm so glad you're back, Dave. I didn't like the other you. It was like being with a twin... a stubborn hard-nosed sarcastic twin who was pretending to love me. It was kinda spooky." She finished her coffee and stood collecting plates. "We're running late this morning. The horses need tending. We were so exhausted last night we hardly had enough energy to feed them." She rinsed the dishes and stacked them in the dishwasher. "We'll leave extra feed just in case we get held up again. Not that we really need to worry too much. We're very high here and, worst-case scenario, if we can't drive home, we'll ask Wolfe to drop us in from the chopper."

"Getting back to me acting kinda spooky..." Kane scratched his stubble. "Yeah, I know when I arrived I was a little tense but I've mellowed some since, haven't I?" He slipped his arms around her waist. "It was a big change for me. I'm military born and bred. Being in charge of missions and protecting people with my body is what I'm trained to do. It's who I am at my core, and what I fall back into, I guess. Maybe it's my safe place. Anyway, I'm sure glad you didn't give up on me, Jenna."

"Never." She giggled. "Did you really want me to handcuff you to the porch railing? I had images of you turning into a werewolf or something."

Relieved, she'd forgiven him, Kane nodded. "I've never gone batshit crazy, but it's been known to happen with head injuries, and PTSD is a nasty thing to suffer, as you know. If I do act out of character again, tie me up and call Wolfe."

"Oh, sure." Jenna raised both eyebrows. "Me... tie you up... if you go crazy? Good luck with that. You'd kill me and you know it."

Kane shook his head. "I doubt it. If you ordered me to stand down. I'd likely obey you. Anyway, you know darn well I don't hurt anyone who doesn't deserve it."

"Now you're sounding like a serial killer." Jenna stared dramatically into his eyes and then laughed. "Where is Dave and what have you done with him?"

Rain pelted down in an unrelenting torrent as they drove to the office. Kane listened to the weather warnings on the radio and took in the water surging alongside the road and overflowing into the lowlands. The weather event had hit hard and unexpected after a drier than usual summer. It was as if the world had turned upside down. With reports of snow in Texas and wildfires in California, it seemed that no one was safe from the peculiar weather conditions. Not being able to recall visiting Bison Ridge or outrunning a mudslide, he understood why his muscles ached. Hauling sandbags for hours the previous evening does that to a person. He glanced at Jenna. "Give me everything you have on the current case." After Jenna explained, he frowned. "Cyanide, huh? That's not something you can pick up at the general store."

"Exactly. I figure we should drop by Wolfe's office first. He might have more information by now. Knowing him, he'd have spent half the night working." Jenna was scrolling through the file of updates from her deputies. "Rowley and Rio are updating the files, so they're already at the office. It was a late night for everyone. I can trust Rio to handle any incoming information, and with Rowley and Anderson on the hotline, our time is better spent chasing down information." She pulled out her phone. "I'll call in and tell them we'll be in later."

Kane nodded and turned onto the highway leading to town. Evidence of the wall of water that had rushed through town was everywhere. Mud covered parts of the blacktop and every fence they passed was strewn with grass and other debris. Dirty water covered the lowlands as far as the eye could see. The highway was elevated with deep gullies on either side all the way from Black Rock Falls to Blackwater, but in the distance he made out road closure signs. The river running from one town to the other had burst its banks, and until the rain stopped, Black Rock Falls would be isolated from the rest of the county. From the weather forecast, that wasn't going to happen anytime soon. "It seems to me our town was lucky to avoid major flooding after the mudslide."

"Yeah, it's amazing how the townsfolk come together in an emergency." Jenna looked up from her iPad. "I don't recall ever seeing so many people out in the pouring rain when we were building that retaining wall. How does Rio know that stuff? I mean he just took charge and was directing everyone. He moved into action immediately after I called him and he had very little time to divert the water away from town."

Kane shrugged. "He retains a ton of knowledge. I guess he must have read it somewhere and I'm sure glad he did." He smiled at her. "I can't believe you managed to get Mayor Petersham to spring into action so fast. From my experience with him, if he hasn't gotten ten signatures on a piece of paper, he doesn't make a move."

"Oh, I can be pretty persuasive when I have to." Jenna grinned. "Although I didn't have too much luck with Duke this morning, did I? When I opened the front door, he took one look at the pouring rain and decided to go back to bed. He must have waited until he was fit to bust to go outside. I'm surprised he wanted to come with us today."

Water pooled in the road outside the ME's office and Kane drove around to the back entrance and parked under cover beside Wolfe's van. "If I'd had the choice, I figure I would have gone back to bed too. Duke will be fine in the Beast. It's under cover and he'll feel safer than in Wolfe's office. He'll sleep while we're away. I guess being dragged around in the rain yesterday, with someone who didn't recognize him disturbed him. He kept looking at me this morning as if I'd forgotten to do something." He turned in his seat and gave Duke's ears a rub. "Stay here, we'll be back soon." He tucked a blanket around the dog and Duke let out a long sigh. "See, he's good."

"Aw, look he's asleep already. He was so pleased to see you this morning. Animals are very forgiving." Jenna collected her things. "Let's hope Wolfe has something for us." She slid from the truck and headed for the back door.

THIRTEEN

Wolfe glanced up from his computer screen at the sound of footsteps coming down the tiled hallway outside his office. It wasn't his daughter Emily or assistant Colt Webber. They were busy in the lab. He recognized the voices and stood to slide coffee pods into his coffeemaking machine. It was a miserable day outside and Jenna and Kane would appreciate a hot beverage. He set the cups under the machine just as they reached his door. "Hey there, what brings you here at this time of the morning?" Concerned, he examined Kane's expression. "How are you feeling this morning, Dave?"

"I'm fine." Kane removed his hat and dropped into a chair. "I can't remember yesterday but everything else is back. Jenna explained about the amnesia and the fact I turned into an ass. Do I need to apologize to you for anything I did yesterday?"

Wolfe added fixings to the cups and placed them on the table. "No, but don't be surprised if yesterday doesn't come back at all. It's very common not to remember a traumatic head injury. I believe you've suffered two types of amnesia, one is from the electric shock, which I considered would be very short term. The other is called anterograde amnesia, when a person is unable to form memories for a time after a traumatic injury." He smiled at Kane. "Your brain was working on autopilot. It didn't like what was happening, considered it too traumatic for you to cope with, so erased it." He opened his hands wide. "Don't worry about it. Unless you start having blackouts, you'll be fine, and the chances of that are minimal. You had a shock, is all. It happens to the best of us." He looked at Jenna. "I'm glad you dropped by. I wanted to discuss my findings with you. I stayed on the case until late and it was worth it."

"Yeah, that's why we're here." Jenna picked up her cup and sipped. "Although, I might wish I had—what was it?—antero- grade amnesia? I'm sure going to have nightmares about driving down the mountain yesterday with a mudslide on our tail, now I know that Dave was on autopilot." She gave Kane a look of horror. "We could have been killed."

"Unlikely." Kane grinned at her. "I figure I'm on autopilot every time I drop into the zone. You should be used to it by now." He poked her in the ribs and Jenna slapped his hand away. "One thing for sure. Life with me isn't boring."

Enjoying the byplay between his friends, Wolfe cleared his throat. "Getting back to the case. If your files have been updated this morning, you'll know Rio hunted down Dianne Gilbert's ex-husband and a cousin late last night. As we had a positive ID and you were out sandbagging the town, I contacted them with the bad news this morning."

"I checked some of the files on the way here." Jenna leaned forward in her chair. "I didn't get Rio's notes about the next of kin. The ex-husband is usually the prime suspect in a murder case. Where exactly is Mr. Gilbert?"

Wolfe went to his keyboard and brought up the relevant information. "Alaska. There's absolutely no way he's involved. Her cousin, Jack Sutherland out of Miles Street, East Meadow, Blackwater is a mechanic at the local gas station. He was heading to work when I called and was out most of the night as a search-and-rescue volunteer evacuating people isolated by the floods. I can't see how he can possibly be involved, with the highway being closed and all."

"You said the victim was poisoned with cyanide and you believed it was consumed." Jenna sipped her coffee. "Have you had time to analyze the stomach contents yet?"

"I have." Wolfe smiled at her. "The stomach contents were partly digested, which would indicate that she died within twenty minutes of ingesting the poison. The poison is an interesting concoction and I'm very surprised it was able to be disguised in the meal. The killer used ground peach pits mixed with a good deal of sugar and coconut. However, I would imagine the resulting mixture would have been extremely bitter. Which makes me wonder if the victim only consumed the meal to please her killer."

"The home-cooked meal from hell." Kane placed his coffee cup on the table with a sigh. "We know she went on a blind date. Now we know she went to her killer's home for dinner."

"Is there any indication on the body to discover where she was put into the river?" Jenna was making notes. "Or anything on the playing card we found on the body?"

Wolfe shook his head. "I'm sorry, all the swabs we collected only indicated she'd been in the water from that particular river. The scrapes on her body could easily be consistent with being washed down the mountain. I examined her and found no other trauma to cause her death. There are no signs of sexual activity. Although, I'm convinced the scrapes on her knees and the swollen ligaments to her right ankle could be the result of running away from her killer. The other unusual injury are the scratches on her lower back. This could indicate she was dragged to the river. I found small fragments of pine needles and soil embedded in the flesh."

"Was she alive when they tossed her in the river?" Jenna's forehead creased into a frown.

Shaking his head, Wolfe met her concerned gaze. "Nope, but she would have experienced considerable pain from the effects of the cyanide poisoning. It's not a very nice way to die." He leaned back in his chair. "I'll send you a full report."

"Thanks." Jenna's phone chimed. "It's Rio. I'll put the phone on speaker. Hi, Rio. Problem?"

"I'm not sure. We just had a call on the 911 line. The manager of the Triple Z Roadhouse said one of the drivers found a woman's body in a vehicle in the parking lot—over where the trucks hole up overnight. Do you want me to drop by and take a look?"

Jenna stared into space thinking. "No, you keep on hunting down social media friends of Dianne Gilbert. Wolfe said she was poisoned with cyanide. It was added to a meal, so someone is out there killing their blind dates. Concentrate on dating sites and see if she makes any mention about going on a date in her posts. Anyone spotted her vehicle yet?"

"Nope, but we have a plate number, so I've sent that out with a media release this morning."

Pleased that Rio always took the initiative, she smiled. "Thanks. Okay, we'll head out to the Triple Z Roadhouse with Wolfe now. Let's just hope this one died from natural causes." She disconnected.

Jenna glanced at Kane. He obviously didn't have any other questions for Wolfe. She smiled at him. "Another perfect day in paradise, huh?"

FOURTEEN

Jenna tucked her hair inside the hood of her slicker, pulled on gloves, and followed Kane through the group of people surrounding a pickup truck. As Kane moved through the crowd, taking people's names and speaking to the man who'd discovered the body, she approached the vehicle. Close behind her, Wolfe, Emily, and Colt Webber pushed a gurney over the rough ground. Rain lashed her hood, making pitter-patter noises in her ears. The rain was coming down so hard it was difficult to see inside the vehicle. She stood to one side as Wolfe approached. Having the medical examiner on scene was a bonus. His quick eye and forensic experience would give her an evaluation of the body before anyone contaminated evidence. She turned as Kane approached her with a man at his side. "Is this the guy who found the body?"

"Yeah. This is Collin Howard he's out of Talbot Street, Wild Springs, and on his way south. He spent the night here and was on his way out this morning when he noticed the body in the vehicle." Kane folded his notebook and pushed it inside his pocket. "No one noticed the vehicle when they arrived last night. The crowd is made up of people staying at the motel and the housekeeping staff. None of them noticed it in the rain this morning either."

The man was in his late forties and his disgruntled expression was enhanced by the water dripping off the end of his nose. Jenna gave him a nod. "How come you noticed the body in this weather? I can't see a thing through the windows."

"It wasn't raining when I came out earlier." Howard shrugged. "It wasn't too difficult to see she was dead. Not with the staring eyes and the blue complexion. I called 911 and then went inside to tell the proprietor. I've been standing by my truck for the last forty minutes waiting for someone to arrive. I hope this isn't going to hold me up any longer. I'm hoping the highway will be open to Blackwater soon."

Nodding, Jenna glanced at the pickup. "Then there's no rush. It's still closed due to flooding and it's only going to get worse. Did you touch anything? Anything at all. We need to know to eliminate you from any trace evidence we find on the vehicle or body."

"Me touch that?" Howard pulled a disgusted face. "No way. One look at her was enough to give me nightmares for the rest of my life."

Understanding the man's concern, Jenna nodded. "Seeing a corpse isn't pleasant for anyone. What time did you arrive last night?"

"Six." Howard wiped his face on the sleeve of his slicker. "Before you ask, no the pickup wasn't here when I arrived, but I remember the other eighteen-wheeler. It was here before me."

"I have his details." Kane moved closer. "I've checked his ID and run his plates. He's who he says he is. I figure we can cut him loose."

Satisfied, Jenna nodded. "Okay, thank you, Mr. Howard. If we need anything more, we'll be in touch. We have your details." She turned away and went to stand beside Wolfe and peer through the open door of the pickup. "What have we got?"

"Homicide." Wolfe turned to her and raised both eyebrows. "She has a cord tied around her neck."

Jenna moved closer to the open door of the vehicle and gagged at the smell wafting out. Any ID?"

"Yeah." Wolfe handed Jenna a purse. "From the driver's license, this is Shelby O'Connor out of Wild Plains Ranch. If the driver said the vehicle wasn't here at six, then found the body this morning, from evidence we can place the time of death between six last night and when Howard made the 911 call, but I'll be able to get closer if she exhibits livor mortis. She is in full rigor, so I estimate she was killed approximately six to eight hours ago." He held up another evidence bag. "And this was stuffed down the front of her shirt."

Jenna stared at the jack of hearts playing card and groaned. "Same killer, different MO. This is all we need." She looked at Webber. "Please tell me you found trace evidence?"

"Nothing, not even the victim's prints. It's been wiped clean." Webber held out the scanner. "Do you figure she picked up a hitchhiker? She could've been strangled from the back seat."

"No, the backseat isn't wet and with the downfalls we've been having, anyone getting inside would track water with them." Kane bent into the vehicle and scanned the interior. "She wasn't killed here. Look at the marks on her neck. If someone strangled her from behind, she'd have arched up, making the killer pull down the cord from behind and leaving a downward mark in the flesh. The mark on her is high under the chin and in an upward angle. She was attacked from behind, probably standing and by someone taller than her."

"Her clothes are soaked through." Emily peeked out from under her hood. "Dave's correct. She wasn't murdered inside the vehicle. Strange though, her phone and purse aren't wet."

Looking around, Jenna shrugged. "No signs of a struggle around the pickup. It's wet but the gravel would have been churned up more if someone had strangled her here. We'll go and speak to the manager and see if she was in the bar with anyone last night."

"He was here before and I asked him." Kane moved closer to her side. "No women came into the bar last night. The only people who dropped by stayed and I've spoken to all of them."

"I'll get her back to the lab. I'll run tests on the cord used to strangle her. It looks generic, so tracing it will be impossible, but you'd be surprised what trace evidence a killer can leave behind." Wolfe bent down and pushed the seat as far back as possible. "It's going to be difficult getting her out of here." He looked at Jenna. "Call me when you hunt down her next of kin. They'll want to do a formal ID and view the body. I'll do a preliminary examination now, tidy her up for the viewing, and send over my findings. I'll wait until the viewing before I start the autopsy."

Glad to be away from the stink, Jenna nodded. "I'll get at it. Catch you later."

"Wait up." Kane had the hatch open and waved her over. "There's an overnight bag in here." He pulled it out. "Grab me an evidence bag, Em, and I'll put it in the van."

Jenna waited for Kane and they headed back to the Beast. After straightening the thick towel she'd spread over the leather seats, she climbed inside. "The seats will be ruined. We're soaked through. Maybe we should have taken the cruiser."

"The towels will hold most of it and the leather is treated, so don't worry." Kane patted her knee. "I know my truck will handle the floods. It's always safer in the Beast. The seats are the least of our worries."

Jenna opened her slicker and reached for her iPad. "I'll do a search for Shelby O'Connor, although the name is familiar. I'm sure I've read something about her or met her at one time. Not that the corpse we looked at triggered any memories. That poor woman's face was horrific. I don't think I'd like to be the relative doing the ID." She put the name into the search engine. "Oh, no wonder I recognize the name. I've met her. She gave a generous donation to the Her Broken Wings Foundation. Her mother had been a victim of spousal abuse. She lost her husband last year and owns the Wild Plains cattle ranch. She's wealthy. No kids. No living relatives listed, and from what she told me, she rarely goes out. All the people she knew socially were her husband's friends, and when he died they completely ignored her."

"If she's rich, there'll be some distant relative around to claim her fortune." Kane shrugged. "I guess it all comes down to who she left her estate to in her will." He glanced at her. "She'll be on social media, and we have her phone. I looked at it on scene and it's not locked. She had to have been meeting someone. It will be on her phone for sure."

Jenna tapped her bottom lip thinking. Should they risk heading out of town in this weather? "The Wild Plains Ranch isn't far from here. It's on the other side of the range. If she hasn't any relatives, the manager—or if she has a housekeeper or whatever—they might volunteer to ID the body." She turned to look at him. "She might have told someone there who she was meeting."

"Okay." Kane turned the Beast around and headed away from town. "Punch in the coordinates and check for road closures." He glanced at her. "This Jack of Hearts Killer is targeting widowed or divorced women, but why? I'm not seeing a pattern emerging, or any motive. They're not thrill kills, or he wouldn't have placed the victim back into her vehicle. It would be a more hit-and-run type of kill, and vicious. Poisoning and strangulation from behind are almost clean ways of killing... and well planned. There's something else going on here."

Instantly, Jenna caught onto his meaning. "What do the women have in common apart from their age and marital status?" She scrolled through her notes. "Nothing online to link them. Dianne Gilbert was divorced, but she inherited the house from her father. The family is military. That would be the men in the photographs all around the home." She blew a strand of wet hair from in front of her nose. "My money is on social media. I bet this killer is catfishing. Pretending to be someone else to gain the victim's trust. The MO for the murders is something we need to discover fast."

FIFTEEN

Annoyance shivered down Julian Darnley's spine. Nothing had gone to plan and leaving behind the cord he'd used to strangle Shelby had been a big mistake. Dressed in coveralls, gloves, and rubber boots, he went about cleaning every surface in the house. The vacuum cleaner stopped its infernal humming and his friend walked into the room. "Did you make sure you wiped down every place she'd have been. I know she was snooping in the bedrooms."

"Yeah, every room." His friend shook his head. "Although it was a mistake to allow her free range of the house. We should have left in the dark and not still be here cleaning. What if somebody sees us?"

Wondering why he'd risked involving his best friend in his get-rich-quick scheme, Darnley shook his head. "Don't be a fool. No one can possibly link us to this house."

"Maybe not." His friend idly wiped a cloth over the door handle. "When I arrived last night, I thought I heard footsteps."

Rolling his eyes, Darnley gaped at him. "You did—it was Shelby and me running around the house."

"No, it was like, well, coming from behind me." He wiped

his gloved knuckle under his nose. "I turned but no one was there, and the next minute Shelby came running around the front of the house. It's not just that. When I followed you to dump her body back at the Triple Z Roadhouse, there was a vehicle some ways behind us. I figure someone was following us."

"You're mentioning this to me now? Just as well it was your overactive imagination—adrenalin rush or whatever spooked you." Darnley shrugged and shook his head. "Look, don't give it another thought. If someone had seen me kill the stupid woman, the cops would be all over us by now. Many people use Stanton and after leaving the Triple Z we headed for the airport." He pushed a hand through his hair. "If they did notice us, which I doubt, they'd see a man with a beard and glasses. Stop worrying. Once we remove every trace of being here, we're in the clear."

"The only part of this idea that's safe is the transfer of the cryptocurrency. I had the IP address bouncing all over the world." His friend chuckled. "Not even the FBI could trace the transfer or find our accounts." He shrugged. "We have a fortune and could walk away now. Why do you want to keep going? Is it the killing? I know you enjoy it. I can see it in your eyes."

Smiling, Darnley wet his lips. "I've always enjoyed killing dumb women. It's a rush when they realize I'm going to kill them. It's like a drug and one hit is never enough." He gave him a friendly punch in the arm. "I watched your face last night. You're just like me. Watching them die is addictive, isn't it?"

"Yeah." A smile curled his friend's lips. "Watching her eyes made my heart race like crazy. I want to kill the next one."

"You?" Darnley picked up the cleaner and removed the bag, replacing it with a new one. "I don't think you're ready. You got sick when we dumped her body, like you cared or something."

"I'm more than ready. It was the stink of her that made me

puke. Watching the annoying bitch die was exciting." Annoyance flashed in his friend's eyes. "Don't you trust me to do it?"

How could I possibly relinquish the thrill? Darnley thought for a beat. If he refused the request, he might lose his friend's loyalty. Having someone to share the excitement was nice and it would be so easy to move the blame to him should the need arise. As a born leader he had no allegiance to anyone but himself. "There is a test to see if you're ready."

"Shoot."

Darnley smiled. "What was her name?"

"That's easy." His friend grinned widely. "Shelby."

Shaking his head, Darnley frowned at him. "I'd forgotten her name by the time we'd gotten back here last night. I don't think of them once they've served their purpose. It's on to the next."

"I don't think of the first one." His friend lifted a shoulder in a half shrug. "That was kind of boring once we'd chased her down. Shelby was different. The chase and then the extermination—the way she begged me to help her. Now that was thrilling. I keep rerunning it in my head and getting the same rush of excitement. It's like being on a roller coaster when the cart climbs to the very top and then you fly down the other side out of control helter-skelter." He grinned. "I can't get her look of surprise out of my mind. When you dropped that cord over her head and tightened it, her mouth kinda opened and closed, and then all the veins in her eyes exploded like fireworks. It was magnificent. Although dumping her body was gross. It took all the fun out of it." He dashed a hand through his hair. "How could you forget killing her?"

Seeing the excitement in his friend's face, Darnley nodded. "Oh, I recall killing her. I sometimes keep things from the women and pull them out from time to time when I can't find anyone suitable. Just seeing or smelling something from them brings it all back just like being there. Not their names—who they were doesn't matter—but I relive the rush of them dying by my hand. It's what puts me apart from the others. I remove the women to prevent them from revealing what we do. I don't just kill for the fun of it like some people." He chuckled. "We hit the jackpot with the last one and I guess the money will last for a time, but why waste the opportunity of getting more?"

"I never figured you'd risk doing anything like this in our hometown." His friend sighed. "It's dangerous and I wouldn't like being unable to come home for fear of being thrown in jail."

Laughing, Darnley grabbed him by the shoulders and shook him. "How could anybody find out what we're doing? There's no proof, no cash trail. No one will ever discover where we've hidden the money. The virtual private network we set up masks our devices' IP addresses. They are untraceable, just the same as the accounts we set up for the cryptocurrency."

"You've forgotten about the bodies we're leaving behind." His friend looked troubled. "You know darn well the sheriff in this town has solved every case in the last four years. Not even the most notorious serial killers have gotten away from her."

Dropping his hands, Darnley shook his head slowly. "Yeah, maybe, but they were serial killers. We're businessmen and the women are just collateral damage or fallout from the deals we make with them. I don't force any of them to hand over their money. Their greed was their downfall."

"Well, they didn't get a chance to complain once they'd handed over the money, did they?" His acquaintance's mouth turned down. "Killing them was always part of your plan. Don't you feel any remorse? You worry me sometimes. I'm afraid of becoming collateral damage too."

"Oh, come on." Darnley frowned at him. "I'm not planning on hurting you. What fun would there be in killing my best friend?" Dumbfounded, he shook his head. "The women are different. They've never been friends—they're a means to us getting rich. Once we have their money, what do you suggest we do with them? They have no further value or have I missed something?"

"No, it's just me. I know you do it to protect us." His friend met his gaze. "It was a thrill the last time, but I felt guilty after we'd returned her to her truck." His friend wiped a hand down his face. "She looked and smelled so bad. Not like the first one, rolling her into the river was much easier."

Trying to fathom his friend's misguided thinking, Darnley rubbed his chin. He needed to explain his reasoning and looked at his friend's bewildered expression. "Let me see... ah yeah, when you buy something from the store, what do you do with the receipt?"

"Unless I need it for a tax deduction, I usually throw it in the garbage." His friend gave him a confused look.

"Exactly." Darnley lifted up his arms and dropped them to his sides. "Do you ever think about that receipt as it molds away in the trash?"

"Of course, I don't. Do you think I'm stupid or something?"

"No." Darnley smiled. "The women are just receipts we don't need for tax, so we toss them away. Got it?"

"Yeah, I guess so."

Pleased, Darnley slapped him on the back. "Good! I knew you'd understand and it's just as well because I have another one on the hook already. They're so desperate to find a man, they'll do anything to please me. I figure we hit another two and then split. It's time we started living the high life."

"When?"

Pleased by his enthusiasm, Darnley packed up his laptop and waved him toward the door. "We have a small window of time while people are taking vacations." He walked backward down the passageway grinning at his friend. "Don't worry. I've been working on these women for the last three or four months. They're the same as the last ones and just as eager to give me their cash to make an impossible profit with the bonus of a wealthy love interest thrown in as well. Leave them to me. You go and find us suitable places to use." He collected the garbage bag from beside the front door. "Oh, and make sure your passport is up to date. I made sure to book us a vacation months ago and told everybody how excited we are to be going overseas. No one will care when we disappear—and even if they do, it will be too late. They'll never be able to find us."

SIXTEEN

Relentless and unstoppable, the rain battered the Beast in great gusts of ice-filled wind that sounded like buckshot. It was as if they were living in an endless storm. In all her time in Black Rock Falls, Jenna hadn't experienced such a prolonged and destructive weather event. Turning around in her seat, she pulled the blanket over Duke before glancing at the GPS. The distance to Shelby O'Connor's ranch wasn't far, but as the minutes ticked by, the road conditions deteriorated. Convinced Kane would keep them safe, she continued searching for information on the victim.

"Did you find anything on Shelby O'Connor's husband?" Kane glanced at her and then his attention went back to the road. "It would be a big spread and ranches like that usually employ a ton of people. He would have a manager for sure. I'm sure Mrs. O'Connor would have played some part in the running of the business."

Looking up from the screen, Jenna nodded. "From what I've found about her, she might own one of the biggest cattle ranches in the county, but she leaves the running of things in the hands of a manager and ranch hands. From the images in the articles online, she didn't appear to be the type who liked to get her hands dirty. She's been widowed for a time and there's no mention of anyone else in her life. I'm hoping the manager of the Wild Plains Ranch will be able to give us some more information."

"Seems to me it's unusual no one has reported her missing." Kane slowed to take a left through a wide gate with the name Wild Plains written in wrought iron across the front and onto a long driveway. "Unless they're used to her MIA."

The ranch spread out with freshly painted buildings all over. Cattle roamed over vast open pastures but many huddled under trees, sheltering from the rain. The main house, a two-story red brick square construction, with two sets of steps sweeping up either side of an impressive front door, seemed out of place in the landscape. It reminded Jenna of something she'd seen in a magazine about Georgian houses in the UK. The entire ranch spelled money with a capital M. "Wow, this is some spread." She turned to Kane. "How many people would it take to run a place this size?"

"It's hard to tell, but I figure this is a cow/calf operation. If you look over there to the right, it looks like they breed horses as well." Kane indicated with his chin. "There's a thoroughbred stallion in that pasture and those mares sheltering over yonder sure aren't mustangs. The money would be in the horses, especially if they're bred for racing." He slowed the truck. "I wouldn't mind betting the outbuildings are heated stables." He frowned. "It seems strange to leave valuable horses out in a storm. I hope nothing has happened to the people working here. We know the killer uses poison, so I guess anything is possible."

Jenna pulled up the hood of her slicker, her attention never wavering from the house looming up before them. "We're not equipped for a chemical attack. Maybe you should just give them a blast of the sirens and see if anyone comes out?"

"Okay." Kane flicked the switch and the sirens blasted. "I figure that will get their attention."

Moments later a man dressed in a slicker hustled out of a nearby barn, and a woman in her thirties opened the front door and stared at them. Jenna waited for the man to come toward them before buzzing down her window. "I'm looking for the manager."

"That would be me, Sheriff. What can I do for you?" The man, in his late forties, leaned toward the window and water dripped off the hood of his slicker.

Keeping one hand on her weapon, Jenna nodded. "And you are?"

"I'm Deke Smithers and the woman standing in the doorway is the housekeeper, Penny Olsen." Smithers waved a hand toward the front door.

Not taking her eyes off Smithers, Jenna eased her weapon back into the holster. "Is there somewhere dry we can talk? We'd like to speak to both of you."

"There's my office, but if you drive around back, it would be more comfortable in the kitchen. You look like you'd appreciate a hot drink." Smithers smiled at them. "Penny always has a fresh pot of coffee brewing and I can smell apple turnovers straight out of the oven."

"Do you always invite visitors into the house when the owner is away?" Kane peered through the window at him.

"The lower floors at the back of the building are for the people working here. Mrs. O'Connor rarely comes down to the kitchen. She spends all her time in the front part of the house. She prefers the workers to keep their place, which is out of sight. Although, she does speak to me and Penny from time to time. She has no interest in the running of the ranch whatsoever." He waved a hand toward a road that wrapped itself around the back of the house. "Head around that way to the back door. I'll meet you there."

Jenna buzzed up her window and turned to Kane. "The lives of the rich and powerful, huh? So, what was she doing slumming down at the Triple Z Roadhouse?"

"Maybe she was having an illicit affair with one of the ranch hands." Kane cleared his throat. "It's been known to happen and I'm sure she wouldn't want her employees knowing about it."

"Possible." Jenna thought for a beat. "As she has no close friends, I wonder if the housekeeper knows the name of Mrs. Gilbert's hairstylist? People often chat freely to the person doing their hair. I figure hairstylists and bartenders often get to listen to a person's entire life."

"Good thinking." Kane stopped directly outside the back door. "I'll grab Duke. You go ahead, but wait for me. We can't be sure it's safe."

Grabbing her notebook, Jenna stepped out onto the soaked gravel pathway and walked up the sloping entrance to the back door. The back of the house was almost as grand as the front, but instead of steps to the door, there was a ramp with a gradual slope to make deliveries easier. Above the entrance, four pillars supported a slab of marble to protect visitors from the weather. It reminded Jenna of some of the images she'd seen of Egyptian tombs. The door to the Beast slammed shut and Kane's footsteps came up behind her. She lifted the ornate copper knocker in the form of a lion's head and tapped it a few times. Footfalls headed toward the door and she stood to one side, one hand resting on her weapon under her slicker. There was no knowing if a threat existed and it was good to know Kane was watching her back.

The door opened and the woman she'd noticed at the front door stared at her with an inquiring look on her face. She smiled at her. "Penny Olsen? I'm Sheriff Alton and this is Deputy Kane. We would like to come in and speak to you and Deke Smithers about Mrs. O'Connor."

"She's away for the weekend and I don't think she'd appreciate us discussing her with you." Olsen blanched. "No, she wouldn't—not at all—and it could cost me my job."

"I don't think that will be an issue." Kane removed his hat and hit it against his leg to remove the water before replacing it. "Mrs. O'Connor was found deceased this morning. We need to know where she was going last night and who she was meeting."

"Oh, my stars." Penny Olsen's attention moved over Jenna's shoulder. "Did you hear that Deke? Mrs. Gilbert has passed." She looked at Jenna with her bottom lip quivering and one hand pressed to her chest. "What happened to her? Was she in a wreck?"

Keeping her expression blank, Jenna let out a long sigh. "I'm afraid the cause of death is still under investigation."

"Best we go inside." Smithers came up the ramp. "These folks are wet through. Get them something hot to drink and a bite to eat. We'll talk in the kitchen. It's warm in there."

Waiting as Kane moved in front of her and through the door. Jenna smiled to herself. As usual, Kane had placed his body between her and any threat. She might have been able to turn a highly trained black ops operative into a cowboy, but inside he'd never change. Looking all around, she followed him into a mudroom. At Penny Olsen's request they remove their slickers and hung them on pegs. The woman gave Duke a long look. Jenna met her gaze. "Duke is a patrol dog. He goes where we go. Don't worry. He won't make a nuisance of himself."

"The kitchen is through here." Smithers smiled at them as he removed his slicker before leading the way through a door.

The kitchen looked like the spread from a magazine. It was all sparkling surfaces and modern equipment. Jenna sat down at the kitchen table.

"Coffee?" Penny Olsen poured cups of coffee and slid a plate of apple turnovers toward them. She busied herself with setting down plates and the fixings for coffee before sitting and looking at them expectantly. "Help yourselves. The turnovers are fresh baked from scratch."

Jenna's mouth watered at the smell of the warm puff pastry, wrapped around a filling of spiced apple. "Thank you. That's very kind of you."

She glanced at Kane, it was unusual for them to accept anything when questioning witnesses, especially when one of the victims had been poisoned, but she followed his example and waited for Smithers and Olsen to eat before she took a bite. She looked at Olsen. "You mentioned that Mrs. O'Connor informed you she'd be away for the weekend. Did she mention where she was going?"

"Mrs. O'Connor doesn't discuss her private life with us." Penny Olsen sipped her coffee and gave Jenna a rueful look. "I did overhear her talking to someone on the phone, but it was about investing in something. I recall her mentioning cryptocurrency, but I only heard a snippet of the conversation."

"I've no idea where she was heading either." Smithers pushed a hand through his hair. "I had a few problems with a hay order and wanted to discuss it with her. The price had almost doubled, and I didn't want to commit to spending so much money without asking her first. She blew me off telling me to deal with it."

"What time was this?" Kane helped himself to another turnover.

"Just a minute." Smithers pulled a phone out of his back pocket and scrolled through the screen. "Ten after eight. She was annoyed with me for disturbing her and I could hear the sound of rain, so I figured she was inside her vehicle but not driving. I don't recall hearing the engine and she has a powerful truck." A look of concern came over his face. "I'm the manager and have a lot of hands who rely on their positions here to feed their families. What am I supposed to do? Now Mrs. O'Connor is dead I assume all the accounts for the running of the place will be suspended until the reading of her will."

"Not necessarily. Does she manage the financial side of the running of the ranch herself or does she use an accountant?" Kane took a long drink of his coffee. "Does she sign the checks for everything?"

"No." Smithers shook his head. "I order whatever I need, and the invoices are sent to an accountant who handles all the finances. This was set up by Mr. O'Connor years ago. He always said he never had a head for figures and the accountant handled everything, including the taxes."

"Okay." Kane nodded thoughtfully. "Then you must contact him immediately. I would say he would be able to give you the advice you need. Usually in these cases as livestock are involved the company continues on as normal under the supervision of the accountant until the beneficiary of the will is established. Once the new owner has taken possession, then I would imagine you would have to negotiate with him."

"Thanks." Smithers ran a hand down his face. "I hope they keep the crew on. It will be difficult starting over. I've worked here for the last ten years."

Jenna pushed a strand of hair behind one ear and looked at them. "Has Mrs. O'Connor ever mentioned meeting anyone new?"

Both of them shook their heads and Jenna pulled her notebook out of her pocket. "Do you know where she goes to get her hair styled?"

"Well, there is only one place in town isn't there?" Penny Olsen's lips flattened. "She went there twice a week because she didn't like washing her own hair. She said that holding up the hair dryer made her arms ache."

"Did she go anywhere else regularly?" Kane frowned. "Did she have an active social life? Has she made any new friends recently?"

"When Mr. O'Connor was alive, they used to go out all the time, to The Cattleman's Hotel most times, and they mixed with the horse-racing crowd, but once he died, not one of them contacted her. Apart from going to her stylist, she rarely went out and spent most of her time on social media. She purchased everything online, so if she had any friends, that's where you'll find them. She never discussed her personal life with us and made it quite clear it was none of our business."

"Did she use a laptop?" Kane raised both eyebrows.

"Yes, she did." Olsen nodded. "It wasn't on her desk when I cleaned this morning. I assume she took it with her."

Jenna finished her coffee and stood. "Thank you. Everything you've given us is very helpful." She handed them both one of her cards. "If you think of anything else or if anybody contacts the house looking for her, please get their name and details, so we can follow up." She thought for a beat. "One other thing. Do you know the name of her lawyer?"

"Yeah." Smithers nodded. "Sam Cross, he came by after Mr. O'Connor passed to discuss the will with her, I believe."

Jenna smiled. "I'll give him a rundown of what's happened and ask him to contact you. He will be able to give you some advice going forward."

She led the way to the mudroom. They pulled on their slickers and walked out the door with Duke close behind. After climbing into the Beast, she turned to Kane. "What do you think?"

"We've obtained some valuable information, but we still don't have a motive for why she was murdered." Kane started the engine and headed back down the driveway. "One thing's for sure: those two had nothing to do with it. Mrs. O'Connor's death means their jobs are on the line. I'd say working here would be a dream job if you could tolerate the boss. I didn't get much from them, but it's obvious Mrs. O'Connor had no interest in the running of the place. The ranch was controlled by a company. She lived in her own sheltered world and had surrounded herself with social media friends rather than the real thing. Which made her a perfect target for a catfisher." He shook his head. "Someone lured her to her death, that's for darn sure. I hope Wolfe found a laptop inside her truck. We'll need to search it and her bank accounts. I'd like to know if she's been syphoning off money to give to someone."

Tapping her bottom lip, Jenna allowed the conversation to percolate through her mind. "I'll call Wolfe and ask him; the laptop might hold vital evidence." She nodded thoughtfully. "The cryptocurrency she mentioned might be the clue we need to break this case. It makes me wonder if she was speaking to a financial advisor."

"Or a scammer." Kane turned to look at her. "What's more perfect than transferring someone's fortune into a crypto account. There are so many ways to make money untraceable and that's one of them. Someone working on the dark web could empty a target's bank account online in seconds. It happens all the time. The only time these guys are caught is when someone gives their name to cybercrime. Most of them are in the wind. They might as well be ghosts."

Horrified, Jenna stared at him. "So, the Jack of Hearts Killer could be taking his security one step further by killing his victim and wiping out all trace of their contact." She swallowed hard. "How the hell are we going to catch a ghost?"

SEVENTEEN

On the ride back to the office, Jenna called the lawyer Sam Cross to inform him of Shelby O'Connor's death and asked him to contact Mr. Smithers to advise him. Damp all over, they finally trudged into her office. She shook her wet slicker, hung it on a peg behind her door, eased out of her rubber boots, and slipped on her usual footwear. After updating her files, she smiled and went to read the neat notes on the whiteboard. She looked over at Kane. "They've made progress while we've been away."

"That's the benefit of having an experienced officer on the team." Kane looked up from his laptop and then stood. "If we're having a meeting, I'll fire up the coffee pot."

"Thanks." Jenna stepped onto the landing and called Rio and Rowley upstairs to update them on the case. Impressed by the way Rio could work without instructions, she turned as her deputies filed into the room. "I can see you've been busy." She indicated to the notes on the whiteboard. "The victim in the truck at the Triple Z Roadhouse, from the ID she was carrying, is Shelby O'Connor, a widow who owns the Wild Plains Ranch. From the initial findings this is another homicide. The killer left the cord around the victim's neck and another jack of hearts playing card. We've been out to the ranch and spoken to her employees. Her laptop is missing, so we'll concentrate on searching her bank accounts. We'll need a warrant to search the company files for the ranch as well."

"I'll handle the warrant." Rio looked up from his notes. "The judge and I are just *like that.*" He crossed his fingers. "Although I hear, he's going on vacation soon and his replacement has a reputation of being difficult."

"That's all we need, but get at it ASAP. There's more." Jenna gave them a detailed rundown of the interview at the Wild Plains Ranch. "Wolfe will notify us when he'll be conducting an autopsy. Most likely it will be at ten tomorrow. I'll need you to include Shelby O'Connor in your investigations. The ID will have to be verified, but I'm sure it's her."

"What did Wolfe discover about the death of Dianne Gilbert?" Rowley looked up from his iPad.

"Wolfe has completed his autopsy on her. Cause of death is cyanide poisoning. The source is from a meal made with peach pits. We can't find anything to link the two women, apart from the jack of hearts playing card left on the bodies. The victims could have met in affluent social circles, but O'Connor has dropped her friends since her husband passed. Although Dianne Gilbert is divorced and out of Bison Ridge. She worked as a bank clerk."

"Ah, Dianne Gilbert was wealthy. It was old money from inheritances. I hunted her down through legal documents, wills, and properties that she owned." Rowley stood and added the facts to the board.

Jenna made a note in her book and nodded. "Okay, so there's a tie-in. We've spoken to her neighbor who said she left her house last evening around seven. We visited her residence and there are no signs of forced entry. We found nothing to indicate where she'd gone, but we did notice there was no laptop or computer on the premises. We assume she had one but will confirm it with one of her friends. If it's missing, it could be significant."

"Did the autopsy discover any other injuries?" Rio looked up from his iPad. "Was she forced to eat the poison? Any motive at all for murdering her?"

After pushing wet hair away from her face, Jenna took the cup of coffee Kane offered her and looked at Rio. "No, no other injuries apart from those Wolfe believes happened due to the ride down the river. When we were at the house yesterday, we found nothing to indicate she had a problem with anyone. Wolfe has already hunted down the next of kin. Her ex-husband is in Alaska and her cousin was isolated in Blackwater with the floods. It has to be someone else."

"We've had a chat with the bank manager and spoken to some of the people working at the bank." Rowley leaned back in his chair. "Mrs. Gilbert mentioned meeting a man online, someone who had the same interests as her. I've spoken to everyone she called a friend at the bank. All of them, including the manager's wife, have been friends since high school." He looked at Jenna. "I pushed hard to get any information on this virtual man, but Mrs. Gilbert played her cards close to the vest and didn't divulge many details. The only information they could give me was she'd met him online about four months ago and he has a beard. She apparently had a thing about men with beards."

"I've hunted her down on social media." Rio let out a long sigh. "I had no idea there were so many dating apps out there for this county and surrounds. I messaged her online friends— well the ones that responded—and asked them if she'd mentioned any particular dating service, but got zip. It was as if they were too embarrassed to talk to me about them—or didn't believe I was a badge-holding deputy."

Jenna raised both eyebrows and caught Kane's knowing

smile. "I'm not sure, if I were using one of those services, I'd want to disclose that kind of information either."

"Why?" Rio looked perplexed. "It's quite normal these days." He smiled. "Everything is online. Instant gratification... no wait, no delay."

"The younger generation doesn't seem to worry too much about anything. They live for today. It's not something I'd be interested in doing but I'm old school." Kane sipped his coffee. "Everyone is different. Maybe she didn't want anyone to know she was using one either. Although it's a perfect place for catfishing—men and, I guess, women using false identities and images to scam money out of people."

"How?" Rowley frowned. "How could anyone do that online?"

"They use many ways to extract money from vulnerable people." Kane stretched his legs out in front of him and crossed his feet. "They have a make-believe online romance, which usually ends up with them asking the woman to finance them in one way or another."

"For what?" Rowley leaned forward in his chair with an interested expression.

"Oh, there are so many different types of scams." Kane place his coffee cup on the desk. "After a few months when they've made the woman comfortable with them and convinced them that they are part of their lives, they come up with a scenario to get money from them. For instance, maybe they tell them they need money for a medical procedure or they would really love to come and visit, but they don't have the money for the trip." Kane shrugged. "It's not something that happens overnight as the women don't realize it's a scam. Catfishers spend months grooming a potential person. I've heard of cases where one of these people bleeds a target dry, and then when all their money is exhausted, they break off the relationship and vanish. Then the person often reports the problem to the authorities and they discover the person is fictitious. It's very difficult to find people who are catfishing because many of them are highly skilled in the use of the dark web. They also use various types of public Wi-Fi connections and then bounce them off hundreds or even thousands of different IP addresses, which makes them undetectable."

Recalling various cases they'd dealt with in the past, Jenna nodded. "It must be similar to the pedophile rings that we've uncovered. I'm guessing it would be the same type of network but they wouldn't be able to hide the transfer of assets, would they?"

"They usually deal in cash and they have untraceable offshore accounts to siphon the money into and usually bounce it around. Finding any of these accounts is practically impossible. It would be even easier to hide cryptocurrency." Kane leaned back in his chair and scratched his cheek. "What we're left with is a person who has literally given away all their money to a fictitious person. We have no name to trace them and a very minimal chance of retrieving their cash. If we did find them and the perpetrator insisted she gave them the cash as a gift, we would have no way to disprove it. The scammer could easily refer to their interaction on social media, which is always readily available. It is hard to prove a scam. There's no law against people receiving gifts of money from friends. It happens all the time."

Intrigued by Kane's knowledge of catfishing, Jenna raised both her eyebrows. "How do you know all this? I know about cybercrime and there are scammers out there, but I had no idea they had a name for this particular scam, let alone how it works. This is another first for Black Rock Falls."

"Cybercrime is everywhere and comes in many types." Kane held her gaze and his expression told her not to ask him any more questions. "Something similar came across my desk at my old job, so it's been around for a while."

Of course, as a special agent attached to the White House, cybercrime would have been part of his job. She gave him a slight nod and turned her attention to Rowley. "As you've been researching this all day, what do you know about catfishing?"

"To start with, they use a professional photograph for their fake image on social media. They need something to attract the person they're targeting." Rowley scrolled through social media pages on his iPad. "It happens all the time—particularly to women. Men who want to impress a woman will post an image of a good-looking guy with a yacht or beside an expensive vehicle or inside a prestigious home. They usually list themselves as widowers or divorced and looking for honest and genuine people. There's no way to know how many of these are actually genuine or are people catfishing." He held up his iPad to show a list of potential scammers. "Like I said, it usually happens to women, but lonely men are just as vulnerable." He sighed. "Although the main problem is the victims lose everything and it can never be retrieved. The difference here is I haven't found any cases where the catfisher murdered the women."

Stomach cramping with the implications of what was happening in her town, Jenna stood to refill her coffee cup and then turned and leaned against the counter. "When you think about it, catfishing would be a perfect method for a killer to find his next potential victim. We know this kind of thing works very well. Pedophiles, for instance, have been pretending to be kids online for years. It seems to me that the Jack of Hearts Killer has taken catfishing to a new level."

"Hmm." Kane raised an eyebrow. "I remember one some time ago that created a false identity to lure young women for a job interview. When they arrived, they were kidnapped and forced into the sex slave industry. It was only when one escaped that we discovered the extent of the organization." He opened his hands wide. "This sort of thing would be the perfect way to lure women into a psychopath's clutches."

Jenna snorted. "This has been going on for a long time. It's just called a different name these days. It sounds like the idea first reared its ugly head as the casting couch." She shook her head. "The depths of depravity some people will stoop to never ceases to amaze me." She looked around the table at her deputies. "We have to find the Jack of Hearts Killer. He's only just started and has no idea we're chasing him down. We need a motive. Is he doing this for monetary value or for the fun of killing them?" She sipped her coffee. "First up, we need to examine both victims' bank accounts and phone records. Rio, you get at that now. The bank will need a request from us to release the information. Rowley, search the victims' phones and look for messages. See if you can find a definite link to one of these dating services for these women. I would imagine the killer is using more than one app. I'm guessing he would spread himself out over a number of different sites and be grooming targets on each of them."

Rowley and Rio collected their things and hurried back to their desks.

"What do you want me to do?" Kane smiled at her.

Jenna collected cups and placed them in the sink. "We do the grunt work." She sat down in her chair. "The guys have everything covered for now, and research is all we can do until the phone companies release the information we need." She leaned back in her chair and sighed. "There's a man out there killing women. He has to be on one of these dating sites, so we join up as many as we can. We can do some catfishing ourselves and use a false name. Then we can list our preferences as looking for professional men with beards and see what happens."

"I think we should portray ourselves as the rich business-woman type." Kane smiled. "If they're hunting down unattached rich women, then that's what we'll give them. There are plenty of women working from home who are directors of companies."

Thinking over the best possible bait for her hook, Jenna smiled at him. "I'm going to be a rich widow. Alone with no one in the world to care for me. I'm looking for the strong silent type to spend my life with in decadent luxury."

"Uh-huh." Kane stretched out one hand and pushed the door shut. He gave her a slow smile. "Are you by chance, speaking from the heart, Jenna? Because you already have the strong silent type and if you want to live in decadent luxury, you only have to ask."

EIGHTEEN

The rain still beat against the window at three o'clock and outside the day had continued dim and gray. Eyes weary from scanning endless faces on various dating apps, Jenna looked up at the sound of giggling and clearly suggestive remarks in the hallway. She glanced at Kane and raised one eyebrow in question. "It sounds like Deputy Anderson is at it again." She pushed to her feet and headed for the door. "I'm going down to speak to her."

"I'll go." Kane stood, stretched, and looked at Jenna. "Ah, maybe not. You have that look in your eyes again, Jenna." He cupped her cheek. "Maybe you should just fire her and get rid of the problem once and for all?"

Annoyance flashed over her, heating her cheeks. Yeah, Poppy Anderson irritated her. It was hard not to notice her frequent lunches with Mayor Petersham and her blatant attempt to gain his support to enter the next election for sheriff. Although, Jenna believed she had the townsfolk behind her. It was other things about the woman that grated on her. Poppy persistently tried to force a wedge between her and Kane. She chewed on her fingers. At work, she'd tried very hard to treat Kane the same as she did the other deputies, with respect but while remaining in charge. Going easy on him at work wasn't an option she'd consider. It wasn't professional. Flattening her lips, she stared at him. Firing Poppy now after Kane had encouraged her, even though he'd lost his memory at the time, had thrown a spanner in the works. "No, I'll deal with her, Dave." She smiled at him. "She can twist you around her little finger. I don't know how she does it, no one gets under your guard—not even me. You know, when you lost your memory and were on remote control or whatever, you implied you'd gotten serious with her. I don't believe there was anything between you, but if she does have anything on you, she'll use it against you—or me. You must know that right?"

"Yeah, and if anything had happened between Poppy and me, I'd have told you. I've always been honest with you, Jenna. I'm kinda pumped that you're jealous. It's an ego stroke but not when you're allowing her to get under your skin. That's not like you." Kane shook his head slowly. "Sometimes I'll have to speak to her, Jenna. I'm her superior and I can't exactly ignore her completely."

Chewing on her bottom lip, Jenna looked away, thinking. "That's fine, but she knows how to push my buttons when it comes to you, and I refuse to allow her to win."

"Uh-huh." Kane scratched his cheek, looking concerned. "You've already reacted. I figure you played to her ego by moving me up here. It's almost admitting you're worried about her ability to lure me into her web. It's never going to happen, Jenna. You know that, right?"

Trying to avoid the prickling sensation on the back of her neck, Jenna gave what she hoped was a nonchalant shrug. "Of course I do. Maybe you should move your desk back downstairs? The last thing Anderson needs is an ego boost. If hers gets any bigger, she'll burst."

"No way. I don't want to work in such close proximity with her." Kane held up both hands. "She drives me insane."

Jenna paused with one hand on the doorknob and looked at him. "FYI, I moved you up here because of your seniority and not because we're married. I needed a spare desk and there was no way I was sharing my office with her."

"Maybe you should mention that to her." Kane shrugged. "Although, I do think she's improving, so the therapy is working. Maggie said she's finishing the jobs she gives her and isn't on her phone all day. That has to be a good thing, right?"

"Really? Well, that's good to know. She sure has a champion in you, Dave, but I think I'll make up my own mind about her." Ignoring his abashed expression, she handed him her iPad. "Here is the list of names of the possible suspects I discovered this afternoon. Can you add them to your list and file them, please?"

"Sure." Kane went to the whiteboard. "I'll split them into two lists. One will contain residents of Black Rock Falls and the other for those from surrounding counties. I figure it has to be a local because they know the area." He smiled at her. "Then I'll update everyone's files."

Annoyed by the raucous laughter coming from downstairs in the main office, Jenna nodded and then headed down the steps. Was she jealous? She didn't think so. Jealousy would mean she didn't trust Kane, and trust wasn't an issue. Poppy's unprofessionalism in the office and blatant sexual inuendoes made her hackles rise and it seemed that no amount of therapy would bring her under control.

As she reached the bottom of the stairs the giggles changed to intimate conversation. Poppy sat on Rio's desk with her long legs crossed. Her back was toward Jenna.

"Why are you wasting your time with a college student?" Poppy leaned forward and squeezed Rio's shoulder. "We could have so much fun together. Drop by my place later. It will be our little secret."

"Thanks, but I'm not interested." Rio leaned back in his seat shaking his head.

"Oh, come on." Poppy giggled. "I see the way you look at me." She leaned closer and touched his cheek. "You want me, don't you?"

Disappointed that the three months of counseling had done nothing to improve Poppy's behavior in the office, Jenna stepped from the bottom of the stairs. Rio noticed her at once and straightened in his chair. Rowley was sitting in the next cubicle head down and obviously focused on the job at hand.

Stopping adjacent to Anderson, Jenna cleared her throat. "It's good to see you have both completed your work and have time to sit around laughing with a killer on the loose? I'll convey your lack of empathy to the victims' next of kin." She glared at Rio. "This is the workplace and not the local bar. I'm surprised you're showing such a lack of professionalism. I want to see your uploaded files and suggestions for potential suspects on my laptop by the time I get back upstairs." She turned to Anderson. "You will empty your desk and move your things into Walter's desk behind the front counter. This area is off limits for you until further notice."

"Why?" Anderson slid off the desk like a snake. "I'm taking a break and, surely, I'm allowed to speak to the other members of the team? You need to loosen up a bit, Sheriff. You're no fun at all."

Give them enough rope and they'll hang themselves. Jenna barked a laugh and leveled her gaze on Anderson. "Deputy Anderson, you know I don't accept sexual harassment in the workplace. This and your lack of experience and work ethic will be in my report to Mayor Petersham, along with my recommendation that you be fired. In the three months you've been here, you haven't displayed one ounce of aptitude for fighting crime.

The best I could possibly offer you is a desk job and I need a deputy I can rely on in the field."

"I've proved I'm reliable in the field." Anderson pouted. "I saved all the women in the caves on our last case."

Nodding slowly, Jenna raised one eyebrow and looked at her. "You did what was necessary to save your own skin, is all. You ran away from danger when I had a knife to my throat. The untrained waitress from Aunt Betty's Café put her life on the line, to ensure the killer didn't get away. All you did was try to hamper Kane from saving my life. Someone who only considers themselves is no use to my team. Every one of them, including Emily Wolfe, would stand and fight beside us without a second thought." She shrugged. "I've given you the chance to prove yourself these past three months and you've failed miserably. I'd never give you the opportunity to risk our lives." She glanced at Rowley. "Jake, with me." She headed up the stairs without a backward glance.

The smell of freshly brewed coffee met Jenna as she walked into the office. Kane was scrolling through files on his laptop and glanced up as she sat down at the desk. She waved Rowley into a chair. "Kane has made a list of possible suspects from the dating apps that both women used. I know very little about dating apps or catfishing. Do you have any input to narrow the search down?"

"Me?" Rowley scratched his head. "Only common sense. I figured on social media they wouldn't have too many followers as it's pretty obvious they set up these accounts frequently. I don't know too much about dating apps either. That's Rio's area of expertise. Like Kane said, they usually use professional photographs and I would imagine they'd give an instant response to a match or friend request." He heaved a sigh. "I figure the best way of finding out how these things work would be to join up with a fake profile."

Impressed, Jenna nodded. "Yeah, we've done that already

and set the bait for potential catfishers, but the profiles need to be refined. We'll need to know what the killer is looking for in a woman. I've taken some notes on what both victims wrote in their preferences." She glanced at her notes. "Both wanted a professional man between the ages of thirty-five and forty-five, who enjoys fine dining and good wine." She smiled at Kane. "Hmm, I'd only need to add a black Stetson and cowboy boots for my perfect match."

"Yeah, but I'm already taken, and my wife wouldn't like me messing around." Kane chuckled. "What else did they want in a man?"

"Let me see." Jenna scrolled down the page. "Dianne Gilbert mentioned liking tall men with beards, and Shelby O'Connor believed eyeglasses are sexy."

Jenna looked up at a knock on the door. Rio stepped inside and she waved him to a seat. "We're trying to narrow down the list of possible suspects using the preferences of the two victims on the dating apps."

"That's not necessary." Rio sat down in the seat next to Rowley. "The information came through and I was able to access both victims' phones and have a list of everyone they communicated with over the last three months. Both women had a number of interested men asking them out on dates. From the messages I've read, between them they had quite an online social life. A few of the men are living in town and a few others in neighboring counties. I cross-referenced the list and came up with matches common to both women."

"You did that in a few hours?" Kane looked skeptical. "We've been hunting down men with beards and eyeglasses who work in a profession of some description. Have you matched your proposed suspects with the preferences of the victims?"

"Their preferences are irrelevant." Rio was all business. "All we need to concentrate on is who the victims were communicating with, and I have that information. It's pointless trying to act as bait, these men take months before they act."

Impressed, Jenna waved him toward the whiteboard. "Okay, write it up and let me see what you've got."

"Here lies the problem." Rio stood. "Not everyone using dating apps uses their own names. Some of them might be catfishing, others might be using the app to cheat on their wives or girlfriends. All these variants must be taken into consideration. It's a fact of life not everyone is honest."

"So what you're saying is any of the possible suspects of the Jack of Hearts murders could be someone just cheating on his wife?" Kane dragged a hand down his face. "Oh, this case gets better by the second."

"Yeah." Rio shrugged. "You mentioned using a fictitious name to join a dating app. It's easy to join dating apps and social media platforms using an alias. For instance, celebrities have stage names, authors have pen names, and they're not excluded from social media, are they? It's the same for anyone. They can use a prepaid anonymous card to pay for anything online, use a burner phone, have a fake email address, and that's child's play. You're aware of the depth of anonymity on the dark web, add this to the scammer's arsenal and they are invincible and untraceable."

Jenna stood and went to the counter to fill cups with coffee. It was going to be a long day. "Okay, write up the list and we'll just work through it like we usually do. We'll go and see the real people and try to find a way to trace the fakes."

"If they're not too bright and have used their own computers, we might be able to trace them through their IP addresses, but if they used a public wireless access, we won't have a chance." Kane stood to pass the cups of coffee to the others. "We could call in Bobby Kalo to hunt them down. As we have access to an IT whiz kid with FBI resources, we might as well use him."

"I agree. It makes sense to utilize all available resources." Jenna placed the fixings on the table and then sat down. "I've been thinking this through. The victims weren't murdered where we found them, and Wolfe couldn't connect the killings from the MO. If it weren't for the jack of hearts playing cards, we wouldn't have had any reason to believe these murders were connected. My question is: does this killer want to be caught or is he another psychopath trying to outwit us?" She looked from one deputy to the other, her gaze finally resting on Kane's concerned expression. "Why else would he go to so much trouble to conceal his identity and then leave a card to advertise he's responsible for both murders?"

NINETEEN

The office grew dark as clouds raced across the sky. Lightning flashed and thunder rolled down the mountains like a herd of giant bison. Duke let out a whine and crawled under Kane's legs. He stood to turn on the light before taking his seat again. He bent to give the dog's ears a rub and offered the trembling canine a cookie from the jar on Jenna's desk to soothe his nerves. He'd never known a dog as afraid of storms as Duke. As the printer hummed, spilling out photographs and information sheets on each potential suspect that Rio had compiled, the room filled with the smell of ink. The current case filtered through his mind as he conjured up various killers' profiles and tried to fit them to the photographs Rio was plastering beside names on the whiteboard. A knock on the door broke his concentration and Poppy stood in the doorway, staring at Jenna with an expectant expression. All eyes turned to look at her.

"I need to speak to Dave." Poppy cleared her throat. "It's personal." She looked directly at him. "I'm sure he knows what it's about. We need to talk, Dave."

Not having a clue what she was talking about, Kane shook

his head. "I'm kinda busy right now. It will have to wait for another time when you can discuss it in front of my wife."

"Okay, I'll call you tonight." Poppy backed out of the room and then turned back. "Oh, and Dr. Wolfe called and left a message to say he has a positive ID for Shelby O'Connor. Her ranch manager dropped by his office."

"Thanks. I'll talk to you later." Kane regretted the words the moment they fell from his lips.

His gaze drifted over Jenna. He could sense she wasn't happy and right now she was floating close to the edge of anger. Being in the honeymoon stage of marriage, for him life was all sunshine and rainbows. Seeing Jenna upset troubled him. Dragging his mind back to his job, he cleared his throat. "I've made a list of the guys we figure are using fake names. I did track down a few of them stupid enough to use their own photographs. I cross-matched their images with the drivers' license photographs in the database. I've compiled a separate list of them because they're the most likely suspects."

"Okay, when you're done, I'll send the list of fakes you haven't been able to identify over to Bobby Kalo." Jenna wouldn't meet his gaze and turned over a cookie in her hand inspecting it and then dropping it into her saucer. "If he can't find them, nobody can, but we need to keep moving forward on the case. Without solid IDs we'll keep the fake people on the back burner until we hear back from him. My priority is to speak to anyone in town the victims came in contact with. I figure our killer has to be a local. An out-of-towner would never be able to move around like a shadow. This person knows our town. He knew darn well he wouldn't be seen when he moved Shelby O'Connor's body to her truck, and I'm sure he met her at the roadhouse. It was pouring rain and there'd be no way a woman dressed for dinner would hang out in the rain waiting for him." She looked at her deputies. "Another thing: how many people would know there's no CCTV cameras at the Triple Z

Roadhouse?" She paused a beat and sipped her coffee. "I'd like to concentrate on grilling the woman's friends as well. Not their workmates, their real friends. They might be able to give us some inside information."

Kane stood and, with Duke sticking to him like glue, took the pen and added asterisks to the list of names for men living in Black Rock Falls. "Okay, these are the men we need to interview. The others are using aliases. I've added their profession and any other pertinent details we need to consider:

Patrick Howard, computer science teacher, 4 Edgemont Ave, IT experience, online persona: Peter Shore

Trenton Hyde, data analyst, 26 Pine, IT experience, online persona: Tom Creedy

Branch Drummond, lists his fake occupation as heart specialist

Kane frowned. "I checked him out and there is a cardiac specialist by the name of Branch Drummond, but he's in his eighties and retired. He lives in Texas."

Julian Darnley, forensic accountant, CEO and owner of Darnley Financial

Kane tapped the whiteboard with his pen. "I figure Darnley is using a fake name too. The company isn't registered and this guy even has a phony website, and a ton of women chasing him."

Steven Croxley, company director

Kane stared at the list. "I figure we should send the entire list to Kalo. He'll dig deeper than we can into their backgrounds. It looks like our victims were busy ladies."

"Some of them could have the knowledge to access the dark web." Jenna stood and walked up and down, staring at the images. "Drummond and Darnley fit the catfishing profile. Look at their images. They're professional shots. Add fake companies and professions and it's a slam dunk."

Kane nodded. "They stuck out and fit the profile, even

down to the fact they have only four or five followers on social media. There are no contact details for either of them. If Bobby can track these two down, we'll have two probable suspects. The others, well, are they just men looking for a date or are they serial killers hunting down a new victim?"

"There's only one way to find out." Jenna turned to look at the deputies. "I know it's late but we should make a start on interviewing these men tonight. I don't want anyone visiting them alone." She looked at Kane. "Pick out the two most possible suspects and we'll hunt them down tonight." She pushed both hands through her hair. "We'll work through the others in the morning." She looked at Rio. "Send out a press release and ask if anyone ran into Shelby O'Connor on the day she died. Set up the hotline to run through to our phones but not Rowley's, just you, me and Kane. I don't want his twins disturbed by the calls all night." She drummed her fingers on the desk. "I hope the autopsy at ten will give us more information. Right now, these suspects are nothing more than online acquaintances. If we're going to bring down the Jack of Hearts Killer, we'll need more hard evidence to link the crimes to one of these men."

TWENTY

It's strange but when a person crosses your palm with silver, they open up a rift in time, allowing someone like me to search back and forth through their lives to offer them tidbits of information. I give them just enough to keep their interest and to encourage them to come back for more. As the visits increase, they become more comfortable divulging information they'd never trust with another soul. This is how I came to know about Julian Darnley and his offers of financial assistance to make millions. Not one, but three of the women who'd crossed my palm with silver had mentioned him and his promises. When one client, Dianne was found dead, I knew why. It's very obvious to me that Julian Darnley is scamming money from susceptible women and then killing them. I figure he transfers their entire fortune into offshore accounts and uses the dark web to hide his presence. I shake my head grinning at his ingenuity, but it also takes someone like me to recognize a serial killer.

You see, you'll find me reading palms to peer into the lives of people. I don't exist in the daylight and at night I live in the shadows. It's an enjoyable pastime—an addiction I currently have under control, but if I need anyone special, I just order a suitable candidate. I can see you smiling. How is this possible? Well, my friend, to move around like a shadow I need all the dark web can offer me. I live there and for me it's my own personal shopping network. Why else do you figure I'm lurking around Black Rock Falls? Here it's all about opportunity, but now Julian Darnley and his accomplice have spoiled my plans. I was here first and they've ventured into my space. That's unforgivable. Even serial killers have a code of ethics. Well, after the Boston Strangler and the Green Man murders became entwined in the 1960s, a serial killer's respect of another's zone has been an unspoken courtesy.

You have to think to yourself, how many women have Darnley and his accomplice killed? I mean, they could have taken the women's fortunes and been in the wind, but they chose to kill them, didn't they? Now I hear you asking why I haven't informed the sheriff. Now that would be no fun, would it? I have to admit I enjoyed watching Shelby die.

It had been another wet and miserable day when Shelby came to visit me, and being a prominent person in town, it wasn't too difficult to discover her last name. She'd confided in me about plans to meet Darnley and I'd followed her. The meeting in the Triple Z parking lot had almost fooled me, but thanks to the persistent downpour, Darnley hadn't noticed me following them to the secluded house. The second man hadn't noticed me parked in the bushes and not a soul caught me peering through the house windows. When Shelby exploded from the house, I knew she'd be the next to die and I returned to my vehicle to watch it unfold.

Her mad dash around the house, and Darnley's use of an accomplice and a rental was pure genius. Once the men had dumped her body back at the Triple Z Roadhouse. I followed them to the airport and waited patiently for Darnley to return the rental. The vehicle would be taken through the car wash and steam cleaned inside, leaving no trace of the victim or the murderer. I'd seen the exhilaration on their faces. I'd seen the same in my own reflection. They'd never be able to stop killing now. My heart races with the anticipation of watching them kill again.

I'm breathing heavily when the bell on the store door chimes and a familiar face peeks around my screen. I smile and welcome them. Only the dedicated come and visit me at night, and all readings are made by appointment via my burner phone. "Kristina, lovely to see you again."

"Oh, I had to find out what's going to happen." Kristina sits down and lays her palm upturned on my table. "I'm going to finally meet Julian. We're having dinner tomorrow. He's promised to invest my inheritance but not as a financial advisor. He wants us to start dating and is moving to town." She stares at me, her eyes moist. "Just like you told me he would."

It hadn't been too difficult to imagine his next move and I smile back at her. "That sounds wonderful. Where are you having dinner?"

"At one of his friend's houses—they're away. He's having food delivered for our dinner." Kristina moves around in her seat. "He's flying in this afternoon but hasn't found a place to live in town yet and doesn't want to talk about finances or about our future together in a public place. He likes intimacy, same as me. I can't wait to see him."

A thought strikes me, and I give her a nod of encouragement. "Drop by again tomorrow night at seven and I'll make you a special love potion." I hold a finger to my lips. "It's a secret handed down for generations in my family and it won't cost you a cent. It's freely given to my special friends. I'll explain everything you need to do when I see you. Don't forget to drop by because this will guarantee success."

"You'd do that for me?" Kristina presses a hand to her chest.

"Thank you so much." She raises an eyebrow. "How does it work—the potion?"

I lean forward conspiratorially and lower my voice, but we are alone. No one can hear us. "The potion releases endorphins that entice men and it will make him amorous."

"Oh, how exciting." She grins. "Do you see anything new in my palm?"

I lean forward and touch her hand. The warmth of life sizzles through her. An energy anxious to be released back into the cosmos. How will he take her life? I can almost taste the excitement—the thrill of the kill. It would be building in Darnley now, and his friend—the follower—would do his bidding. Dragging my mind away from the smorgasbord of promised delights, I peer into her palm. "Julian will surprise you. As the night unfolds, he'll release all your doubts and fears."

TWENTY-ONE

Jenna studied the whiteboard. "We'll take Patrick Howard, computer science teacher, out of 4 Edgemont Ave." She made a note about his IT experience and his online persona, Peter Shore. She glanced up at Rowley. "When Rio has finished sending out the press release, go and interview Trenton Hyde, the data analyst out of 26 Pine. He has IT experience and his online persona is Tom Creedy."

"Got it." Rowley made notes and then stood.

Glancing at the clock, Jenna pushed to her feet. "When you're done with the interview, unless there's something that needs to be brought to my attention, bring your files up to date and then head on home. Will discuss what's next in the morning. Tell Sandy I'm sorry to keep you so late and give the twins a kiss for me." She went to the bench and filled two Thermoses with coffee. She handed one to Rowley. "You might need this. The weather is getting nasty. Grab some energy bars as well. We have boxes of them."

"Thanks. I'll give Sandy a call and tell her I'll be late." Rowley tossed a few bars to Rio, and they headed out the door.

The phone buzzed on her desk. It was Maggie. "Yeah, Maggie."

"We've had a call about Dianne Gilbert's silver Buick. It's in the parking lot of the shooters club. The manager just called it in. He didn't take much notice as she's a member, but then he watched the news."

Jenna sighed. "That's great but we have to go and interview a suspect. Call Wolfe and he'll organize a tow truck to take it to the lab."

"Okay." Maggie disconnected.

She looked at Kane. "We have Gilbert's vehicle. I'm handing it over to Wolfe. We need to go."

"I'm not familiar with Edgemont Ave." Kane scratched his chin and stared at her. It's not up in the mountains again, is it?"

Hoping Kane's memory wasn't regressing, Jenna shook her head and placed the Thermos on the desk. "No, it's in the new builds, not far from the hospital. As we have localized flooding, maybe to be safe you should check the road conditions. I sent the others to Pine because that side of town is too high to be flooded." She grabbed her still damp slicker from the peg behind the door and reluctantly pulled it over her head. "Unless anything else happens today, we'll head home after the interview as well. I just hope we can make it. The roads didn't look good when we came through this morning." She filled her pockets with energy bars from a box on the counter and picked up the Thermos.

"I figure the lowlands would flood before that happens. It would need to become an inland sea to flood our road." Kane was searching his phone. "Just give me a second." He scrolled through pages and then nodded. "Yeah, our way home is fine and so is Edgemont Ave." He pocketed his phone and bent to attach Duke's coat. "It's been a long day hasn't it, boy?"

After Kane pulled on his slicker and gathered his things, they headed out the door. Down in the foyer, she stopped at the counter and glanced at Poppy. "You can head home." She turned away to speak to Maggie. "I'm sorry. I've kept you way too long."

"The slow days make up for it and I know you need me here." Maggie smiled at her. "My husband will have dinner cooking by the time I get home. He likes to help now he's retired. I don't mind working late. I'll wait until the deputies leave and then lock up, unless you want me to wait for them to return."

Jenna smiled at her. "No, it's fine. Lock up when you leave. Rowley and Rio have keys to get back into the office."

"Sure thing." Maggie smiled at her. "See you in the morning."

Jenna chuckled. "I'll be here even if I have to swim."

"I'll call you later, Dave." Poppy smiled at Kane and then looked directly at Jenna almost challenging her to say something.

I wouldn't give you the satisfaction. Ignoring her, Jenna followed Kane out of the door and dashed to the Beast. She could hear the rain beating down on Kane's slicker as he secured Duke in the back seat. She turned and looked at him, and he smiled at her with rain dripping off the rim of his Stetson. By the time he'd slipped behind the wheel Jenna had entered the address into the GPS.

"Poppy is pushing your buttons again." Kane looked at her with a concerned expression. "She has nothing to discuss with me." He shrugged. "If I'd wanted to hook up with her, I had plenty of chances and I didn't. If she calls tonight or any other time, I'll block her calls. I'll be adding my own complaint about her to Mayor Petersham. Enough is enough, Jenna. It's time to fire her."

Blowing out a long sigh, Jenna leaned back in her seat. "I'm over talking about Anderson. Can we drop it? What are our plans for dinner tonight?"

"As we're famished, I'm not planning on waiting too long. Frozen pizza, with extra cheese, and I'll defrost one of Aunt Betty's peach pies. I'll slip it into the oven. It comes out just like fresh baked." He started the engine. "By the time we've showered I'll have dinner ready."

Feeling her stomach growl in anticipation, Jenna laughed. "That sounds wonderful." She glanced at the GPS. "Head out toward the hospital. Edgemont Ave. is part of the new building project that Mayor Petersham has been crowing about all year. I'm not aware of the extent of the building in the area but the local professionals seem to like it and they're buying the land like crazy."

The evening was turning ugly. Lightning zigzagged across the darkened sky and thunder rolled down the mountains like giant bowling balls, the noise meeting the next crack of lightning so fast that Jenna expected the trees to fall like ninepins. The entrance to number 4 Edgemont Ave. was little more than a dirt road. To build the house, the ground had been hastily cleared of trees. The driveway had once been covered with gravel, but the constant deluge had washed away most of it, leaving a line of muddy potholes in its wake. "Oh, this doesn't look good."

"No, it doesn't, and with only the headlights, it's impossible to see how deep those holes go. They're probably left from the tree roots." Kane backed away from the driveway and turned onto the blacktop. "I'll drive along the road some and see if there's another way inside the property. This track appears to be the entrance the trucks used during the build. If the owner of the house was sensible, he'd have a separate entrance. I've noticed many of the people living in this area have dual driveways."

Jenna heaved a sigh of relief when a second entrance came into view. Light spilled from the windows of a house about fifty yards ahead through a line of trees. As the Beast's lights moved across the driveway and then illuminated the way ahead, she turned to Kane. "The road looks okay here. From the tracks I would say someone returned to the house recently."

"Yeah, we're good to go." Kane drove through the gates. "When we get there, I'll leave Duke in the truck. He'll be fine."

As they approached the front door, floodlights spilled across the driveway. Jenna collected a notebook out of the glove box and tucked it under her slicker before climbing out. She headed for the door and knocked three times. Footsteps came from inside and she could make out a figure through the glass panels in the door. The door swung open and a man in his thirties wearing a sweater and blue jeans looked from one to the other. His eyes widened behind his glasses, but he said nothing. *No beard like in his online image.* Jenna lifted her chin. "Sheriff's Department. I'm Sheriff Jenna Alton and this is my deputy, Dave Kane. Am I speaking to Patrick Howard?"

"Yes, is there a problem, Sheriff?" Howard pushed a hand through his hair in an agitated manner.

Something was obviously bothering him, and Jenna gave him an encouraging smile. "Not a problem but we need some information. Do you mind if we come in to speak to you?"

"Okay, but would you mind going straight into the mudroom on your left and keeping to the coverings I've laid down against muddy footprints? The contractors only finished the floors a few days ago and the rain has been a real problem. I'm trying to keep everything dry."

"We'll be happy to speak to you in the mudroom." Kane removed his Stetson and slapped it against his leg to remove the raindrops. "This won't take long."

The smell of fresh paint and cooking hung in the air. Jenna scanned the hallway, peering into as many rooms as possible. The sparse furnishings indicated that he hadn't occupied the house for very long. She pulled out the notebook and her pen. "I believe you're a member of a number of dating sites using the online persona Peter Shore."

"How do you know that?" Howard became immediately defensive and narrowed his eyes at Jenna.

"Oh, we know everything that goes on in Black Rock Falls, Mr. Howard." Kane slowly replaced his Stetson and stared at him. "Why the need to use an alias?"

"I'm a computer science teacher at the high school." Howard rubbed the back of his neck. "Can you imagine what would happen if the students discovered I was using an online dating app? I would lose every ounce of respect I've gained over the last five years working here."

His excuse sounded reasonable, and Jenna made a few notes before looking up at him. "I'm sure you've heard on the news by now about the deaths of Dianne Gilbert and Shelby O'Connor? We know that you were in contact with both of these women over the last few months. We're trying to establish a timeframe between when they were last seen and when they were found deceased. When did you last speak to them?"

"I'm assuming from what you're saying that Dianne and Shelby have been murdered." Howard looked from one to the other. "Is that correct?"

Keeping her expression bland, Jenna met his eyes. "The cause of death is undetermined at this time. Will you please answer the question, Mr. Howard?"

"Do I need to call my lawyer?" Howard's hands trembled as he reached into his back pocket for his phone.

"The Sheriff only asked when you'd last spoken to them." Kane inclined his head and raised one eyebrow. "I can't imagine the answer would give us enough evidence to prosecute you for murder, but if you want to call your lawyer, go ahead. It's your dime."

Jenna cleared her throat to get Howard's attention. "We can obtain the transcripts of the messages you sent to both women, but if you cooperate, it will save valuable time. We're already in possession of a court order to do this. How do you think we tracked you down?"

"I didn't think I could be tracked using an alias and a phony email address." Howard looked astounded. "I used a burner phone to speak to them and they're untraceable."

"We have ways of tracking down everybody." Kane shrugged nonchalantly. "Especially when you used your own laptop and wireless. I found you through your IP address."

Starting to get irritated by the delay, Jenna raised her voice. "Okay, Mr. Howard, you have two choices: answer the question now or we'll take you down to the office and wait for your lawyer to drop by."

"Okay, okay. Give me a minute." Howard started to pace up and down the small room becoming more and more agitated. "I spoke to Dianne on the phone maybe two weeks ago. She seemed reluctant to want to meet me after I told her I'd shaved off my beard, although I offered to take her to dinner at Antlers." He stopped pacing and turned the phone over in his hand. "I spoke to Shelby weeks ago. She was never really interested once I told her my occupation. It seemed that she was more interested in somebody on a higher income, like a doctor or lawyer." He snorted. "I didn't come up to her standard." He looked at Kane. "Haven't you noticed how some women act like that? They come over all nice at the start and then turn into vipers?" He barked a laugh. "No, I guess someone like you wouldn't understand what it's like for us mere mortals."

"I think I do." Kane straightened. "Life isn't a bed of roses for all of us, you know."

Jenna looked at her notes. "Can you account for your whereabouts around eight on Sunday and last night?"

"I was here." Howard chewed on his bottom lip. "I live alone, and now that means I don't have an alibi for when they were murdered, doesn't it?"

Jenna raised an eyebrow. "I don't recall mentioning they were murdered." She closed her notepad and tucked it back under her slicker. "That's all for now, Mr. Howard. I suggest you don't leave town. I might need to speak to you again."

As they drove home, Jenna turned to Kane. "What did you make of Howard?"

"Way too nervous. Hearing about their deaths on the TV might have softened the blow, but he showed no empathy for the dead women. I figure he knows something he's not telling us, but my gut is telling me he's not responsible." Kane headed through town, throwing up great sprays of water as the Beast charged through the puddles. "We'll need to go over the bank accounts of the victims. Having the phone records isn't enough. The targets are all wealthy. That has to be a motive."

Jenna nodded. "I'll talk to the banks again in the morning." She sighed. "So you think the murders were to keep them quiet?"

"Nah." Kane's mouth flattened into a thin line. "That was personal and the killer enjoyed it."

TWENTY-TWO

After calling his wife, Sandy, Rowley pulled on his slicker and peered out the glass doors of the office. Mother Nature was dancing with Thor by the sound of the thunder, and a lightshow stretched from one end of town to the other and beyond. He turned to Rio. "It's nasty out there. I figure we should go in my truck. I'll drop you by here to pick up your vehicle after the interview."

"Yeah, that's fine by me." Rio pushed on his Stetson and smiled. "Especially as you have the coffee." He turned and gave Maggie a wave. "See you in the morning."

"Drive safe now." Maggie smiled at them.

Bending his head against the rain, Rowley ran to his truck with Rio splashing along behind out of the parking space. "How do you want to play this?"

"You take the lead and I'll just jump in if necessary." Rio pulled an energy bar from his pocket and slowly unwrapped it. "I've been doing a deal of research on serial killers, and don't you think it's unusual for them to be killing during this unusual weather event?"

Dragging his thoughts away from his wife and the twins

waiting for him at home, Rowley shrugged. "It's a compulsion to kill, so maybe the weather doesn't make much difference. Ask Kane. He has details like that at his fingertips."

"I analyzed the conditions behind some of the cases that I was researching and came up with two different conclusions." Rio had that faraway look he always had when he was analyzing situations. "The first one is that a killer might believe that heavy rain destroys evidence." He waved a hand. "When sometimes it's the complete opposite. Footprints in soft dirt, evidence on the victim's clothes can give a positive identification of the location of the murder." He held up two fingers. "The second is that bad weather would keep witnesses away from the murder scene. These people are very smart and they'd know it's unusual for foot patrols to be conducted during a storm. Most cops would be sticking to their patrol cars."

Rowley turned his truck onto Pine. "Yeah, all of that makes sense, but it wouldn't work for a thrill killer. They're opportunistic and not many people are walking the streets during thunderstorms like we've been having over the last week. I figure whoever's committing these murders has it planned down to the last second."

He slowed the truck and searched for number twenty-six. The rusty gate hung open on a jaunty angle, one end resting heavily against a pine tree. Ahead, a dark driveway vanished into a maze of trees and vegetation. Vines wrapped around every tree, forming a canopy that blocked out the last rays of daylight. Rowley unconsciously touched the butt of his weapon. Driving onto a person's property at dusk always posed a risk. Even without a TRESPASSERS WILL BE SHOT sign, the "castle law" in Montana gave residents the right to defend themselves against intruders walking onto their property. In fact, all Montanans had the right to defend themselves anywhere if they believed they were in danger. He flicked on his wigwag lights and red and blue lit up the trees around them. He glanced at Rio. "Just in case the owner views us as a threat."

"They all consider law enforcement as a threat." Rio grinned at him. "Everyone has something to hide." He glanced around. "This place is spooky. I'm sure glad it's not Halloween. In this town trick-or-treat has a whole new meaning."

Laughing, Rowley looked at him. "Oh, it's not that bad. So we've had a few murders around Halloween. Nothing has happened when the kids were out in their costumes."

"Not yet anyway." Rio peered ahead. "It looks like the owner has come out to greet us. I'm glad he's pointing that shotgun at you rather than me."

Rowley sucked in a breath. "At this range it wouldn't make much difference. Send a message to Jenna just in case he decides to shoot."

"Okay." The message went and Jenna replied. Rio glanced over to him. "They're on their way." He let out a long sigh and pushed open the door. "I'll speak to him." He stepped into the rain. "Trenton Hyde?"

"The one and only." Hyde lowered his weapon a few inches as if deciding which one of them to shoot first. "What do you want? This is private property."

"I need to ask you a few questions about Tom Creedy." Rio stood behind the truck door with his weapon drawn. "Can we come onto the porch? It's kinda wet out here."

"I guess so." Hyde dropped the shotgun alongside his leg.

"Drive up closer." Rio dropped back into the seat. "He's not a threat now. If he tries anything, I'll drop him before he raises his weapon. I'll send a message to Jenna."

Still doubtful, Rowley drove to the front porch and, keeping a close eye on Hyde, moved slowly up the steps. Under his slicker, he rested his hand on his pistol, just in case. The man didn't resemble the image he used online. Hyde was older than the thirty years he'd listed for his alias Tom Creedy by ten years or so, but he did have a beard. He was finding it hard to believe this man was a data analyst. "Mr. Hyde? We traced an online persona as Tom Creedy to a computer owned by you at this address. Do you live alone?"

"No." Hyde closed the front door behind him and lowered his voice. "My wife is inside."

"So, I assume you wouldn't want her to know about Tom Creedy?" Rio moved up the steps to Rowley's side. "I guess searching the internet for another woman would be difficult to explain."

"There's no law against it, is there?" Hyde's eyes flashed with anger. "What business is it of yours anyhow?" The man's hand moved on the shotgun, and he raised it slightly as if in warning.

Standing his ground, Rowley straightened. He pointed to the swing on the stoop. "Put down the gun, Mr. Hyde. We're not a threat to you and all we want to do is to get this interview over and get back to our families."

"So what do you want?" Hyde reluctantly laid down the shotgun. "My wife is impaired. She had a stroke five years ago. I have my needs and she doesn't need to know about it. So what, I meet women online. After, I come back and care for her."

"Who cares for your wife when you're out with other women?" Rio's eyebrows raised in question.

"Her sister drops by to stay overnight." Hyde wiped a hand down his face. "If you were in my position, you'd understand."

Unable to contemplate cheating on his wife, Rowley cleared his throat. "I believe you were in contact with Dianne Gilbert and Shelby O'Connor. From the messages we obtained from their phones, you've known both of them for over three months. When was the last time you met either of them?"

"What makes you think I've met either of them?" Hyde narrowed his gaze and looked from one to the other. "I wanted to, but I figure they were too classy for me. They expected the

best restaurants and when I mentioned booking a room somewhere they both insisted on the Cattleman's Hotel. I ended up
having to make excuses. You see, there are plenty of women out
there happy to just go for a drink. I never meet up with them
more than once." He shrugged. "I'm not interested in forming a
relationship." He stared at Rowley. "Don't give me that conde-
scending look. It's better than cheating on my wife with hook-
ers, isn't it?"

Shaking his head, Rowley blanked his expression. "Are you
aware that Dianne Gilbert and Shelby O'Connor were found
dead?"

"Nope." Hyde shrugged. "Like I said, I didn't have too
much to do with them. A few text messages, one phone call, is
all. What happened to them? Did they drown in the floods?"

"That's yet to be determined." Rio pulled out his notebook.
"Where were you on Sunday night and last night around eight-
thirty?"

"I was here with my wife." Hyde stared at them as if daring
them to question her about his whereabouts.

The man's expression didn't faze Rowley. "So she'll be able
to verify you were here? Is she capable of speech?"

"She understands everything you say but she can't say
much. I don't want you to question her unless you plan on
hauling me in for murdering two women I've never met." Hyde
shook his head. "If this is the case, then my sister-in-law will be
able to give you the days I went out. I can't leave my wife alone
—and I don't."

"Okay, give me her details." Rio frowned. "We'll only
contact her if necessary. Or is she aware you go out to meet
women?"

"No. I tell her I go visit my brother in Blackwater and stay
over." Hyde was radiating something like anger. "He has my
back." He gave Rio the information and then looked at Rowley.
"Women don't understand the needs of a man. They start off

sweet and then become a burden." He let out a low growl. "Don't suggest that divorce is a solution because it's not."

Disturbed by the man's rising anger, Rowley shook his head. "I can't advise you on marriage, Mr. Hyde." Interested in how he supported his lifestyle, he pushed on. "You're a data analyst, right? How do you manage to work and stay home to care for your wife?"

"Yeah, I'm a data analyst. Everything is done online these days. You don't need a fancy office just for someone to employ you." Hyde leaned against the wall. "Tons of people work from home these days. It's nothing unusual." A sound came from behind him and he glanced over one shoulder. "Is that all? I need to get back inside."

Having no other questions, Rowley glanced at Rio. At his nod, he smiled at Mr. Hyde. "That's all we need. Thank you for your cooperation."

Rowley walked down the steps and back to his truck. The back of his neck prickled, knowing that Hyde would only need a few seconds to grab and aim his shotgun. As he started the engine, he glanced at Rio. "That guy gives me the creeps."

"He hasn't a reliable witness to say he was at home when the murders took place." Rio dropped into the passenger seat. "If his wife is as incapacitated as he said, she might not be a reliable witness. Another thing, why the alias? How could his wife find out he was running around town with other women? She never goes out and I'll bet my last dime she can't use a computer. Who would tell her? Not her sister, that's for darn sure. She's already covering up for him."

Running the information through his mind, Rowley nodded. "That's if his wife is incapacitated. He made sure we didn't see her, didn't he?" He thought for a beat. "I'll run it past Jenna. Usually, people in similar situations require some type of outside assistance. A doctor or social worker would usually be checking in on them from time to time. Maybe she has a nurse drop by. She must be on medication." He stared back at the house in his rear-vision mirror. "I'm finding it hard to believe women want to hook up with him on dates."

"I can just imagine their faces when they see he's not the guy in the photograph. Although if what he says is true, they don't seem to mind." Rio shook his head. "I figured some of the dating apps are used to arrange booty calls and he's proved me right. I guess when you think about it, with the booty calls and the catfishing, there's not many people on them actually looking for a perfect match."

Thinking of his own precious wife, Rowley smiled. "I'm glad I'll never have to use one of them." He glanced at Rio. "Would you?"

"Me?" Rio chuckled. "Nah—not yet anyway. I'm taking baby steps toward a relationship with Emily Wolfe. She doesn't want to jeopardize her career right now, so we're not planning on getting serious." He rubbed his chin ruefully. "The waiting I can handle, but then there's her dad—at least he hasn't tried to kill me yet."

Rowley headed back to town. "I like Emily. She's smart and beautiful, but beware of the big bad Wolfe. One wrong step and he'll blow your house down."

TWENTY-THREE

WEDNESDAY

Kane gave his black stallion a friendly slap on the rump, walked out of the stall and shut the gate. He'd checked him over with great care to make sure he hadn't suffered any side effects from the lightning strike. Jenna's recounting of the incident came to mind. Warrior, although rolling his eyes in fear, had led her to him. He'd bonded with Warrior from the first day they'd met. He'd had a choice of a few available horses, but Warrior had nosed him in the back as if to say, "I'm coming home with you." The fact he'd stayed around rather than heading back to the barn proved his loyalty, but Warrior was *his* horse and his alone. Others found him a little wild. Shaking his head in disbelief that he'd actually expected Jenna to tend Warrior after such a traumatic experience troubled him. What had he been thinking? He thanked God that Rowley had been on hand to tend the horses. Warrior needed a firm hand most times and although he'd walked him through fire, any stallion would be skittish after what had happened. He tried to find the memory of that day and came up empty. It was like it hadn't happened—as if he'd slept through an entire day—and yet he'd been driving the Beast!

Glad he'd gone to the expense and extended the barn to incorporate larger than normal stalls for the horses, he leaned on the gate to watch Warrior dip his head into the carrots he'd left as treats. Not being able to ride the horses as much as they'd liked was fine when the weather was good but turning them out into a storm wasn't an option. At least with the larger stalls they wouldn't go stir crazy. He'd been leaving a radio on all day. The talkback station played a few tunes and seemed to keep the horses placid. He turned as Jenna came into the barn pushing the wheelbarrow. She'd insisted on taking the dung outside to the pile after delivering an impressive kick to his groin earlier during their workout. He smiled to himself. She'd actually struck him on the bruised thigh he'd received falling from Warrior, and he'd groaned and rolled away from her. She'd been horrified at hurting him, but he'd lapped up the attention she'd offered. It was something he'd never want to get used to. "I'm just about done here. Why don't you head in for a shower?"

"Okay." Jenna went on tiptoes to kiss him, her cheeks wet from the rain. "Are you okay?"

Kane pulled her close and pushed a strand of wet hair under her hood. "Yeah, I'm fine. I'm in excellent physical condition and I tend to recover faster than most people. I could have taken out the dung."

"Yeah, no doubt, but I needed the exercise." Jenna bounced away from him. "I'll cook this morning. There are still hotcakes left over from yesterday and I can't do too much damage to strips of bacon."

Wiping a hand down his face, he grinned at her. "Okay. I'll be there soon." He turned to pull out wads of hay from a bale and dropped them into the mangers.

His phone buzzed and he answered using his wireless earbuds. "Kane."

"Hi there, Kane." FBI Agent Ty Carter's distinctive drawl came through the earpiece. "I've been looking over the names *you sent to Kalo. We haven't found a trace of the real name of Julian Darnley. To most people, his company appears to be legit. It takes some kind of skill to create backup information to support a phony company. Kalo is still searching, but he said it was like chasing smoke."*

Kane leaned against the stall and stared at the sheets of rain creating small streams that headed down the steep driveway and disappeared. "Why am I not surprised? We're waiting on the banks to release the victims' bank accounts. I can smell a scam here, and when one of the witnesses mentioned cryptocurrency, it started to fit together."

"Yeah, but without Darnley's ID, you have nothing." Carter sighed. "The interesting thing is that Kalo found a gamer link between two of your suspects and decided to hunt down the people they played with over the last few months. Surprisingly, he discovered all the people you sent us to investigate are gamers and play in the same community. Kalo mentioned they're in the same clan, gamer talk for their own group, I guess. He figures Darnley is one of the gamers. He has to be. It would be too much of a coincidence that the killer isn't one of the clan. All of them have a similar skill set and knowledge of the dark web. He fits. There's another guy in the same clan you might want to hunt down as well. This is an oddball case. They look like a bunch of harmless nerds. Is this all the suspects you have right now?"

"We're interviewing two in town. There's zip solid evidence. We're hoping the autopsy this morning and the bank records will give us more information." Kane scratched his cheek. "I'm in the barn. Can you send me the details? Do any of them have priors?"

"Nah, nothing on file. A few juvie offences but nothing to cause alarm, People use an alias for different reasons and gamers in particular have avatars as well—I mean some of them are wizards or dragons." Carter snorted. "That doesn't mean they're not capable of murder. We all know that killers come in every

flavor. We're not giving up on Darnley. He's fixed himself so deep in the dark web it's going to take time to unravel his ID. He's up to no good, that's for darn sure. Maybe not murder but you might have unearthed a cryptocurrency scam and we need to take him down." He blew out a long breath. *"Okay, I'm sending through the info now. If we find anything else, I'll call you."*

Pushing away from the wall, Kane headed for the barn door. "Thanks, I'd appreciate it." He disconnected, pushed his Stetson down hard over his head, hit the keypad to close the barn door behind him, and then dashed to the house.

Over breakfast Kane brought Jenna up to speed with the information Carter had supplied. He opened the file on his phone. "Steven Croxley is Steven Finch. He's an herbalist and recently opened a new store in town. It's called the Black Rock Falls Wellness Center." He searched for the store online and found the website. "He's a seller of medicinal herbs. Hmm, so he'd know all about naturally occurring poisons."

"How long has he been in business? I don't recall seeing his store." Jenna crunched on a strip of bacon.

Kane scanned the page. "About six months, I guess. His store is down the alleyway beside the bank. From what I can make out, he's refurbished the storage shed beside the beauty parlor. With the mist coming from the river every night, that would be a perfect place to have a store that sells potions." He grinned at her. "Come Halloween, there'll be a lineup outside his store for love potions and good luck charms, just in case we have another serial killer running the streets this year."

"Okay, who else?" Jenna refilled the cups with coffee and idly added the fixings.

Kane scrolled down the list. "Branch Drummond. He lists his fake occupation as a heart specialist." He looked at Jenna and raised both eyebrows. "I'm not sure what hearts he specializes in but they're not human. His current occupation is listed as a cleaner at the meat-processing plant. His real name is Bruce

Campion, a gamer. After looking at the other suspects Kalo traced him through his online gaming ID. He's using the same laptop for both gaming and the dating app. It seems this group of people prefers to use the public wireless connection in town at the computer shop."

"That would make sense." Jenna sipped her coffee and looked at him over the rim. "I recall Wolfe mentioning if you use public wireless, you're able to create an untraceable chain of connections. I remember him mentioning something about bouncing signals around the world or something?"

"Yeah, then this would make his dark web page difficult to trace." Kane leaned back in his chair, making the wood creek. "Okay next on the list is Wyatt Kennedy out of Riverside Road, Black Rock Falls. The interesting thing about this man is he's using a dark web identity and his real profession is financial advisor. He raised a red flag for Kalo for those reasons alone, so I figured we should check him out."

"Maybe he's Julian Darnley." Jenna poured more syrup on her hotcakes. "Have we got an image of him?"

Turning his laptop around to face her, Kane displayed the picture of the man on the screen. "No beard and no glasses but those could be just props he's using to fool the women he meets. I figure if he's planning on killing them, he wouldn't want to scare them off."

"Who else?" Jenna sighed. "This is becoming a marathon."

Kane turned his laptop back around and scrolled through the files. "This is one of the clan of gamers Kalo discovered and added to the list. His name is Jack Sutherland out of 22 Miles Street, East Meadow. Online persona: Keats. He is an English literature teacher in middle school. The other one he added is Nathan Stevens, a pathologist out of 5 Elm Street, and his online persona is Bloodlust. You gotta love that—he lives on *Elm Street*. Now that's spooky." He grinned at her. "I guess we'll break this list down between us and work through it." He frowned as he scrolled through the crime scene photographs. "Without evidence, it's all grunt work. We have two dead women, and you know darn well it's only a matter of time before the killer strikes again."

"This is why I don't want to jump on these men too early and spook them. We'll need more information before we question them." Jenna pushed a strand of hair behind one ear and looked at him. "I figure we wait and see what Wolfe finds in the autopsy and then see what the bank statements reveal. We need to know what we're dealing with, and right now we're grabbing at straws."

TWENTY-FOUR

Julian Darnley arrived before dawn at the house and moved through the rooms, taking shots with his phone. He wanted to make sure everything was back in its right place when he left. His friend had found another perfect kill house. It was on the edge of the forest with no close neighbors. His next date could scream and run for miles and no one would hear or see her.

Once finished, he removed the framed photographs from the family room and the kids' drawings plastered all over the refrigerator. He'd explained to his date, they'd be dining at a friend's house and hoped she wouldn't snoop around. It would make way too much extra work for them once she'd gone. Checking for her fingerprints and the hairs she might have shed meant meticulously cleaning every surface—but it was worth it. The anticipation of the next kill shivered through him. Knowing what was to come outweighed the expected increase in his finances. He had more than he could ever spend but he'd never be able to stop killing. Watching the next overly entitled woman die in fear was an addiction and he couldn't get enough.

A tremble of excitement rippled through him as he called

his friend. "I'm here and everything is in place. I'll leave for work soon."

"Have you considered my request?" His friend gave an excited chuckle. *"I can't stop thinking about it. I want it so bad."*

Darnley leaned against the doorframe. "I'll give you a cut of everything I take, but I need the kill. It makes it complete for me. You understand that, right?"

"Yeah, maybe." His friend paused for a beat. *"I figure you owe me this one. I did find her for you after all."*

Annoyed, Darnley pushed away from the wall and headed for the front door. He struggled into his coat and reached for the knob. He'd wrapped tape around the lock, to make his entrance easier the next time he arrived, although picking locks was his specialty. "Do you know how long it took me to convince her to meet with me? I had to give her ten grand to make the investment look legit."

"Just this one." His friend cleared his throat. *"Agree or I walk. I'm over watching you have all the fun."*

Ignoring the soaking rain, Darnley stopped in the driveway. "If you want to kill women—hire yourself a hooker."

"Really? It doesn't work that way and you know it. What fun would there be in killing a hooker? It's all about the chase and you know it." His friend snorted in disgust. *"You need me, and we work well together."*

Sliding into the rental, Darnley stared into the forest. Water dripped from pines darkened by the constant deluge, sending small rivulets running down the driveway in a spiderweb of veins. Shadows filled the forest and it screamed danger. Seeing it like this excited him. His fingers itched to be cutting a slender throat and watching the blood spill onto the rain-soaked driveway and wash away.

"Are you listening to me?"

The voice in his ear brought him out of his fantasy. "Yeah,

I'm here. I'm in the Yukon and heading for work. Okay, I guess you can have this one. We'll work out the details later."

"You won't be disappointed." His friend chuckled. *"I'll make her suffer."*

TWENTY-FIVE

Heavy clouds slipped down the mountains and hung over the town like a white tablecloth. The reports of more landslides came almost daily. So far, they'd been high in the mountains but the back road to the Glacial Heights Ski Resort was blocked. Jenna stared at the soaked lowlands. Cattle stood huddled under trees, some surrounded by the rising floodwater. The brown swirling menace was everywhere. She turned to Kane. "I'll get Maggie to chase down the owner of those cows. I figure he moved them here to be safe and the water has risen overnight."

"I'm not sure how he's going to move them." Kane's brow wrinkled into a frown. "The water has come up to the top of the fenceposts over yonder. His access might be better from this side. A horse should get through okay, but forcing cattle to walk through deep water won't be easy."

Strategizing her day ahead, Jenna scanned her files. Her deputies had filed reports on their interview with Trenton Hyde. She relayed the information to Kane. "Rowley doubts Hyde is involved. Rio's take is the same. Hyde is a data analyst and Rio believes he's capable of hiding his activities on the dark web but figures he's more of a gamer than someone catfishing. His notes about gamers are interesting. He thinks they live in an alternate world and like to keep their real identity secret."

"Hyde doesn't sound like a man capable of murder." Kane flicked her a glance.

Considering the obstacles preventing the investigation moving forward, Jenna chewed on her bottom lip, thinking. "I hope we'll be able to search the victims' bank accounts soon. I sent Rio with all the necessary paperwork and there's a note saying that the bank manager will get back to us this morning."

"We'll get it." Kane snorted. "If I know Kalo, he wouldn't wait for a bank manager to get off his butt. He'd just hold on to it until it was legal to release the information."

Nodding, Jenna grimaced. "He skates a fine line between legal and illegal. I guess once a hacker always a hacker. Although, I know Jo watches him like a hawk. She is a stickler for the rules."

"I don't understand the bank manager's hesitancy." Kane shook his head. "The women are dead and maybe more will follow if we can't follow leads. Delays like this end up costing lives."

Jenna nodded. "He's the assistant manager, the other guy is away for three months visiting his family in California."

As they turned onto Main the emptiness of the usually busy town surprised her. "Where is everyone?"

"Staying home, I guess." Kane drove into his slot outside the office. "Rio and Rowley are keen to start work today. I'm surprised they made it here before us this morning."

Jenna led the way inside and smiled at Maggie behind the front counter. "Morning, Maggie. Any calls on the hotline?"

"Nothing as yet." Maggie smiled back. "I'm sure glad you got through the floodwater today. The latest road reports are just in. There's some local flooding here. I'll give you a list—oh, and Blackwater is still isolated. Now there's water across the highway in that low patch near Elk Crossing."

"Thanks." Jenna glanced around the office. "Did everyone come in early today?"

"Anderson hasn't arrived yet." Maggie peered over the counter. "And where is my foot warmer today?"

"At home. He's sharing his basket with Pumpkin now and went back to bed after breakfast. We turned up the heat for them before we left. They're good company for each other and won't even miss us." Kane leaned on the counter, his hands clasped. "I did ask Duke to come with us, but he just buried his nose under the cat and pretended to be asleep."

Jenna laughed. "He'll be fine. He has food, water, and a doggy door."

She gave Maggie a wave and headed through the office. She went to Rio's and Rowley's desks. "We'll discuss the case in my office." She turned to Rio. "When we're done, go and chase down the bank accounts of the two victims. Surely the assistant manager has released them by now. This waiting is getting ridiculous. We've never had such a delay before he arrived."

"The guy isn't at all approachable, Sheriff. If he hasn't signed the paperwork, I can try and explain that we can't proceed with the investigation until we get to view the bank accounts." Rio glanced at his watch. "I figure he won't be in the office until at least nine. I'll head over then to speak to him." He met her gaze. "Are you sure you want me to do this? I figure Kane might have more influence over him?"

Slightly confused, Jenna frowned. "I'm sure you are quite capable of talking to a bank manager. From what I'm hearing about him, he lacks confidence. Maybe if you explain that we're dealing with a probable psychopathic killer you may be able to get him to hand over the files. The entire case hinges on the fact that we believe the motive for these murders has something to do with cryptocurrency. Without being able to peruse the victim's bank accounts, we've got no proof."

"I'll make sure to tell him." Rio gathered his things from the table. "Did you make any headway with Patrick Howard?"

Jenna turned and headed for the stairs with Rowley and Rio close behind. "Yes and no, but we do have a list of potential suspects that Kalo hunted down for us. We'll need to interview them today."

As she climbed the stairs the smell of brewing coffee drifted toward her. Kane had gone upstairs on arrival and filled the coffee machine. As she walked through the door, she giggled. He was going through the cabinets hunting down cookies. It was less than an hour since breakfast and he was hungry again already. "Thanks for making the coffee."

"We'll need it if we're going to be out most of the day." Kane pulled out the Thermos flasks and nodded to Rowley and Rio as they arrived. "Grab what you need. It's going to be a long day."

"I'm just hoping we don't get a call about another body." Rowley walked to the counter and filled a cup. "They never stop at two." He cleared his throat. "I dropped by the beauty parlor this morning on my way here. They open at eight and I asked about Shelby O'Connor. I spoke to her stylist, and she doesn't recall her ever speaking about her personal life. Their conversations were usually about fashion and online shopping."

"Well, it was worth asking. Thanks." Jenna, went to the whiteboard, took the pen from the holder, and with her iPad in one hand added names to the list of suspects. She turned to look at her team. "I'm not convinced Patrick Howard or Trenton Hyde are main suspects. I'm not dismissing them completely, but Kalo sent us a few interesting people to add to our list of possibilities."

"Wouldn't it save time if we waited for the bank records before we interview these men?" Rio stared at the whiteboard.

"At least we'll be able to concentrate on people who might have a possible motive."

Jenna paused writing and turned to him. "No. I need the information these people might be able to give us ASAP."

"All these people are connected." Kane sat down at the desk and stared at Rio. "They're all gamers."

Jenna nodded. "Which means they know each other. Maybe not by name but by their player ID." She added more names to the board and underlined them. "All these men are gamers in what Kalo referred to as a clan. Not all of them are using a dating app, which is to our advantage because it narrows the field."

She looked at the list on the board.

Steven Croxley. Online name: Steven Finch. Herbalist at the Black Rock Falls Wellness Center. Dating app.

Bruce Campion. Online name: Dr. Branch Drummond. Gamer ID: Dr. Death. Fake occupation: heart specialist. Real occupation: janitor at the meat-processing plant. Dating app.

Wyatt Kennedy. Riverside Road, Black Rock Falls. Online name: Fall Guy. Not on dating app. Gamer.

Jenna stared at her team. "We've no reason to believe Kennedy is involved, but as Kalo recognized his name from the dark web and discovered his profession as a financial advisor, if we discover the murders revolve around a scam, I figure we should see what he has to say. You'll also notice Julian Darnley, the CEO of Darnley Enterprises, is missing. This is because Kalo couldn't identify him. He believes he's one of the men in the group of gamers but has created an impenetrable maze around himself. It's as if he is a ghost. Kalo mentioned it was like chasing smoke. He finds a trail and then it vanishes. He could be using a ton of different IDs on online accounts, and then when anyone gets close, he deletes them and moves on. This being the case, we leave no stone unturned. We assume one of these men is the killer and use caution. Darnley is on both women's lists of potential dates, but so are the others, so don't get sidetracked. Any one of them could be the killer." She glanced around, glad to see their heads nodding. "Okay, next we have:"

Nathan Stevens. 5 Elm Street. Pathologist. Gamer name: Bloodlust.

Jack Sutherland. 22 Miles Street, East Meadow. English literature teacher at middle school. Gamer ID: Keats.

"Kennedy, Stevens, and Sutherland are the three we need to lean on to see if they'll give us information about the others' online playing times." Kane cracked his knuckles. "The other two are catfishing. We'll start with them and see what a little digging will unearth."

"What are you trying to achieve by speaking to these men?" Rowley looked up from his iPad.

Seeing Rowley's overwhelmed expression, Jenna nodded. "We only need to find one of them willing to cooperate with us. Gamers usually play at the same time and compete against each other or play as a team. One of them would be able to tell us if the others were online or missing at the time of the murders."

"It only takes one to cooperate with us." Kane opened his hands. "The person in the clan missing at the time of the murders will give us a head start. If Kalo can track him down on the dark web, he might find a money trail. I'm convinced the Jack of Hearts Killer is catfishing online and scamming vulnerable women."

Jenna returned to her seat. "We need a motive for killing the women. So far, we know the suspects are tied up with the dating apps. It's too much of a coincidence for two women with practically the same list of potential dates to be murdered."

"This is where I get confused." Rowley's eyebrows met together in a frown. "One of these men is using a dating app to meet women, and then he kills them. It seems simple to me. What makes you think there is a scam going on as well? Isn't catfishing just someone pretending to be someone else online to get a date?"

Jenna waved a hand at Kane. "This is why we have a profiler on the team."

"Looking at the dating apps and the online information, these women were cautious. From the messages and other information we hunted down, they both had long conversations with the suspects before they committed to going on a date." Kane leaned back in his chair. "If this is a serial killer who plans his kills over months, it would be unusual. They might follow a woman around and then kill them, but long conversations would suggest empathy. So, this guy has something else he's after. We're both convinced the only way a killer would wait for his kill was for a special reason. Both our victims were wealthy. The reason is money. We just have to prove it." He looked from Rowley to Rio. "The money trail will lead us to the killer."

"Good luck with that if they're converting it into cryptocurrency and using the dark web to hide the transactions." Rio didn't look convinced. "It might be a solid motive, but how do we prove it?"

Jenna leaned forward and twirled her pen in her fingers. "We don't have to prove motive. We just need it to point us to the killer. Kalo was a black hat hacker. He hacked the Pentagon and just about every so-called impenetrable system. This is why the FBI employed him. He'll get the information we need."

"If the killer is convincing women to give up their cash and then killing them to hide his involvement"—Kane shrugged—"then the motive is clear."

Jenna stared directly at Rio. "Head over to the bank now. We must get those files."

TWENTY-SIX

Kane stared out of the office window, willing the rain to stop. The dark days dragged on forever and confused his internal clock. He always had some idea of the time, but after a week of torrential rain, the only thing keeping time was his stomach.

After Jenna had divided the list of suspects between them, it hadn't taken long to discover the men's locations. Rio and Rowley would head out to speak to Wyatt Kennedy, the financial advisor who worked for the local bank, and then visit Branch Drummond. Footsteps on the stairs had everyone staring at the door.

"How did it go?" Jenna stood as Rio came into the room.

"I have the last three months of the victim's accounts." Rio grinned and handed her a flash drive.

"I'll send them to Kalo. You head off to interview the suspects and watch your backs. We're on our way to the autopsy." Jenna tapped her bottom lip. "When we're done, I'll call you. But if you're through before I call, go and see Wyatt Kennedy." She turned away to make the call. "Bobby, we have a green light." She listened for a beat. "Thank you. Call anytime day or night." She looked at Kane. "Let's get at it. We're already late."

Kane nodded and turned to the deputies. "Take a break to eat at the usual time. It's nasty weather out there. When we're through, we'll be heading out to see Nathan Stevens and then dropping by the Wellness Center to have a chat with Steven Croxley." He stood, filled a Thermos with coffee and handed it to Rowley. "Call in when you arrive and leave."

"Copy that." Rowley pushed his hat firmly on his head, took the Thermos, and followed Rio out the door.

"Wow! This case is overwhelming." Jenna pushed her hands through her hair. "So many suspects and not one of them stands out as a possible."

Kane handed her a Thermos before pulling on his jacket. He slid both hands down Jenna's arms. "We'll need to eliminate each one as soon as possible to narrow the search. I don't figure it will take Kalo too long to get back to us. Once we've gotten the information from the bank statements, we'll have a better idea of which way to take the investigation. At the moment I'm assuming the motive is money." He dropped his hands and reached for his slicker. "If this proves not to be the case, then we're looking at a type of psychopathic behavior we haven't dealt with before. If necessary, I'll consult with Jo. Apart from being friends, Jo and Carter are valuable resources. Jo has been interviewing tons of psychopaths for her research and might have come across something like this before. Unless you have a problem asking the FBI for assistance in this case? It's only two murders. Three give us a serial killer... but I figure it's only a matter of time."

"You once told me that a good leader utilizes all their resources, so why would I mind? Only someone with the brains of a worm would suggest that utilizing every possible source of information at hand is a weakness of character or leadership. I mean, really? It's like suggesting POTUS doesn't discuss things with his advisors but just goes it alone." Jenna handed him his hat. "What are your main concerns with the profile? It's just not like you not to have some type of idea by now."

Kane smiled at her. "Oh, I do have some idea of a profile but it's vague because the crime scenes are confusing." He pushed on his black Stetson. "First, Dianne Gilbert was poisoned. That's a hands-off method of murder typically favored by women." He collected his notebook from the table and pushed it inside his pocket. "Then we have a complete turnaround with O'Connor."

"How so?" Jenna leaned one hip against the desk and raised an eyebrow in question.

Kane shrugged. "Strangulation takes strength. It's very personal and hands on. It's not what it looks like in the movies. It's a horrific thing to witness. Anyone who hasn't done it before often makes the mistake of not continuing the pressure for at least four minutes. When you're killing someone, four minutes is a very long time. Any less and the victim will regain consciousness. From what I noticed at the scene, O'Connor was attacked from behind and by someone much taller than her. The body was moved. O'Connor wasn't a small woman, and it would take a reasonably strong person to lift a dead body into a truck, push it behind the wheel, and sit it up."

"The Triple Z Roadhouse is busy all the time, day and night." Jenna stared into space. "They wouldn't have had too much time to move the body before being seen by someone. What else have you got in that head of yours?"

Smothering a smile, Kane wondered if she could read his mind. "There are glaring anomalies between the cases and if it wasn't for the jack of hearts card left at the scene, I wouldn't have considered them as being by the same hand. Very few psychopaths have breaks between kills. Some do because they have no choice, like being in jail, but once the bloodlust is rampaging, it's unusual for them to stop killing. These murders were meticulously planned, and from what we know from the phone records and social media of the victims, the killer took months of preparation getting to know them—this in itself goes against everything we know about psychopaths. It's the same method of grooming we see in pedophiles—this is why I need to know why they took so long. There must be another reason other than the lust to kill—usually psychopathic killers aren't so patient. It's not their first kill either. It's too clean. I figure something is preventing this man from killing."

"So do you believe a woman is involved?" Jenna chewed on her bottom lip. She glanced up at him. "Have you considered two killers, one male and one female?"

Kane nodded. "Yeah, the thought has crossed my mind. That would be something, wouldn't it? A woman allowing her partner to go on a dating app so he can supply kills for her." He glanced at his watch. "Oh, we are so late for the autopsy."

He followed Jenna down the steps and they dashed to the Beast. Five minutes later, they arrived at the back entrance of the medical examiner's office. This entrance offered a covered parking lot used to move corpses back and forth from examination to undertaker with privacy. It also meant they wouldn't get soaked getting inside.

He waited for Jenna to slide her card through the reader, and as they stepped inside, they almost collided with Emily Wolfe. Wolfe's daughter was coming out of the pathology lab, her attention fixed on an iPad.

"Oh sorry." Emily looked at them. "A few results just came in. I'm taking them to Dad."

"How are the studies going?" Jenna fell into step beside her.

"Great." Emily smiled. "Studying to become a doctor takes time, but I'm well ahead. Interning with Dad makes it so much easier. Others have to wait until we do practical examinations on cadavers to gain the knowledge I have already."

Trying to ignore the smell of antiseptic and death, Kane

smiled at her. Emily's fascination with dead bodies never ceased to amaze him. "We're late. The case is weighing us down with red tape."

"Yeah." Jenna frowned. "We're getting nowhere fast."

A whooshing sound came from along the hallway, and Wolfe stepped out of an examination room. Kane lifted one hand in an apologetic wave. "I'm sorry we're late."

"It's okay." Wolfe waved away the apology. "I was speaking to Jo just before and she mentioned the new judge is a thorn in your side."

"He sure is." Jenna pulled off her coat and reached for a pair of scrubs from the alcove beside the examination room. She tossed a pair to Kane. "In a murder investigation, the last thing we need is delays."

"I won't hold you up." Wolfe turned to Emily. "Do you have results for me?"

"I do." Emily handed over the tablet.

Inquisitive to know what the results would reveal, Kane hurried to remove his jacket and pulled on scrubs, mask, and gloves. He followed Wolfe into the examination room. The smell of death and the sudden drop in temperature raised goosebumps on his flesh. His gaze moved over the body of Shelby O'Connor. Once a vibrant woman and now an empty, decaying vessel. He nodded to Webber and waited for Jenna and Emily to join them before peering at the screen array. "What have we got?"

"Any drugs or poisons in her system?" Jenna moved to his side.

"Nope, not a thing pertinent to her murder. I found contraceptives and an antihistamine, is all. She'd had approximately two glasses of red wine before her death. I found no residual food in her stomach at all." Wolfe's eyebrows rose. "She wasn't murdered in her truck. Every indication suggests the killer attacked her outside in the rain and then transported her body back to her truck. What happened between the time she left her vehicle at the Triple Z Roadhouse parking lot and returned is a mystery, but I'm working on it." He lifted a shoulder. "Usually with two deaths this close together, we assume it's the same killer and find a pattern. In the previous case, I discovered wine and a meal containing poison. As there wasn't a trace of food and no poison in the wine, the only connection is the Jack of Hearts card."

Pinching the face mask tighter over his nose, Kane moved his attention to the X-rays. After so many autopsies he'd gained a wide knowledge of injuries resulting in death. "The hyoid bone is crushed."

"Yeah, and that takes some force." Wolfe walked to the body on the gurney and indicated to the dissected throat. "Shelby O'Connor didn't go down easy. The rope burns are in two different places." He pointed to the red welts around the neck. She was struggling hard." He moved to the victim's arms. "Y'all should look at this. See these half-moon marks on the top of each arm? They indicate there are two people involved. Someone was holding her as she was being strangled. I know it happened at the time of death due to the lack of bruising. Someone held her hard enough to leave nail marks in her flesh. I found DNA traces from the nails and I'm running them through the databases. No hits as yet but we're still searching."

"We had our suspicions, mainly because of the different MOs." Jenna peered at them over her mask. "This sure makes this case interesting. Two sadistic killers with patience, go figure."

Kane nodded. "Yeah, two people with the same psychopathy is unusual. Did you find anything else?"

"I've swabbed the area for latent DNA but she was soaked through, anything viable would've been washed away." Wolfe narrowed his gaze. "Nothing under her nails, no defensive marks. This was an attack from behind, as I've established."

Kane walked slowly around the body, scanning the victim's arms and legs. "Considering the killer or killers are clean freaks and don't leave any trace evidence, why didn't they wash her before dumping her in the truck?"

"Yeah." Jenna stared closely at the victim's legs. "She has dirt and scratches all over. Her feet are cut up, as if she's been running through bushes or on gravel."

"Her arms and cheeks too." Wolfe indicated with one gloved finger. "This would indicate she ran for her life." He went to the screen. "I've taken samples of everything. The soil is local."

Kane leaned back against the cabinet. "Do you figure she met with one guy and the second one showed, maybe acting as backup?"

"That would make sense." Jenna paced up and down. "Maybe something about him spooked her and she made a run for it." She stopped pacing and looked at Kane. "Can you imagine how terrified she must have been?"

Kane allowed the scenario to drift through his mind. "Then the other guy shows and she runs to him for help. He holds on to her so his friend can kill her."

"That's what the evidence proves." Jenna nodded. "Two guys moving a body would be easier." She turned to Wolfe. "She might be carrying fibers from a second vehicle on her. Did you find anything?"

"I did." Wolfe indicated to the screen. "Carpet and fabric fibers consistent with being dragged across the back seat or floor of a vehicle. I also found fragments of what could be a brick wall in the grazes on her knuckles. I'm running an analysis on them now. What is good about finding fibers from vehicles is that many can be traced back to a make and model. The bricks, well most brick houses are red brick in town. One thing is for sure, she wasn't running around a cabin. I figure a red-brick house with a gravel pathway." He indicated to the rope in an evidence bag. "The rope can be purchased anywhere. It had only the victim's DNA, nothing else. The killer was wearing gloves."

Relieved Wolfe had found some answers, Kane nodded. "The information on the make and model of a vehicle will narrow down our list of suspects."

"Did you find evidence of sexual activity?" Jenna frowned.

"Nope." Wolfe reverently covered the corpse with a sheet. "It seems to me the killers wanted these women dead as soon as possible. I know you're thinking psychopath but I'm not seeing the craziness that usually goes with murders of that type." He stared at Kane. "Both these murders are too clean. I'm seeing unrushed and a well-planned disposal of someone rather than the usual slash and thrill kill we usually see." He looked at Jenna. "I agree with Kane that there's an underlying motive to these murders."

"What I can't understand is why they identified themselves with both victims." Jenna folded her arms across her chest. "If it hadn't been for the jack of hearts card, we'd never have connected the murders." She stared at Kane. "What does this mean? Do these killers want us to catch them?"

Kane straightened. "It's confusing. I'm figuring one killer and one follower. The main player changes his MO to throw us off his track and removes all evidence, so he doesn't want to be caught. I figure by leaving his calling card he's marking them as his kills." He slowly removed his gloves, balled them, and tossed them into the trash. "He's clean because this isn't his first rodeo. Two kills close together means he's escalating. I've no doubt he's a psychopath and maybe a little different than others because of his accomplice. Maybe the accomplice is slowing him down or making him more cautious." He removed his mask and wrinkled his nose at the increasing stink. "It's only a matter of time before he loses control and then no one will be able to stop him. I figure the next kill will be brutal."

TWENTY-SEVEN

A blast of cold damp air hit Jenna as she stepped outside. She took a few deep breaths to clear the smell of the morgue from her head and then climbed into the truck. She turned to Kane. "I've been running the potential suspects through my mind. I think we should talk to Steven Croxley at the Wellness Center first. He'd have knowledge of poisons."

"Some of the herbalists act like they're all about candles and natural oils, but he'd have a variety of medicinal herbs and fungi at his store. Many people swear by them for alternative cures." Kane backed out of the parking slot and headed toward Main. "Although cyanide from peach pits isn't the type of poison someone like him would use. He'd have so many better alternatives."

Jenna stared out of the window. Townsfolk braving the downpour trudged along the sidewalk like a procession of brightly colored drowned rats. She turned to Kane. "Yeah, but maybe that's what he'd expect us to believe." She smiled at him. "I'm thinking outside the box."

"Uh-huh." Kane chuckled. "Trying to think like a psychopath... mmm, interesting." He glanced at her. "We can't think like them or we'd be them, Jenna. They don't think logically or illogically. They have a logic of their own controlled by their own individual psychosis. They're all different." He shrugged. "But I happen to agree with you. He could easily be using peach pits to throw us off the track. I guess we'll find out soon enough." He pulled to the curb outside the Wellness Center.

Jenna pushed open the truck's door. Beneath her feet, brown water rushed along the gutter carrying twigs and leaves and spilling onto the sidewalk. She stared at the swirling mass, not wanting to get her feet wet. The next moment Kane swung her from the seat and deposited her on the sidewalk. She looked up at him. "I could have jumped."

"Unlikely, the door doesn't open wide enough." Kane frowned. "That's not being overprotective, Jenna. It's being practical. It would take time to go back to the office and change if you fell flat on your face in the water."

"Oh, I guess." Jenna pulled up her hood against the driving rain and hurried toward the Wellness Center door.

"Jenna." Kane stopped beside her. "I help you because I care. Not because I think you're incapable. It's the way I was raised. Opening doors and helping is what I do. After so long together, it shouldn't concern you."

Jenna stared at him. "These days, some women take it as an insult, like we're incapable of opening a door by ourselves."

"You don't think that, do you? Who in Black Rock Falls would care? Or is your head still in DC? Because the people around here see being gentlemanly as having good character, not as demeaning to women."

Holding one hand up as if to control traffic, Jenna cleared her throat. "Okay fine, but I'm not discussing this here in the pouring rain, Dave. We have work to do. Let's get at it."

She pushed open the door to the store. Inside, the smell of incense mixed with a miasma of scents. She pressed a hand to her nose as a sickly sweet aroma impregnated her nostrils. "Oh, that smell is nasty." She glanced at Kane. "Do people really burn that stuff to relax?"

"It's suffocating." Kane's nostrils flared. "I prefer pine-scented fresh mountain air."

Jenna made her way through the displays of candles, soaps, and herbal remedies. A man came out of the back room and smiled at them. He appeared to be in his late thirties, with a beard and glasses. He fitted the victims' ideal man. She walked to the counter. "Mr. Croxley?"

"Yeah, I'm Steven Croxley." He rested his hands on the counter. "What can I do for you, Sheriff?"

Jenna pulled out her notebook and placed it on the counter. "I believe you were in contact with Dianne Gilbert and Shelby O'Connor. We found your profile on their dating app. Have you been in contact with them lately?"

"Not this week." Croxley narrowed his gaze. "How did you find me? I don't use my real identity online."

"People using social media are very easy to trace." Kane leaned on the counter. "Do you have a reason for not using your real name?"

"Yes, I do." Croxley waved a hand around the store. "Well, I mentioned I was an herbalist in my bio, but I didn't want strange women just rolling up and expecting me to give them free consultations."

Jenna made a few notes and lifted her head to look at him. "I see, and where exactly do you hold these consultations?"

"I have a place in the back." Croxley moved from around the counter. "Through here." He waved them through a curtain and into a small room.

Inside was pleasant enough. Jenna scanned the room. In the middle sat a table covered with a red velvet tablecloth. Wall hangings depicted lists of various types of medieval medicines and an acupuncture chart. The flame on a fat fragrant candle placed in the middle of the table wavered as they entered. She turned to Croxley. "It's like stepping back in time."

"This is where I do my consultations and, yes, that's the illusion I try to portray—the medicine I dispense has been used since ancient times." Croxley smiled. "People who come here enjoy the dramatic side of what I do. When I make them special concoctions to cure what ails them, they believe they'll work, and believing is part of the cure." He suddenly frowned. "I send them to their doctor if I believe there's something to worry about. I'm not a fraud. The cures I use have been handed down for generations."

Jenna backed out of the suddenly claustrophobic room. "That's all very interesting. Can you recall what you were doing on Sunday and Monday nights?" She glanced at her notebook. "Say around the hours of six and midnight?"

"Sunday night I went to Antlers." Croxley, rubbed his chin, thinking. "I figure I arrived there around six-thirty. I'd hoped to see Kristina. She owns Antlers and sometimes stays in the apartment above the restaurant."

Jenna nodded. "When did you leave? Did you see anybody that you know?"

"Around eight-thirty, I guess, and then I went home and played games." Croxley eyed them with suspicion. "George Miller was in the next table with his family. I'd just had my truck serviced, so I'm sure he'd have recognized me. When I dropped by to collect my truck we spoke about his rheumatism."

"And Monday?" Kane removed his Stetson and smoothed his hair before replacing it. "Around the same time?"

"I was here until six-thirty." Croxley pulled out a book from under the counter. "I have an appointments book. I like to have a hard copy." He suddenly smiled. "It's all part of the charm, you know, writing the customer's name in a parchment book. Not having computer screens polluting the air is all part of the holistic approach. Many of my customers blame the wireless network for their sickness." He ran his finger down the list on the page. "I spoke to Lillian Green about her indigestion. She held me up for half an hour. I left, dropped by Aunt Betty's for supper, and headed home. I was home in time to watch the second game on *Monday Night Football*, so around eight I guess." He let out a long sigh. "I can give you a rundown of the game if you like." He looked from one to the other. "I do watch the news. I know Dianne and Shelby are dead, but what would I possibly gain from killing them? They were nice women and had been a welcome change from the women I've dated in the past. I'm saddened by the news of their deaths."

Nothing about Steven Croxley's behavior made Jenna believe he was responsible for killing the women, although he did fit their perfect match as a soft-spoken good-looking man. The hairs on her neck prickled a warning and she swallowed hard. Psychopaths were masters of deceit, and if he was the killer, he'd almost fooled her. The moment they left the store, she'd check out his alibi. She turned to Kane, glad to have him at her side. "Did you have any questions for Mr. Croxley?"

"Do you believe the wireless network causes illness?" Kane raised one eyebrow.

"No, I don't." Croxley shrugged. "I use a computer to keep my accounts and stock levels. I use my phone for the dating apps." He looked at Jenna and smiled. "Ah, that's how you traced me. Well, I'm glad most people don't have the technology to trace people via their phones."

Jenna handed him a card. "If you think of anything else that might help us in our inquiries, call me. Thank you for your time."

"My pleasure." Croxley smiled.

Relieved to be out of the store, Jenna stood under the awning for a few seconds just breathing. "The smell in that place makes my head spin." She glanced at Kane and chuckled.

"I can't believe I'm saying this, but I think I prefer the smell of the morgue."

"He fits the profile." Kane walked beside her to the truck and then swung her back inside. "We need to speak to George Miller."

Jenna waited for him to slip behind the wheel. "My thoughts exactly."

When Kane's stomach growled like a pack of wolves, Jenna glanced at her watch. "Oh, is it that late? Stop by Aunt Betty's. I figure we eat now and then hunt down our next suspect."

"I thought you'd never ask. I'm famished." Kane grinned at her and headed for the diner.

Inside, the aroma of fresh-baked pie pushed away the smell of the herbalist's store. People sat at just about every table. When the manager, Susie Hartwig, waved her over to the counter, she eased through a line of people with Kane at her heels.

"We're rushed off our feet today. I'll take your orders so you jump ahead of the line." Susie smiled brightly. "What can I get you?"

Jenna looked at the board of specials. Seeing it was a pulled-pork burger with special sauce, fries, and cherry pie, Kane's favorites, she smiled. "One regular special for me, two burgers and a large serving of pie for Dave, and coffee. Thanks, Susie. Put it on the office tab as usual."

"Here, take a pot of coffee with you." Susie turned and pulled one from the coffeemaker and handed it to Jenna. "I'll bring another with the meal."

Jenna led the way to the table with Kane's stomach still growling like an angry dog behind her. She placed the coffee pot on the table and shucked her coat. After sitting down at the table reserved for the sheriff's department, she turned to him. "I hope you don't mind me ordering for you. I know it's your favorite."

"You sure it won't make me look incapable of making up my mind by having a woman order for me?" Kane gave her a wry smile, his eyes dancing with amusement.

Snorting, Jenna laughed. "Ouch! Okay, there's no need to explain. I understand. Turn it around and it does seem a little silly."

"Exactly." Kane took her hand and squeezed it. "You did that because you care, no ulterior motive. So, are we good now?"

"We're perfect." Jenna poured the coffee and added the fixings. "What's your take on Croxley?"

"We know the same person or persons murdered both women, so if George Miller recalls him at Antlers, he's clean." Kane pulled out his phone. "I'll call him."

Jenna sipped her coffee while Kane made the call. Her mind moved to the next possible suspect on their list: Nathan Stevens, a pathologist out of 5 Elm Street. His online persona was Bloodlust and she found his name on a list of pathologists working out of the Black Rock Falls Pathology Clinic. The clinic was housed in a new build at the other end of town and employed four pathologists and three nurses. She hadn't realized so many people in town needed blood tests. She glanced up as Suzie arrived with a tray. She helped her move the plates and coffee pot onto the table. "Thanks, Susie."

"Enjoy." Susie hurried back to the counter, weaving between the tables.

"George recalls seeing and speaking to Croxley." Kane looked at his plate and sighed. "We can take him off the list." He pushed his phone into his jacket pocket and attacked one of his burgers.

Jenna watched him eat. Like everything in Kane's life, it was methodical and neat. She'd never seen him drip mayo on his chin. She'd seen him angry and sad. He had a heart as big as Texas and never hid his love for her. It was just as well because, at times, she'd had the awful thought he was a government science project and she'd married a cyborg. She swallowed her last bite of burger and washed it down with coffee. "I've been looking over the info on Nathan Stevens. He's the guy Kalo suggested we look at as he's a member of the clan of gamers with the other suspects."

"Yeah, I recall him." Kane grinned. "Gamer ID Bloodlust and he's out of Elm Street. If he's a pathologist, then that's where he's gotten the name. I figure we'll ask him if the others were online at the time of the murders. He might tell us if he's got nothing to hide, although he's not on any dating apps I could find or involved with the victims on any social media platforms."

Jenna lifted her fork and pressed it into the crumbly delight. Cherries oozed out and she raised it to her mouth and groaned. Flavor exploded over her tastebuds. "Now I know why you love this pie."

"I love all pies." Kane chuckled. "Aunt Betty's cherry pie is mouthwatering. It's the best I've ever eaten. It's because they make it from scratch."

Jenna's phone interrupted them and she checked the caller ID. "It's Bobby Kalo." She put the phone on speaker but dropped the volume, so no one would overhear the conversation and held it between them. "Hey, Bobby, what have you got for me?"

"The victims' bank records show a massive drain on the day the women were murdered. As in the money has vanished into the ether. I couldn't find a trace of the transfers. They were completed online and there's no evidence of hacking. The correct passwords and security were used in both cases. It's as if the women gave up their fortunes voluntarily. To whom is what I'm still trying to discover, but everything leads to the dark web and all pathways have been destroyed. Whoever is doing this is an expert."

Pushing a hand through her hair, Jenna stared at Kane's

unreadable expression. "Okay, thanks. Keep trying. We don't think this guy has finished yet. Send me the amounts, times, and all the details you have, please."

"They're on their way to you now. I'll keep searching. Bye for now." Kalo disconnected.

Baffled, Jenna slowly lifted her gaze from the screen and looked at Kane. "If they willingly gave away their fortunes, why kill them? It's not against the law to give away money or to accept money freely given, as long as people pay their taxes."

"That's because the killer swindled them out of their money." Kane sipped his coffee and leaned back in his chair looking contented. "I figure he created a phony get-rich-quick scheme and convinced them to transfer their accounts. He killed them because committing fraud means jailtime—or it's just part of his game." He peered over the rim of his cup at her. "Leaving a calling card tells me it's all a game to him—the hunting them down online, the convincing them to trust him, and then seeing the fear in their eyes as he murders them."

The warmth in the diner didn't stop the shiver running through Jenna. She nodded. "You're sure he's murdered before, so this isn't just the start, is it?"

"No way." Kane placed his cup on the table and sighed. "I figure he'll have one planned for tonight, maybe tomorrow. We're not going to be able to stop him until he makes a mistake, and they all make mistakes eventually."

TWENTY-EIGHT

Reluctant to leave the cozy diner and head out into the miserable weather, Jenna stood and pulled on her jacket. The cold damp weather made her bones ache and she stretched. "I guess we'd better get at it, but I'd rather be anywhere but out in the rain right now."

"Me too." Kane's mouth lifted in a half smile. "Look on the bright side. At least we have a motive for the murders now. Where to, the office or the pathologists?"

Wanting to collect as much information as possible, Jenna gathered her things. "The pathologists. If he gives up information on the others in his clan, we'll be able to narrow down the suspects." Her phone chimed and she stared at the caller ID. It was Maggie. "Yeah, Maggie. What's up?"

"There's a brawl at the Triple Z Bar. Rio and Rowley are there but called in for backup. There's a man down and Wolfe is on his way with Webber."

"That's all we need." Jenna turned toward the door. "We're on our way." She disconnected and looked at Kane. "Triple Z bar ruckus."

"Can't the others handle it? They're on that side of town." Kane ran around the hood and climbed into his truck.

Staring at the gray clouds and shaking her head in dismay, Jenna buckled up. "They're already on scene and Wolfe is on his way. There's a man down."

As they headed along Main with lights flashing and sirens blaring, vehicles moved out of their way. Rain thundered on the roof like buckshot and the wipers' speed increased as the Beast splashed through deep puddles stretching across the blacktop. The soaked forest looked forlorn as they sped past. Bushes and foliage hung limp, heavy with rain. Soil filled with pine needles spilled onto the road. The earth between the trees had blackened and the smell of mold wafted into the cab. They slowed to drive into the entrance of the Triple Z Roadhouse. Overflowing potholes littered the parking lot like small holes cut into an ice-covered lake for fishing. As they rounded the eighteen-wheelers and pulled into the curb some ways from lines of motorcycles surrounding the entrance to the bar, Jenna stared at a group of men fighting outside in the rain. People spilled out from the front to watch them. Many openly carried weapons, but that was nothing unusual.

She pulled up her hood. Glad that her jacket had SHERIFF in bold print across the front, she slid from the truck. "Sheriff's department. What's this all about?"

Some of the men dispersed at the sight of them, but what had happened to Rio and Rowley? The sound of fighting and breaking glass came from inside, along with the reek of stale beer and cigarettes.

"Break it up." Kane was already in the thick of it, pulling men apart and thrusting them against the wall. "Don't move or I'll cuff you."

Jenna glared at them. Some were already shaping up to continue the fight. "Don't even think about it." She touched the weapon at her waist. "Start up again and I'll give you all a ride to the cells to cool down." She looked along the line. "Your choice. Leave now or I'll book you."

Muttering under their breaths, the men complied, and once they'd walked away, she followed Kane inside and found bedlam. Loud music and the shouts of men greeted her. A chair sailed past her head and she ducked a flying bottle. The bar stunk of unwashed male and garbage. Broken glass crunched under her boots as she pushed through the crowd and peered around the dim room. Near the bar, she made out Rio and Rowley doing their best to break up the fights. Ahead of her Kane was pushing his way through a group of onlookers. As her eyes adjusted to the light, she noticed the colors on the backs of the fighting men's jackets. Two rival biker gangs, neither from Black Rock Falls, had clashed. She wanted to pull her weapon but with so many armed men, doing so would be like lighting the fuse of a stick of dynamite. The group had split into two and both sides yelled encouragements to the men fighting like wild animals. Jenna pushed through the onlookers and tried to raise her voice over the noise. "Sheriff's department. Exit the building. Anyone still standing here in five minutes will be charged with inciting a riot."

Some of the men close to her slowly turned to leave. The next moment Wolfe was at her side. Glad of the support, she turned to him. "Thanks for coming."

"There's a body here somewhere." Wolfe pushed a guy aiming a bottle at Kane's head to one side and glared at him with a look to freeze time. "Y'all wouldn't want to do that, now would you? Why don't y'all leave now, before the sheriff arrests you for an attempted assault on a law enforcement officer."

To Jenna's surprise the man dropped the bottle and backed away with a few of his friends. She repeated the orders several times and the crowd around the fight slowly dispersed, but a group of bikers hovered near the front entrance. They looked subdued enough and she turned to watch her deputies. In front of the bar the fight was still out of control.

"Watch my bag. I'll go and help." Wolfe dropped his bag onto a table and turned to wave Webber forward. "It's been a time since I've been in a fight." He smiled at Jenna and the two men ran forward to assist her deputies.

Without warning, someone grabbed Jenna's arm. She turned and stared into a smiling face. "Take your hand off me and leave the premises."

"I don't think so." Another man came up behind her, grabbed her other arm, and snatched her weapon.

Twisting, Jenna kicked out hard but found only air. The next moment, the men from the entrance had surrounded her and they were dragging her toward the door. Rain splattered her face as they propelled her along. "Take your hands off me right now. Have you lost your minds?"

"We're just having a little fun, Sheriff." One man with dirty black hair hanging in his face grinned at her. "This is on our bucket list for today." He looked around. "Isn't it guys?"

Trapped in the men's steel grips, Jenna went limp. They'd have to drag her. She wouldn't cooperate, and Kane or one of her team would notice her missing soon enough—but would they hear her screams above the noise inside the bar? She looked desperately around at the sea of faces. "Hey. Can't you see what's happening here? Help me."

She fought and yelled at the top of her voice, but the men had trapped her in a sea of black leather jackets. To her horror, she realized they all belonged to the same biker club. The fight was a setup to get her alone. Screaming and kicking, she fought like a crazed animal, biting into leather-clad arms and tasting the sourness of old leather on her tongue. As they dragged her toward the motel rooms out back of the roadhouse, two men took hold of her kicking legs and they carried her. There was no escape. A door to a room was flung open and she was tossed onto a bed. Scrambling to her feet, she pressed her tracker ring and hoped to God that Kane would hear his phone.

The black-haired man came toward her and she kicked out, landing a solid blow to his chest. He staggered back, but the smile never left his face. She balled her fists ready to fight. "You won't get away with kidnapping me."

"I was told you were a feisty one. You caused embarrassment to my family by making a public spectacle of my cousin when he was teaching his wife a lesson. We came to town to put things right." He waved to the six men who'd followed him into the room. "You planning on taking down all of us, Sheriff?"

Jenna stared at him. "I'll hurt you if you come any closer." She hoped Kane would be listening. "Motel room number four will be unlucky for you today. I don't go down easy."

"I don't think so. We've invited you to a party. We're here to have fun." He smiled. "Now lie down and be a good sheriff." His smile faded into a thin line. "Or we'll just tie you to the bed. It don't matter to us if you cooperate or not. In fact, we like it when they scream."

Heart thundering in her chest, Jenna snorted. "Rape will get you life. Kidnapping a sheriff as well." She laughed. "You'll never see the light of day again. That's if you live out the day. My deputies will show no mercy." *Dave will kill you.*

"You figure those weaklings under a woman's thumb are gonna stop us?" The dark-haired man waved a hand around the room. "We're armed. No one will disturb us."

Anger welled and Jenna took a fighting stance. Even if they planned on shooting her, she'd go down fighting. When Kane arrived, she wouldn't be able to control him. He'd take them all down without hesitation. She bared her teeth at them. "Don't say I didn't warn you. Bring it on."

TWENTY-NINE

Phones sounding Jenna's distress call went off all around Kane. He pushed one of the fighting men toward Rowley and grabbed for his phone, running for the door at the sound of her voice with Wolfe at his side. He glanced to one side as Rio rushed up beside him and the three of them bolted for the motel. A group of men stood outside the door to room number four. Inside Jenna's screams dug deep into his soul.

"Drop your weapons." Wolfe was beside him, Glock drawn. "Okay, now hands on your heads fingers linked."

"Kick them this way." Rio had his weapon drawn. "On your knees. Now!"

Not waiting, Kane aimed a kick beside the lock of number four. Wood splintered in a scream of destruction as the door flew open and ricocheted off the interior wall. He drew his weapon and scanned the room, taking in the situation in an instant. "Sheriff's department, draw down on me and you're dead."

Six armed men all stared at him in shock with their mouths hanging open. One man jumped away from the bed, eyes wide.

Another was struggling to contain Jenna, but she was screaming and fighting like a wild cat. He had seconds to get the jump on the others and acted without a second thought. His first shot took out Jenna's attacker's left leg just behind the knee. The man screamed like an injured wolf and fell onto the bed in a splatter of blood. *Target neutralized.*

As he swung his gaze around, men fumbled for their weapons—big mistake. His mind slowed, calculating each threat as it presented itself. He could see every minute detail—each twitch of a finger, each potential last breath. The fastest and slowest draw seemed to fall into an order of potential threat. As the bikers' minds urged their bodies into action, their reaction time was like watching an old Western shoot-out movie in slow motion. He had time to disarm them all before their brains registered they were facing the Grim Reaper. Six deafening shots rang out, filling the room with the stink of gunpowder. The men fell to the floor screaming in agony and holding their injured arms. It was their lucky day. He'd aimed to disarm not kill. In two steps he closed a hand around a greasy collar and dragged the man off Jenna. Ice-cold rage shuddered through him at her torn shirt and the scratches on her flesh. He wanted to rip out the man's throat but tossed him into the wall and slid his gaze over Jenna. She was as pale as a ghost and a dark bruise marred the perfect skin on her cheek. Her eyes looked up at him, wide and filled with fear, as she tried to pull her torn shirt and jacket over her exposed flesh. Rage had him by the throat and he spun around, willing her attacker to go for his weapon. Part of him, the male animal avenging his mate, wanted to take the threat down but years of training gave him clarity. Killing him wouldn't be enough punishment. He wanted him to feel the fear he'd inflicted on Jenna. Kane stared down his nose at the sprawling, whining trash at his feet. "You dared to put hands on my wife." He holstered his weapon. "You do understand street justice, right? I'll give you the chance to draw your weapon before I kill you."

"You busted my knee, and she almost blinded me." The man shook his head and cradled his ruined leg. He pointed to the long gouges to his face. "I need a doctor. You're a cop. You have to help me. Duty of care, man." His attention moved past him and over to Jenna. "He can't just gun me down, Sheriff. I have witnesses."

"Dave." Jenna's voice slipped into his brain. "I'm okay."

Pushing down the overpowering need to turn, hug her close, and give her comfort, Kane kept his attention fixed on the men. "Stay behind me, Jenna."

He moved to shield her from the wounded men—all still armed with pistols and hunting knives, all a threat. He noticed Rio slide into the room, but he didn't need backup. His body would protect Jenna from harm. Her being safe was all that mattered. He smiled at her attacker. "Yeah, I figured you're the typical coward who attacks women and then begs them for help. A rabid dog that runs with a pack. You haven't got the guts to take on a man, have you?"

A split-second later, Jenna's attacker growled and went for his weapon. Instinctively, Kane spun and landed a kick to the biker's head before he had time to slide his pistol from its holster. As the man slid unconscious to the floor, Kane flicked a glance at Rio. "Disarm and secure them and then call the paramedics. While we're waiting for them to arrive, get their details."

"Maybe you should check Jenna?" Rio looked anxiously around him at her. "That's a nasty bruise on her cheek."

Falling into the zone to control his emotions, Kane nodded. "Yeah, I noticed." His gaze moved over the men lying in pools of blood on the stained filthy carpet. "Which one of you has the sheriff's weapon?"

"That would be me. In my belt." One of the bikers staggered to his feet clutching his arm and turned to allow Rio to collect the weapon.

Kane assisted Rio to secure the prisoners with zip ties. He ground his teeth as he rolled the black greasy-haired man over and shook him conscious. Anger shimmered just under the surface as he bent close to the groaning man's ear. "Just give me an excuse to take you out."

"Dave." Jenna touched his arm.

His gaze slid over her and his stomach clenched. A tremble went through her, but she took her weapon from Rio, holstered it, and raised her chin as if being kidnapped by bikers happened regularly. He forced his hands to remain by his sides and not clasp her to him. The last thing she'd appreciate would be a damsel in distress scene in front of the men who'd attacked her.

"With me, Kane." Jenna turned and walked into the bathroom.

He followed her and pushed the door shut behind them. With gentle care, he held her, breathing in her honeysuckle scent and allowing the world to slip back into place. "You're okay. You fought well, and I'm proud of you."

"I'm angry." Jenna's mouth turned down. "They disarmed me. That never should have happened."

Kane pushed the hair from her face and stared into her eyes. "There was a crowd, I shouldn't have left you alone. You didn't stand a chance. There must have been fifteen men surrounding you." He swallowed hard. "It was my fault. I misread the situation and figured the problem was with the fight not the onlookers."

"Really?" Jenna touched her cheek and winced. "You'd have to be able to read minds to know they were planning to attack me." She waved a hand toward the door. "This was a setup to get to me—it wasn't the cartel. That guy planning to rape me has a beef with me. It was personal. He figures I disrespected his cousin when he was 'disciplining his wife.'" She lifted her fingers to indicate a quote and snorted. "Do you believe men actually say that these days?"

Kane opened the door and peered at the man bleeding on the floor. "I don't recognize him."

"Not him, his cousin." Jenna's eyes blazed. "I recall a group of hunters from another town causing a ruckus and one was abusing his wife. I dropped the wife beater on his butt. Remember? I asked you and Rowley to stay back and allow me to deal with him?" She snorted with disgust and pointed to her attacker. "That guy out there couldn't take me down alone. He needed his buddies for backup."

Kane smiled at her. She was still ferocious and wild from the fight. She hadn't been beaten down in mind or spirit. He'd married a warrior. "Take a few deep breaths. It's over. Wolfe is outside. He'll need to bag your hands. You're covered in evidence."

"Yeah." Jenna stared at her bloodied fingers. "I tried to get as much under my nails as possible." She grimaced. "I bit them too. I'll need blood tests and samples from the ones I've bitten as well, in case they're carrying anything nasty."

Kane nodded. "When Wolfe is through with you, I'm taking you home." He gave her a long "don't argue with me" stare. "If you're okay, we'll catch up with Bloodlust first thing in the morning."

"Okay, as soon as we have the prisoners squared away." Jenna rubbed her arms. "I sure need to take a shower. I can still feel his hands all over me."

"What happened?" Rowley burst into the room. "Are you okay, Jenna?"

"I'm fine." Jenna cleared her throat. "I'll need you to make arrangements with the sheriff at Louan to send some of his deputies to take over at the hospital." She turned to Kane. "Contact the DA. We need a bus to take these men straight to county.

I want everyone involved charged. Make that clear. Nobody is walking away this time. We'll need to step away and ask Rio to take over. They'll be screaming conflict of interest if either of us gets involved."

Kane smiled at her and pulled out his phone. "You got it."

THIRTY

I'm waiting for her to arrive. The wine is spiked with a special drug. I need more information on this man spoiling my hunting ground. I look at my reflection. I'm much like Kristina, the same hair color and eyes. We could almost be sisters—would it be like watching myself die? *How intriguing.* My thoughts are wandering to the thrill of the night ahead, but I must prepare the draft for Kristina and gather the potions I need. Time rushes by as I pound ingredients in the mortar and I'm surprised when the doorbell chimes. It's Kristina and seeing her again sends a strange excitement through me. I walk from my room to greet her. "I'm so glad you came to see me before you went to see Julian. Come in and sit down. I'm making a love potion for you. I'll be one minute." I hastily add the ingredients to wine and pour them into a small bottle and shake it. "This is for you." I hand her the bottle. "I'll explain what to do before you leave, so you don't forget."

"You are such a good friend to me." Kristina smiles. She sits obediently at my red velvet-covered table and her fingers caress the fabric. "I know I can trust you and I don't trust many people. It took me so long to agree to meet with Julian."

I offer her a glass of the wine, liberally laced with my special mixture of herbs. I've used them before to loosen a person's tongue or to make them sleep for a few minutes. I lean forward conspiratorially. "I'm worried about you meeting a stranger on your lonesome. As your friend, tell me your plans for this evening, and if you get into trouble, you only need to call me and I'll come and get you. If anything should happen to you, I'd be mortified."

"You needn't worry. I'm meeting Julian at the library parking lot. It's safe there, so I'll be fine. We'll be taking his vehicle to his friend's place for dinner." Kristina's enthusiastic expression beams at me.

I frown and clasp her hands. "Doesn't this idea concern you. He might be a rapist—how would you know? Why not dine at a local restaurant?"

"No, no, he's nice, and he's helping me. He's a financial advisor, so we're discussing my finances. He wanted to do that in private." Her cheeks pink. "He's so nice. We talk on the phone all the time. I'd have met him earlier, but he's been working in another state. He's meeting me straight from the airport."

I give her my best cynical stare. "What could possibly be so private he needs to be alone with you? It's just an investment plan, isn't it?"

"I shouldn't be telling you this. Julian swore me to secrecy, but he wants to transfer some of my money into cryptocurrency and we don't want anyone snooping. He's doing this just for me. I was worried at first, so I invested a small amount and made ten thousand in the first week." Kristina grinned and pulled her hand away to touch her purse. "I have all my account numbers and online passwords with me. Once we've talked business, then we're having dinner and discussing our future together."

I smile and pat her hand. She hadn't needed any encouragement to tell me everything, but I had to be sure. If I wanted to watch her die, I needed all the details of her rendezvous with Julian. "Well, I'm glad I've given you something to help." I chuckle. She trusts me and I can't hide my amusement. "This potion will make you irresistible to him, but you must follow my instructions to the letter."

"You know I will." Kristina nods solemnly.

I tap the small bottle she's placed on the table. "Drink this one hour before you're due to leave. Lie down, close your eyes, and picture your future—everything you want to happen with Julian." I lean forward and stare into her gullible eyes. "You will see the future. Call me in the morning and tell me what happened."

"Oh, I sure will." Kristina swallows her small glass of wine in one gulp. She opens her hands palms up and smiles. "If Julian doesn't work out, what future do you see for me?"

We make small talk, discussing her hopes and dreams. Soon her voice slurs, her eyes flutter, and she slumps forward on the table. I take her purse and peer inside. Her phone opens using her thumb print and I take the time to remove my number and delete the messages from my burner phone. It's better there's no link to me, however small. I spend time carefully reading the messages from Julian to discover the mask he hides behind and then move to handwritten notes in a little book. As she'd said, I find all the information on the fortune she'd accumulated. All the inheritances and business deals over the past ten years had built into millions. I can't resist taking photographs of the pages. The temptation to take it all makes my fingers itch. With this information and my knowledge of the dark web, I have the chance to walk away with a fortune. I'd never be found, never be suspected. I am no one—I don't exist. I smile and shake my head, undecided. One thing was for sure, soon I'd be watching Julian killing another of my customers. He believed no one knew his identity, but I did, and watching his insatiable hunger for murder had become an enjoyable sport.

I wait, watching the time, and then I check her pulse. The slow steady beat is typical of a drug-induced state. How easily I could kill her, and although it's tempting, the thrill would come later and not by my hand. I take the smelling salts from my pocket and wave them under her nose, watch her jerk awake and laugh. "Goodness me, one small glass of wine and you're dropping asleep. Do you want me to give you a ride home?"

"No thanks." Kristina yawns. "I walked. I'm staying in my apartment over Antlers. Owning a restaurant in town sounded like fun at the time but it's more work than I anticipated. The manager is running things now, but I still use the apartment a few times a week to keep an eye on my investment." She stood, pushed the potion into her pocket, and smiled. "I'll take this one hour before I need to dress for my date, just in case it makes me sleepy."

I squeeze her arm and smile. "Don't worry. Once you've taken it, the hour's rest will make you feel fresh and invigorated. You'll be irresistible to him." I stand to pull back the curtain to my room. "Have fun with Julian."

"I will. I'll call you in the morning and tell you all about it." Kristina heads for the door with a wave.

I watched her go, knowing she'd never walk through my door again. It's strange how people move in and out of my life and then vanish like shadows... Maybe the only shadow I can ever keep is my own? My gaze moves to the clock on the wall. I like to keep timepieces five minutes ahead and watch as the second hand makes rhythmic clicks as it moves into the future. It's hypnotizing in the dark scented room and I could watch it all night, but it's time for me to go. All good things must come to an end and my time in Black Rock Falls will soon be over —for now.

THIRTY-ONE

Shaken by the attack but determined not to show any emotion, Jenna leaned against the vanity in the motel's bathroom and held a bag of ice to her cheek. It had seemed as if she'd waited forever, but once Wolfe had bagged her hands, she'd had no choice. With the number of men involved, she needed all her deputies, including Wolfe and Colt Webber, to load men into buses or ambulances. She looked up as Rowley knocked on the door. "Ma'am, you up to talking?"

The idea of talking made her legs tremble but, making an attempt to cover her need to scream and never stop, Jenna nodded. "Sure, I'm fine." She waved at her cheek, ignoring her aching back and bruised flesh. "It's only a bruise and my pride is a little dented, is all."

"I've organized deputies from Louan. They're at the hospital to guard the prisoners and we have more coming later to run shifts until the injured men are cleared to go to county. They were happy for the overtime and it will leave us free to work on our current caseload." Rowley cleared his throat. "Kane said he'll be taking you to the morgue soon and Wolfe will do the examination."

Nodding, Jenna sucked in a deep breath. "Yeah, I'd like that. I don't need to be explaining what happened to anyone else." She needed to think ahead. Keeping on top of the murder cases was paramount. She didn't need her deputies distracted. Forcing her mind to think straight, she concentrated on police procedure, and everything slipped back into place. "Have you completed the paperwork on the prisoners? Read them their rights? Arranged attorneys?"

"Yeah. Don't worry. We have everything under control." Rowley leaned against the bathroom door and stared at her. "Another thing, there's no body. I figure it was all part of their plan. They called it in to make sure you'd arrive on scene." His shoulders lifted. "The fight stopped all at once and when we turned around the place was almost empty. That must have been when you pressed your tracker ring." He glanced at his feet. "Now seeing what happened, maybe I shouldn't have let those guys involved in the fight leave. I did take names and warned they'd be expected to pay restitution to the owner."

Jenna put down the icebag and awkwardly sipped from a bottle of water Kane had given her. The plastic bags on her hands were like huge air-filled gloves, her head ached, and every muscle in her body was screaming. She willed herself to keep going as if nothing had happened. Right now her deputies needed to see a strong leader. "That's all you could do in the circumstances. We have bigger fish to fry. The men who attacked me have taken two valuable deputies away from a murder investigation." She shook her head. "Did you make any headway with the men you spoke to?"

"We interviewed Wyatt Kennedy out on Riverside." Rowley pulled out his notebook. "Kalo mentioned he discovered this man—another member of the gaming clan—is using his gamer ID as his dark web identity." He lifted his gaze to her. "I checked him out and spoke to him and he really is a financial advisor. Now that we know the killer is draining the victims' bank accounts, he seemed to fit the profile. He admitted to using the dark web, saying the business dealings intrigued him and being there was academic and not for illegal purposes."

Jenna snorted. "Really? He must figure we're a new kind of stupid."

"Yeah, we thought the same, so we spoke to Kalo again and he believes that Kennedy is what he calls 'a watcher,' someone who's looking around rather than conducting business... but if he was doing something illegal, it would be easy to hide. It's impossible to discover every place he went. He covers his tracks." Rowley cleared his throat. "Rio pushed him real hard and discovered he was online playing with his clan at the time of the murders. He recalls chatting to Branch Drummond, known online as Bruce Campion, and Steven Croxley, known as Finch, the herbalist at the Black Rock Falls Wellness Center, around that time on Sunday."

Running the information through her head, Jenna nodded. "Any proof?"

"Yeah, Rio asked him for that and Kennedy showed us the messages." Rowley shrugged. "I don't figure any of them are involved. That's if you're sure the same man killed both women."

"I'm sure. The problem is that many gamers use laptops and they can take them anywhere. As Wolfe established, two men are involved. They could be covering for each other but criminals don't go to the trouble of inventing a story so easily checked." Jenna pressed the ice to her bruised cheek. "There's a group of players, and if two of them stop playing long enough to kill someone, they'd be missed. We'll take them off the probable suspect list, but I'm not discounting anyone just yet."

"That's what we figured." Rowley folded his notebook and pushed it inside his pocket.

Jenna nodded. "You'll have your hands full with the men outside. We'll follow up with Jack Sutherland and Nathan

Stevens in the morning. If we had a suspect that was screaming at us to check them out, I'd keep going. I feel like I'm playing chess with this killer and he's taking forever to make his next move." She stared at the door. "What's happening out there?"

"The men are all gone now. We called in Walters, and Colt Webber is riding with the injured ones to the hospital; they'll be locked up in the secure ward with the Louan deputies guarding them until they're ready to be transported to county. The six Kane shot in the arms aren't badly injured and will be moved tonight. The guy that attacked you will need surgery. Rio is taking down Kane's statement for the record. He wanted to make sure he had his account of the shootings and Rio's down for the DA." Rowley pulled a statement book from under one arm. "I need to take your statement. Did you witness the shootings?"

A shiver went through Jenna as the image of Kane's expression slipped into her mind. His eyes had flashed with a rage she'd never witnessed before, but his expression was like ice. In that few minutes the iceman had returned—the cybernetic killer she'd only glimpsed before. How Kane had controlled himself, and only nicked the men's arms to make them drop their weapons, must have taken an immense amount of mental willpower. She nodded. "Yeah. He gave warnings, made them aware he was a peace officer. The man attacking me, he shot in the knee. I didn't see that because the man was on top of me, but I did witness the others. They went for their weapons. He had to make a split-second decision—to disarm or kill. It's just as well he never misses. Those guys don't know how lucky they are to be alive." She met Rowley's troubled gaze. "Rio came into the room about that time as well. It was a righteous shoot. Self-defense."

"Yeah, believe it or not, two of the injured men mentioned Kane had identified himself before he shot anyone. They're saying it wasn't necessary for him to shoot the man attacking you. Rio told them that won't fly, as he was confronted with six armed men and someone attacking the sheriff. Taking out the threat is procedure, then move to the next one. Kane followed it to the letter of the law. In the circumstances, many would have shot to kill. Seven to one. I'm surprised either of you are alive."

She looked past Rowley as Rio came into the room.

"If I hadn't seen it, I wouldn't have believed it." Rio smiled at her. "I figured I'm fast and accurate, but he leaves me for dead."

"Leaves who for dead?" Kane walked into the crowded room, shouldering his way past Rio and Rowley to get to her side. Raindrops dripped from the rim of his Stetson and covered his shoulders.

Forcing her mouth into a smile, Jenna looked at his troubled expression. She couldn't hide anything from him. "You've impressed Rio with your shooting."

"Practice, practice, practice." Kane slid a hand around her waist. "Time to go. Wolfe has gone ahead and he'll meet us at the morgue. The Beast is right outside the door." He turned to the deputies. "You'd better get at it. The paperwork needs to be with the DA now."

Suddenly able to breathe again, she watched them go and then looked up at Kane. "Are you okay?"

"Uh-huh." Kane lifted her chin with one finger and stared into her eyes. "The need to protect you and get bloody revenge rose up like a fire-breathing dragon, but I controlled it." He brushed his thumb over her lips. "Once I could see you were handling the situation, sanity came back. I can see you're not handling it, are you?"

Jenna leaned into him. "I'm shaken but I'll be okay. I thought you had lost it for a moment."

"Nah." He ran both hands down her arms. "People will have to deal with me if they hurt you, but it will be within the law. I'm not a psychopath, Jenna, and I know I worry you sometimes, but the difference between me and them is I really don't want to hurt anyone. In law enforcement we often have to do things we don't like." He shrugged. "I so want to kiss you, but Wolfe would give me a lecture about contaminating evidence." He squeezed her gently. "Come on, let's go."

THIRTY-TWO

On the way to the morgue, Jenna tried to keep her mind away from the incident by bringing Kane up to date with Rowley and Rio's interview with Wyatt Kennedy. "What do you think?"

"We know two men are involved. They could be covering up for each other." Kane turned into the driveway behind the ME's office. "I wouldn't discount them just yet."

Inside the morgue, exhaustion swamped Jenna as she made her way to an examination room. She wished she could rub the frown line from Kane's forehead. Something was worrying him and he was playing his cards close to the vest. As Wolfe took the required samples from her mouth and hands, Emily came to the door. "Hi, Em."

"Hi." Emily looked at her father. "A batch of results just came in, I figured you'd want them."

"Yeah, thanks. I'll need you to stay behind. We'll need to process the samples from Jenna and the others tonight." Wolfe nodded to Emily. "Can you get started now?"

"Yeah, I'm on it." Emily looked at Jenna. "We'll talk later. I want to know everything that happened." She headed for the door.

"Maybe tomorrow night. She'll need her rest tonight." Wolfe checked the bruise on Jenna's face and examined her head. He smiled at her. "Remove all your outer clothing and place them in an evidence bag." He glanced at Kane and took a camera from the counter. "Take photographs of any damage on her, check her all over for bruises and scrapes. Make them close-up shots and make a note of each one in the book on the counter with the image number." He turned back to Jenna. "I figured y'all would be more comfortable if I left Dave to take the images. When he's done, you can take a shower. There's a set of scrubs on the counter you can wear. I'll check your clothes for hair and trace evidence. The bikers will have left something behind on you and the DA will need everything I can find to bring a case against them."

Jenna stared at him in disbelief. "It's open and shut."

"No, it's your word and Dave's against seven witnesses." Wolfe frowned at her over his mask. "They're innocent unless proven guilty. I've taken swabs from everyone involved. Luckily their leather jackets were wet from the downpour, so you did a considerable amount of damage to them. They have bite marks all over. You broke the skin on your attacker's hand, and human teeth transmit over one hundred million organisms per milliliter. Trust me, I'll find something to identify you in that bite, including the pattern from your teeth. He, on the other hand, could carry a multitude of diseases: hepatitis, herpes simplex, tuberculosis, and tetanus to name a few. I'll run tests on all of the bikers and let you know ASAP." He glanced down at the results Emily had handed him. "I'll take a look at these. Come down to my office when you're done here." He headed out the door, closing it behind him.

Slowly undressing, Jenna frowned at Kane. "I hope we're not looking at a long, drawn-out court case."

"Nah." Kane snapped on gloves and opened the plastic bag for her. "Wolfe is just being realistic. In any case he's involved with, he's neutral and always gives an unbiased opinion. When he takes the stand, he'll give the evidence he found with no frills. That's what I like about him. He is incorruptible. He also tells the truth no matter how difficult it is to hear."

Jenna peeled off her clothes, folded them, and dropped them into the bag. He was right but she'd always seen Wolfe as being on her side, come what may. She looked at Kane. "We don't have anything to worry about. That biker gang kidnapped me and planned to rape me to teach me a lesson. I have enough evidence on me to prove it and you—"

"Don't worry about me." Kane smiled at her, sealed the bag, and then picked up the camera. "Rio witnessed the shooting, and I didn't kill anyone. They're all going down, Jenna, including the men in the bar fight. Rowley took photographs of their driver's licenses to save time. I've spoken to the DA. Apart from the damage to the bar, he's going to prosecute them for their part in the kidnapping. He figures once he has solid evidence against the men who kidnapped you, the others will go for conspiracy to kidnap a peace officer with the intent to rape and attempted murder. I trust Wolfe. He'll be working all night gathering evidence to take these men down. The fact he is unbiased works in our favor not against us." He smiled and pushed her toward the bathroom door. "I'm done here. Go take a shower." His phone buzzed a message and he glanced at the screen. "Take your time. I'll be back before you're done."

Jenna stood under the hot water for a long time. Tremors wracked her body and she slid down the wall to sit on the floor and watch the blood swirl down the drain. It took some time to get her head around what had happened. She figured she must be in shock and waited until the shivering eased before getting slowly to her feet. After brushing the blood from under her nails and scrubbing her flesh until it turned red, Jenna stared at the bruises on her arms and shins. The nail marks on her chest, where her attacker had tried to rip her bra, stood out red and raw. She straightened and pressed both hands on the vanity and stared into the mirror, examining the mark where a fist had connected with her cheek. Moving her tongue over the split inside her mouth and tasting blood, she shuddered. She'd come so close to being raped. The helplessness of being overpowered tore into her, tumbling her mind into bad memories she'd believed had been buried for good. She'd fought back harder than ever before and yet they'd still managed to pin her to the bed—two men, not the seven in the room—and she'd been helpless... useless. All the daily morning training sessions with Kane and she'd still failed. A tear ran down her cheek and she hastily wiped it away. She refused to break down. If she let them win, they'd always win. She had to be strong—stronger than ever before. No one, not even Kane, would ever know how terrified she'd been. The voice inside her head wished he'd killed them all, so she wouldn't have to face them in court, but she had a responsibility to be an example for all abused women. Being afraid was okay, but allowing these animals to get away with rape and abuse was never going to happen on her watch. Grinding her teeth together so hard her jaw ached, she scrubbed the towel over her skin and used the hair dryer attached to the wall to dry her hair. She shivered and wrapped the towel around her, but the moment she opened the bathroom door the sound of Poppy Anderson's voice came from the hallway. *What the heck is she doing here?*

Jenna went to the examination room door and inched it open a crack. There was Kane leaning against the wall laughing and smiling at something Poppy had said. As usual, she had her hand on his arm and was leaning in way too close. As Poppy's perfume crawled up the hallway toward her like a snake, she opened the door and slammed it shut. The sound echoed down the tiled hallway as she turned and reached for the scrubs on the bench. A few moments later the door opened and Kane stuck his head around, his face etched in concern. She turned her back on him unable to form words.

"Here, I asked Poppy to grab you a change of clothes from the office." He deposited an evidence bag on the bench. "It's way too cold to drive home in scrubs."

Jenna kept her eyes on the bag. "I'm glad you both found my being kidnapped and attacked so funny." She turned to look at him. "Why didn't you ask Maggie to bring them. I hate the thought of Anderson touching my things."

"I didn't think." Kane stepped toward her. "I'm sorry."

Jenna held up a hand to ward him off. "Don't come any closer. The stink of her perfume on you is making me sick to my stomach."

"Stop it!" Kane wrapped her in his arms. "She doesn't know about the attack. I told her you were soaked through, is all. She said she stepped into a pothole the other day and ended up on her butt in a puddle." He let out a long sigh. "I was laughing at her—not you. Yeah, she touched my arm, but she touches everyone. She's a touchy-feely person and I don't encourage her. I know you're mad at me, but I couldn't just grab the clothes and run or she'd figure something was up, so I played it cool." He stared into her eyes. "Have I ever lied to you?"

Shaking her head, she leaned into him. "Nope. I don't and can't ever trust her. She has no respect for me or the fact we're married. As her superior I've done everything possible to help her, but my patience is wearing thin." Her knees went to Jell-O. "I don't feel so good."

"It's emotional shock." Kane lifted her onto the bench. "I'll help you dress and then we'll get a hot drink into you." He pulled out her clothes and looked at her. "Talk to me, Jenna. Has this caused a PTSD episode?"

Reluctant to talk, Jenna shook her head. "Not really. I know I'm here but the feeling of being completely overpowered won't go away." She pushed her arms into a sweater and looked at him. "Deep down, I wanted you to kill them, and as sheriff that's against everything I believe in." She lifted her legs to push them into her pants and then slid from the bench to pull them up. "I'm glad now you didn't, but in the moment I wanted them all dead." She stepped into her boots and Kane bent to lace them. "I'd forgotten how easily a man can overpower a woman of my size. Even with the skills I have, I'm still vulnerable and I hate it. I had a knife on my ankle, and I couldn't get him off me long enough to reach it." She touched her face, pressing the bruise carefully. "They slid my weapon from its holster so easily. I figured I was bombproof and I'm not."

"That's easily fixed." Kane straightened. "I have a Ruger LCP II at home. It's small and easily concealed. You could carry it in a pocket or a light shoulder holster. It's a good backup weapon."

Jenna nodded. "The extra weight would be worth it for peace of mind."

Once fully dressed, she walked beside Kane to Wolfe's office. Inside, a cup of coffee was pressed into her hands and a plate of cookies pushed toward her. She dropped into a chair. "Thanks. Did the results come in for Shelby O'Connor?"

"Yeah. Once we've discussed them, I want you to go home and rest. It's after six and you have no reason to return to the office. Everything is under control. Do we have a deal?" Wolfe handed a cup to Kane and sat in his office chair.

Jenna nodded. She wanted nothing more than to crawl into bed and sleep. "Deal."

"I ran the DNA from the marks from Shelby's arms through every database we know and found no match. Kalo is on the case and is trying a few other places, some of the ancestry sites that offer DNA to find relatives." Wolfe leaned back in his chair. "I do have some good news. The fibers and trace elements I discovered on her body are significant. The carpet fibers match a specific make of truck available for rental at the airport

—a GMC Yukon. They were fitted especially for durability because of the constant cleaning. This, and I found a match for the cleaning fluid used inside the vehicles. It is specific to them, and not available in stores. I can prove without doubt that the vehicle used to transport her body was an airport rental."

"So good and bad news." Kane reached for a cookie, holding it between thumb and finger. "Good because we know where the vehicle came from, but bad because there won't be any trace evidence left inside or out once it's been cleaned."

Jenna raised both eyebrows. "Maybe, but it's good because rental companies keep records, and we'll be able to trace everyone who drove that truck. Or one of those trucks. I gather they have more than one?" She waved a hand dismissively. "Never mind if it's one or twenty. It might take a few days to narrow it down, but we have him." She smiled at Kane. "Like you said, sooner or later they all make mistakes."

THIRTY-THREE

Confident he had his plans in order, Julian headed to the library to meet Kristina. The house was snug and warm. The wine spiked and ready to pour. His decision to drug her might upset his friend, but he didn't care. The result would be the same: Kristina would give him her fortune and then die. Aware of the CCTV surveillance over the library entrance, Julian made sure to park in the shadows. He'd informed Kristina of the make and model of the truck he'd be driving. When he'd arrived, only a white Chevrolet Equinox sat in the lot. He shook his head. She'd said her vehicle was white. Maybe he'd been mistaken about the make but, surely, she'd recognize his GMC Yukon. He flashed his lights and the door to the vehicle opened, the interior light showing a dark-haired woman. He drove closer and leaned over to open the passenger door. "Kristina?"

"Of course, it's me." Kristina smiled warmly. "Who else would be out in this weather and carrying a very good bottle of vintage wine. You enjoy a good red, I believe?" She climbed inside his truck and looked him over. "It's nice to meet you at last."

Taken aback by the vibrant woman beside him, Julian stared at her. "Your photograph doesn't do you justice."

"The camera hates me." Kristina laughed and patted her purse. "I have everything we need to do business in here. I can't wait to get it over with and have dinner. I'm famished." She fastened her seatbelt. "Have you prepared the meal yourself?"

Frowning, Julian shook his head. "No, I ordered takeout. The delivery is coming in about an hour. We should be ready by then. I don't know my way around my friend's kitchen. I did find the toaster and the microwave, and that will have to do me for now. I'm looking at real estate in the morning. I'm hoping to have a house before my friends return from their vacation over-seas—but I have three months, so I don't need to rush into buying a property." He headed out of the parking lot and took Maple to avoid the CCTV cameras along Main.

They made idle chatter until they arrived at the house. He helped her from his rental, taking the bottle of wine and smil-ing. "I shall enjoy this, but I've opened a bottle of your favorite. It's breathing in the kitchen." He led the way to the front door.

"Well, we'll open both of them." Kristina chuckled. "I'll drink the white and you can enjoy the red. There's nothing like a good glass of wine with dinner."

"I'm looking forward to tasting it." He ushered her into the kitchen. His laptop sat open on the table. "I hope you don't mind working in the kitchen. I didn't want to use my friend's office. It seemed like an invasion of his privacy."

"I understand completely." Kristina removed her coat and hung it on the back of the chair before sitting down. She looked at him. "How do you remember all your account numbers?" She opened her purse and removed a small red leather-bound note-book. "All mine are in here. I don't trust anything people can hack."

Julian smiled at her. Her perfume drifted over him. It was unusual, musky and rich—almost hypnotic. He pointed to his own notebook open on the table. "I don't trust anyone either. We're a good match. All my accounts are in here and all the details I need to access them. It's just for my own records. I keep my clients' details in the company files. I'm happy to add yours to my little black book." He chuckled. "It remains close to my heart at all times, and at night, it's locked in my safe."

"Oh, I do the same." She pushed her notebook toward him. "My personal accounts are all here. Do you mind if I watch you transfer the funds? It's not that I don't trust you, but we have only just met."

"Of course." Julian sat beside her and pulled his laptop toward them. "It's easy. I just access your accounts and transfer our agreed amount into my personal account and from there I can transfer funds to just about anywhere." He tapped away on the keyboard, moving money so fast she couldn't have stopped the transactions if she'd wanted too.

"So how do you know it's arrived in your account?" Kristina stared at the screen with a blank expression.

"I access my cryptocurrency accounts. They're not on a banking website. They're in a different place." He accessed the dark web and went to his account and converted the money into cryptocurrency. As her money transferred from one account to the other it showed on the screen as a downloading file. It was completed in seconds. Her fortune drained and hidden where no one could find it without his access codes. "See how easy it is? This is the same as we did last time but you deposited the cash into my company account. You recall after only one week I was able to deposit the full amount back into your account plus $10,000 profit?" He smiled at her. "This transfer is off the books. It's a private transaction between you and me. It means everything you earn is yours, without paying my company a commission or taxes like before."

"The page looks so strange. Not like any website I've seen before. Is it safe?" Kristina gave him a concerned stare.

Everything had gone to plan and the next stage would be so easy he couldn't contain his amusement and laughed. "As safe as houses." He stood and poured her a glass of wine. "Now we'll drink to our arrangement."

He'd sacrifice the thrill of strangling her. They'd be so many more to come and he needed time to get away without her DNA all over him. Now all he had to do was avoid drinking the wine he'd poisoned. He'd already created an excuse and planted it in her mind during one of their many phone conversations. "White wine isn't something I enjoy. I'll just take a sip."

"No, please don't. It might be unlucky as you hate white wine. You must open my gift and join me in celebrating." Kristina took the glass from him and inhaled the bouquet. "I insist."

Julian could not believe his luck. "I will, thanks." He lifted the bottle and stared at the label. "This is far too extravagant." He stared at her determined expression, and after all, he did have something to celebrate. "I'll need a corkscrew." He opened a drawer. "Ah, here's one." He opened the bottle and poured a glass. He took a sip. "Oh, that's divine."

"To our success." Kristina stood and raised her glass.

Julian finished his wine and poured another. He looked at Kristina, she'd only taken a sip. "Dinner will be here soon."

"Oh, then may I use the bathroom?" Kristina smiled at him.

Julian nodded. "Yes, first door along the hallway." He pointed the way.

Pleased at seeing his plan unfold so successfully, he waited, leaning against the counter, but she wasn't gone for more than a few minutes. He smiled to himself, seeing the empty glass in her hand, and when she sat back at the table, he refilled it. "How do you like the wine?"

"Delicious but it's going to my head already." Kristina smiled at him and blinked a few times as if trying to focus.

"Maybe I drank it a little too fast. I was so excited about our deal."

Good, it's working already. Julian chuckled. "I did as well. This is my second glass." He inhaled the rich aroma. "You've spoiled me. I'll want this vintage all the time now."

"Oh, I feel all wobbly." Kristina held her head.

As she slumped sideways, he stepped forward to grab her, leaning her forward and laying her head on the table. His thoughts went to his friend, and he grinned into the silent room as the sound of a vehicle approached the house. Julian hurried outside just as the impressive antique grandfather clock in the hallway chimed the half-hour. His friend drove toward him, bathing him with headlights, and parked beside the walled garden. Julian pulled on his coat and gloves before venturing out into the stormy night to meet him. Rain ran down his cheeks like teardrops as he peered into the window. "Leave the engine running. Grab the food out the back and I'll move it and then drive my rental closer to the door so we can move the body."

"You haven't killed her yet, have you?" An angry line etched his friend's mouth. "You promised I'd have this one."

Shaking his head, Julian stared at him. "No, of course I haven't killed her yet. Now do as I say. She's in the bathroom and we haven't got much time. Grab the food and head inside. She's expecting you."

"I can't wait." His friend headed for the back of the truck.

Excitement shivered through Julian as he slid behind the wheel and disengaged the handbrake. Heart thumping, he waited, watching in the rear-vision mirror for his friend to open the hatch and lean inside. Moving fast, he slid the truck into reverse and hit the gas. A muffled cry cut through the silence as his friend fell under the wheels. Julian turned the wheel sharp to the left and heard the crunch of bones as the front wheel bumped over the silent body crushed beneath him. As planned, the truck came to rest against the brick wall surrounding the driveway.

Laughing with glee, he stepped out and took a minute to enjoy the bloody mess. He stared into the unseeing eyes, grinning. "You were a liability and now the cops are going to believe you murdered the three women and then had a terrible accident. They'll call it divine justice or providence. I can't wait to watch it on the news."

Careful not to leave any trace of himself behind. He took the food and dropped it into his rental. It would be easy to dispose of the takeout in any garbage pail in town. He so wanted to be able to wake Kristina and bring her out to see what he'd done. The idea of tasting her fear thrilled him, but it was too late for her now. Staring at the pool of blood, he wiped the rain from his face and headed inside. It was time to remove his fingerprints from the house and make sure everything was in place before his final move. Unfamiliar tiredness dragged at him and he shook his head, confused. Perhaps the adrenalin high his body had expected hadn't arrived and he'd slipped into the slump that always followed. He needed to get this over with. He had everything he wanted now. His friend's money—or should he say "ex-friend's" money—would be his in a few clicks of his keyboard. He'd clean up and then use the rope in his pocket to strangle Kristina—she wouldn't feel a thing, but the cops would expect some part of what he did to be the same. *Fools.*

He'd leave his card and get the hell out of Dodge. The cops would come by eventually, find the dead woman and her killer, stupid enough to be run down by his own truck. No one would be looking for him. He'd be home free. He smiled. *A perfect crime.*

Strolling down the passageway, he shrugged out of his wet coat and tossed it on the table. He downed the glass of wine and resealed it with a cap for the purpose, found in one of the drawers. He'd take the wine with him. Why waste a superb bottle of wine? He wiped the corkscrew and tossed it back into the drawer. There was one more thing he needed to do before he left and he sat at his laptop to transfer his friend's money into his dark web accounts. His vision blurred and he pressed the heels of his hands into his eyes.

"How are you feeling, Julian?" Kristina lifted her head, clear eyed and smiling. In one hand she held a pistol aimed at his chest. "You've been a very naughty boy, haven't you?"

Shocked at seeing her conscious, Julian moved saliva around his mouth trying to moisten his dry throat. "I don't know what you mean."

"Well, extortion comes to mind." Kristina smiled at him. "Oh, and for your information, the blurred vision you're experiencing right now is caused by a slow-acting toxin. I have the antidote with me and my Glock as backup in case you decide to do something stupid. Nice trick with the truck by the way, I'll have to remember that one."

Baffled how she'd managed to remain conscious after drinking enough poison to fell a bear, Julian stared at her. His stomach clenched and panic gripped him. "What do you mean, toxin? I opened that bottle myself. There's no way you could have poisoned the wine."

"Oh, it was easy." Kristina aimed the gun at his head. "I used a syringe and injected it into the bottle through the cork. I used a very fine needle. It's undetectable." She sighed. "Now here's the deal. Refund my money, right now, and I'll give you the antidote. Turn the screen around so I can watch the transaction."

Stomach gripping, Julian nodded. "Okay, okay. How did you know?" He transferred cash from his private account, leaving the cryptocurrency in his account.

"I've been watching you for a time." Kristina pushed a number written on a piece of paper toward him. "Now all your cryptocurrency into this account."

Anger welled and he shook his head. "I've refunded your money, now give me the antidote. Are you insane?"

"It seems to me you have two choices." Kristina smiled at him with confidence. "Either do it and live, or die and I'll do it myself. I've been manipulating accounts on the dark web all my life." She snorted. "Oh, don't look so mad. You can start up again. It's a great scheme you have here. Catfishing and then bleeding women dry. I like the twist—killing them to avoid any throwback to you—but I found you, didn't I? I *know* who you are."

A choking sensation gripped Julian's throat. He swallowed hard trying to rid the blockage. His heart pounded and then missed beats. Horrified by her smiling face, he stared at his laptop screen. She'd poisoned him and he had no choice but to comply with her wishes if he wanted to live. He lifted his pounding head and tried to focus on her. "Okay, I'll do as you say."

"I'm watching you. Make one false move and I'll shoot you in the head." Kristina moved behind him. "I figure you have maybe four minutes before you die."

He fought to keep his vision clear as he made the transfers. "There, it's done." He turned slowly to look at her. He tried to lift his leaden arms and now each breath was an effort. Terror closed in on him, surrounding him with helplessness. "Kristina... please... you said if I did what you wanted, you'd give me the antidote."

"I lied." Kristina leaned against the counter watching him. Her soulless brown eyes fixed on his face; her mouth held in a slight red grin.

Panic surged through Julian as he fought for each breath. "*Please,* Kristina."

"I'm not Kristina." She smiled and bent closer to look at him. "That sweet deluded woman is safe in her bed. Now hurry up and die. I have to clean up and then get your rental back to the airport."

Her pupils had grown huge like an owl's at night. It was so quiet in the house and all he could hear was the *tick, tick, tick* of the grandfather clock, counting down the minutes to his death.

Julian stared at her face. It had distorted into the image of a grinning carnival clown. *"Please."*

Terror gripped him. His limbs trembled but he couldn't feel his legs. As the toxin crawled up his body, paralyzing his lungs, he gasped for breath. Her laughter was the last thing he heard as his sight faded to black. *This is what it's like to die.*

THIRTY-FOUR

THURSDAY

Sun streamed through the gaps in the drapes when Jenna woke and stared at the digital readout on her clock and groaned. It was past eight and she had a ton of work to do today. She sat up dislodging her black cat, Pumpkin, from her chest. The spell in the hot tub had eased the stiffness in her muscles. The long sleep had made her feel much better. "Dave, are you here?"

Nails sounded on the wooden floor and Duke bounded into the room; his paws landed on the side of the bed and his entire body wiggled with happiness as his thick tail fanned the air. "Hello, Duke. Where's Dave?"

"Right here." Kane came into the room carrying a cup of steaming coffee. "You look rested. Do you feel okay?"

Jenna smiled at him, then winced as her sore mouth and cheek reminded her of the attack. "I'll be okay. It shook me up some, is all."

"Do you want to go into the office?" Kane eyed her critically. "We can work from home. I have all the files up to date."

"We'll need a warrant to look at the books at the airport car rental." She took the cup from the bedside table and blew across the beverage. "Then we'll go and speak to the pathologist and see what he can give us on the other gamers."

"I requested a warrant last night." Kane smiled at her and sat on the edge of the bed. "Maggie took it over to the judge's house on the way home from the office. She called to say he's read it through and signed it. We just need to drop by the office and collect it before we head to the airport."

Jenna relaxed against the pillows. "Is it really sunny outside?"

"Yeah, not a cloud in the sky." He chuckled. "The horses went a little crazy when I let them out into the corral. The grass in there is up to my knees, although its flattened now they all had a rolling contest." He rubbed Duke's ears. "I'll leave you to dress and go and start breakfast. I've already spoken to Rio, and everything is under control. Jim Talbert, the biker who attacked you, will be moved to county sometime this morning, so once we get the list from the car rental place, we'll have everyone working on it."

Jenna sipped her coffee and looked at him. "Kalo has the images of our potential suspects. Can't he use the FBI facial recognition software to search for a match? The Jack of Hearts Killer has to be the person who hired the Yukon or his accomplice."

"Soon as we get the list, we'll send it to him." Kane backed out of the room. "Get ready."

After eating breakfast and carefully applying makeup over her bruised cheek, Jenna climbed into the Beast, with Duke in the back seat, and they headed for the office. It was so good to see the sun, but the smell from the floods still tainted the air, and everything seemed to be covered with a coating of mud. The water level had fallen but had left massive damage in its wake. Fences were down and others bore the results of the flood surge, with dead grass and other debris, including dead animals, caught in the railings and wire. "It's a mess out there and look at the potholes. It will take the council forever to repair them all."

"I guess now the water level is dropping, the full extent of the damage will be clear." Kane turned onto the highway and accelerated. "I checked the road alert, and some roads are still closed. A bridge was washed away in Blackwater. We're lucky the highway was open yesterday or we would have been on our own."

Jenna shrugged. "Maybe the bikers wouldn't have gotten into town if the roads had been closed." She stared out of the window. "If it hadn't been yesterday, it would have been another day. They'd planned to take me down and we couldn't have stopped it, but next time we'll stick together."

"Amen to that." Kane headed along Main past Aunt Betty's Café and pulled into his parking slot outside the office. "Wait here. I'll pick up the paperwork." He slid from the truck and bounded up the steps.

Moments later, he returned and they were on their way. When they arrived at the airport, they parked out front of the car rental office. Jenna dropped the search warrant on the front desk and smiled. "I'm Sheriff Alton. I have a warrant to collect the names of anyone renting a GMC Yukon two weeks either side of today."

The woman behind the counter's mouth dropped open. "Do you believe one of our vehicles was used in a crime?"

Jenna straightened. "That has yet to be established. Can you give me a printout of the details of the people, please? We're in a hurry."

"Yes, of course." The woman looked over the warrant and went to the computer. "I do recall a man who rented a Yukon yesterday." She looked up at them. "Ah, here he is. His name is Nathan Stevens, out of 5 Elm Street." The printer whirred. "There are others, but this man is a regular." She stood to collect the papers and handed them to Jenna. "Is there anything else you need?"

Jenna gave Kane a meaningful stare. She had proof that the pathologist gamer known as Bloodlust was involved in the murders. She scanned the pages mentally matching the dates he hired the trucks to the deaths of the victims. "He hired one yesterday?"

"Yeah, but it was returned last night. It's already been detailed and is back out in the lot. We have a fast turnaround here." The receptionist tapped at her computer. "It was returned around nine-thirty last night and went through the carwash at seven this morning. The guys steam-cleaned the interior right after. They are required to log each process and it's all here from the get-go."

"How do you know what time it was returned?" Kane narrowed his gaze at her. "Don't you have a drop-off area out back?"

"Yes, we do." She smiled at him. "The vehicles have a tag on them that allows them to enter the gate. It has a time-and-date stamp. The driver locks the vehicle and places the keys inside a locked box and leaves by a side entrance. Each vehicle is insured by the driver. If there's any damage, we contact them and make a claim, but it doesn't happen very often. If people return a vehicle late, we add a payment to their credit card."

"Do you recall what he looked like?" Kane straightened. "My height, smaller?"

"Oh, yes, I'd say smaller, maybe five-ten, and he had a beard and spectacles." She smiled. "Softspoken and very charming."

That was the description of Julian Darnley. Wanting to punch the air, Jenna nodded at the woman. "Thank you." She almost ran out of the door and, breathless with excitement, turned to Kane. "Do you think Nathan Stevens is the elusive Julian Darnley, and he's the Jack of Hearts Killer?"

"There's only one way to find out." Kane started the engine. "We'll go and pay him a visit. He should be at work by now."

Concerned, Jenna reached for her phone. "I'm calling for backup. I'm not taking any chances. If we corner this guy, we don't know what he's capable of doing."

"Hold up." Kane glanced at her. "We know there's two of them, so we might miss the opportunity of catching the other killer if we go in all guns blazing. Call the clinic and see if he's there. Ask as a private citizen. Think of an excuse to see him, maybe to clarify a result or something."

Nodding, Jenna searched through her phone for the number of the pathologists. "Good idea. It will give us time to check the entrances and exits of the building." She thought for a beat. "He returned the Yukon last night. I sure hope he didn't kill anyone." She made the call, disconnected, and turned to Kane. "He's not there. The receptionist said he didn't show for work and hasn't called in. Head for his home." She checked her notebook. "Five Elm Street."

"Okay." Kane turned the Beast around and then glanced down at the GPS screen. "That's near the hospital."

Jenna's mind was working overtime. She ran down the list of suspects. "What about the other members of the gamer clan Kalo discovered? Can we link them to Nathan Stevens?"

"I recall one possible." Kane accelerated. "Jack Sutherland. We don't know what we're walking into. Call it in and put a hold on Rio and Rowley's interview. Give them a heads-up that Sutherland might be the accomplice. He was the other gamer in the clan, flying under the radar, and from Kalo's notes they chatted online often during the games. We have to assume they're friends."

As they arrived at the small house a short time later and parked some way from the entrance, Jenna scanned the area. Only a fool would walk into an unknown situation. Water droplets fell from the trees as she made her way along the sidewalk. Behind her, Kane walked in silence and Duke followed, alert as always. The yard was empty, no flowerbeds or trees, just a strip of grass each side of a paved walkway. The gravel driveway offered a view to the backyard, where a solitary tree took up most of the small space. Jenna turned to Kane. "It's kind of a small place for someone extorting money from lonely women."

"It's perfect." Kane moved to her side. "He's playing it low key. He wouldn't want to call attention to himself, and I figure his ride is an older vehicle as well. I doubt any of the women he meets see his true self. He hires a truck and likely has a story to make an excuse to cover the reason he doesn't take them to his home." His head moved slightly as he scanned the area. "No sign of any cameras. He doesn't expect to be found. Typical psychopath."

Easing her weapon from the holster, Jenna edged along the perimeter of the neighboring property. "The drapes are drawn but there's a light burning on the porch. I don't figure he's home." She glanced at Kane. "Let's do this."

Moving swiftly, they dashed to the front door. Jenna took one side and Kane the other, their backs to the wall. She knocked on the door. "Sheriff's department."

Nothing.

"Sheriff's department." Kane hammered his fist on the wooden door, making it shake. "Open up, Mr. Stevens."

Nothing.

Jenna looked at him. "Go round back. I'll wait here."

"Okay. Duke, stay." Kane slipped away without a sound.

Keeping her back to the wall, Jenna stepped silently to the front window. The drapes were drawn but a light showed through a crack. She moved closer and peered through the gap. The room was empty and she could see right through the house to the kitchen. The next moment Kane was at her side. She shook her head. "He's not here."

"Nope. I looked through all the windows, no one is home."
He frowned. "We need to look inside and track his phone. I'll
pull up his driver's license and see if it matches the image we
have of Julian Darnley. We know he had contact with both
victims before their deaths. If we can prove it's the same person,
we have one of our killers." He turned and headed back to the
Beast.

"I'll call Kalo." Jenna pulled out her phone and hurried
after him. "Hi, Bobby. We think we have a match for Julian
Darnley and one of the gamers, the pathologist by the name of
Nathan Stevens. If we send you the images, will you do a facial
recognition match of the two men? We need probable cause for
a warrant."

*"Yeah sure. Carter is here. He wants to speak to you. I'll
transfer you to his desk."* The line went dead for a few minutes
before Carter picked up.

*"Hi, Jenna. Kalo has been keeping us informed. What else do
you have on this Nathan Stevens?"*

Jenna gave him a rundown of the evidence. "If we can prove
they're the same person, Stevens could be murdering someone
right now. We need to find him ASAP. The phone location and
search will give us his accomplice."

"Okay." Carter paused for a beat. *"Then go for the phone
first, as the judge in your town is difficult. If you can prove he's
involved, then he'll have no choice but to give you the warrant to
search his house."* He cleared his throat. *"I'll write it up and
send it through as an urgent FBI request the moment Kalo
confirms. I have the images in front of me now, and looking at the
eyes, shape of head, eyebrows, it's the same guy. I'll get at it and
have a copy of the paperwork in your inbox by the time you get
back to the office."*

Grinning, Jenna hurried after Kane. "Thanks. I'll talk to
you later."

"My pleasure." Carter disconnected.

The muddy footpath squelched under her feet as she ran to the Beast. She wiped them on the blacktop before climbing inside. The screen of the mobile data terminal displayed two images and it didn't take facial recognition software to see they were the same man. She clicked in her seatbelt and turned to Kane. "Carter is going to push through the phone trace and a search of his records. He figures we should find him first and then go for the house."

"That makes sense." Kane started the engine and headed back to the office. "What we need is a list of the women Stevens was grooming. He could be doing this all over the state." He frowned. "As Darnley doesn't legally exist, he doesn't have privacy rights. As we're sure he's committing crimes by luring women to their deaths, we can access his social media accounts under that name." He smiled at Jenna. "I don't need Kalo to do that. I can run a search when we get back to the office."

THIRTY-FIVE

It had been some time since Kane had used his codes to access social media. Prior to this, when he worked in DC, cybercrime fell under the umbrella of his work in the Secret Service. He cracked his knuckles and entered the codes. To his surprise the files opened without a problem and he made short work of tracing the list of women and their contact details. He saved the details to a file and shared it with Jenna. He took a long drink of his coffee and then a bite of a sandwich that had appeared like magic at his elbow. He looked up at Jenna, working opposite him, and a curl of worry wrapped around his heart. She had a traumatic time ahead. With the news Jenna's DNA had been found on three of the four men responsible for her kidnapping, including her attacker's DNA under her nails, the DA threw the book at the bikers. It would be a time before she'd need to go to court, but everything had consequences. Jenna had suffered great hardships in her life. First the spousal abuse and then coming close to death after being kidnapped by psychopaths had left invisible scars, and she'd struggled with PTSD for over two years. Now the attempted rape and kidnap would have stirred up bad memories and started the horrific cycle again.

"You keep looking at me and frowning." Jenna reached for her cup of coffee and sipped. "Do I smell bad or something?"

Kane chuckled. "You smell like sunshine and honeysuckle." He sucked in a deep breath. "I've been concerned about the kidnapping, is all."

"Oh, don't worry. No one is going to bring charges against you for excessive force." Jenna leaned back and stared at him. "More like not enough force. Most in your position would have made sure they didn't draw down on them—like permanently."

He liked that she cared about him. It was hard to get used to after so long being alone and living a new life. He could tell her everything—well, apart from his real name and his missions. He smiled. "I've been concerned about PTSD. You hide things very well. Just don't hide them from me. If you're worried about anything, we'll work through it together. You're not alone anymore, Jenna."

"I know that and, yeah, I had flashbacks at the time, but I'm okay." She met his gaze. "I'll tell you if that changes, promise." She sipped again and then placed her cup back on the table. "Did you find anything?"

Nodding, Kane leaned forward on the desk. "Darnley was in contact, as we know, with the victims prior to their deaths. We know by their phone records he was obviously using a burner as the calls are untraceable. The two victims are wealthy. They owned businesses and had no man in their lives. I've sent the list to your files. If he's killed again, it will likely be one of those women."

A knock came on the door and Rowley poked his head inside. "We just had a call from the judge's secretary. She said she has a signed warrant for us to collect. Do you want me to go and get it?"

"Send Maggie. I'll need you here. The moment we get a location we'll be moving out." Jenna's phone chimed and she stared at the screen. "It's Carter. I'll put it on speaker. Hi, Ty. Thanks for the warrant. The judge has signed it."

"My pleasure. We've confirmed the ID and Kalo has pinpointed the location of Stevens' phone. It's stationary out at 3 West Lane, Eastern Heights. This is your man. I'd pack for bear. The house looks isolated. It's surrounded by acres of trees. I'll text you the address and send the arial shot of the house."

"Thanks, we're on our way." Jenna disconnected and stood. "Grab what we need from the gun safe. I'll go and organize the others. I'll meet you downstairs." She took her jacket from the peg behind the door and ran down the stairs.

Kane selected the rifles he needed and headed after her. As he reached the main office, Rio and Rowley were slipping into their Kevlar vests and helmets. He handed them each a rifle. "Use these. This is a psychopath, and you can't talk him down. Disable if possible. It's likely there are two of them and maybe a victim. Use caution."

"Let's go. We'll take all the vehicles. A show of force is an advantage." Jenna headed for the door.

"Who do I ride with?" Poppy walked up to Kane. "Can I come with you, Dave?"

Kane strapped on his helmet and shook his head. "No."

"You're on desk duty." Jenna stared at her. "You're not an active member of my team. You'd be a liability in the field. You don't have the experience to take down a serial killer."

"And I never will if you keep me locked up inside like a naughty child." Poppy glared at her. "Give me a break. What's wrong with you? Do I intimidate you? Is that it?"

"Fine, go with Rio. Let's see how you cope under fire." Jenna waved her away. "Get her a vest, will you?"

"Sure." Rio turned back to the equipment closet and dragged one out and tossed it to Poppy. "You follow orders or you can stay in the truck, understand?" He led the way out the door.

Kane pushed Duke into his basket under the front counter. "You stay with Maggie. I'll be back soon." He patted the dog's head and followed Jenna out to the Beast.

Without delay they set off in a convoy and shot through town and up into the hills surrounding Black Rock Falls. The roads had potholes but were clear from any other damage from the recent deluge. The temperature fell sharply inside the cab as they entered the dense forest roads, winding upward. Sunlight pierced the canopy, the shadows turning the blacktop into a mirage of jigsaw pieces, dark and light shadows. Trickles of water crossed the road as they ran from the hillside, slithering like snakes to join a small stream alongside the forest. A calmness surrounded Kane. Unlike others, his response to action was calm clarity. In his mind, he had the image of the house and the access points. The long tree-lined driveway offered them a way to get close without being seen. If they parked out of sight, he'd go ahead with Jenna and scope out the area and have the others as backup. If it looked safe, they'd surround the house.

"You're the expert, what's the best way into the house?" Jenna was checking her weapon.

Kane explained. "Call the others on the phone and tell them our plan. This guy is smart and he might have a scanner."

"Okay." Jenna holstered her weapon and pulled out her phone. She made a conference call. "Follow us in with stealth. We'll park some ways from the house. Use your coms. We'll be entering from the front and back."

Kane turned into the driveway and slowed, stopping twenty yards from the house. In the driveway he could make out a blue truck, the hatch open. The front door to the house was ajar. He pressed his com. "Someone must be outside. The front door is open, and I'm seeing a truck. Keep out of sight. I'll go ahead and check it out." He could feel Jenna beside him and turned to her. "I'll go."

"No!" She shook her head. "*We'll* go. I can move as silently as you." She pushed him in the back. "Move out."

Kane moved through the trees. The ground was soft under his boots and they reached the house without making a sound. The truck was parked at a strange angle with the rear hatch open, and the engine was running. As they moved closer the smell of death reached him on the wind. "I figure we're too late."

"Let's take a look." Jenna slipped through the trees and stared all around. "Oh, that doesn't look good. Someone is under the wheels."

As they approached the vehicle the pool of blood on the gravel glistened in the sunlight. Congealed and dark, it had been there for hours. With Jenna covering him, Kane moved around the vehicle. A body of a man, eyes cloudy in death and covered with insects lay beneath the truck. It was obvious from his injuries the truck had run over him. Kane holstered his weapon and pulled on gloves before shutting down the engine.

"That's not Stevens." Jenna peered at the body. "This guy has blue eyes and blond hair." She spun around, weapon aimed at the door. "Which means Stevens is probably inside."

Kane shook his head. "Unlikely. He took the Yukon back to the rental place. This guy is probably his accomplice. It looks like he was getting something out of the back and left the vehicle in reverse." He shook his head. "The reversing lights are on. It doesn't make sense but things happen."

"We'll check the house." Jenna used her com to call the others forward. "Watch our backs while we clear the house."

Inside, the smell of death hit them again. In silence, Kane moved along one side of the hallway, Jenna the other, clearing the rooms as they went. They both paused at the kitchen door. The smell was stronger here and he gave her a nod and stepped inside. He raised his weapon, aiming at the man sitting at the table and then lowered it. A face frozen in death stared at him, flesh blue and eyes bulging from behind spectacles. The corpse had a beard, but he had no doubt it was Stevens masquerading as Julian Darnley. He looked over his shoulder at Jenna. "I wasn't expecting this, that's for darn sure."

"Murder, suicide?" Jenna holstered her weapon and pulled on a face mask and then gloves. "Look at him. He's been foaming at the mouth. That's poison." She moved closer. "That has to be a fake beard. Look, it's come away where he's drooled." She spoke to the others using her com. "Stand down. We have two bodies. Rio call Wolfe and stay clear. We don't want any contamination." She moved closer to the body. "Oh, don't tell me we've been wrong about Stevens." She pointed to a card sticking out of the front of Stevens' shirt.

Kane pulled out the card and flipped it over on the table. He'd seen it before, and his gut tightened. A shiver slid down his spine at the implications. "The Grim Reaper. It's the thirteenth card in the tarot deck, known as the death card."

"Does this mean we have another player on the team of crazies?" Jenna turned suddenly and looked around her. "Oh, I just felt an ice-cold breeze. This place is giving me the creeps." She rubbed her arms and stared at him. "Now you're frightening me. You're wearing your combat face again. Okay, what do you know?"

Pushing back the memories of cases too gruesome to discuss, he frowned. "This is the calling card of a killer some cops believe is a myth. The FBI has been on this case for years and no one has ever found a trace of them. The murders they committed would give the toughest cop nightmares. Insiders called them the Tarot Killer but the name was never revealed. We've never discovered if they're male or female and the murders go back ten years or so. Unpredictable and like smoke, they prefer to kill psychopaths, but we figure they've killed others as well—people we've found that have committed atrocious crimes. It was one of the cases discussed at the conference

I attended with Wolfe, Jo, and Carter." He took a deep breath, ignoring the stench and looked at her over his face mask. "If this person is in town, no one is safe. This is the work of the psychopath's psychopath. This person could convince the devil himself to take his own life."

THIRTY-SIX

Jenna took in the entire scene. A laptop sat open on the table, and beside it a small black book with its pages pressed wide to display a list of numbers. "I figure the killer is a woman, and Stevens, masquerading as Darnley, tried to extort the wrong person this time. She somehow turned the tables on him—well, both of them, I guess—and then took the Yukon back to the airport. What are the chances of a psychopath choosing a psychopath like the Tarot Killer as a victim?"

"Infinitesimal." Kane moved around with his phone recording the scene in detail. "They say it takes one to know one, so she probably figured Darnley was catfishing, and when he became interested in her money, she played along and then killed him."

"I think you're wrong this time." Jenna balled her hands on her hips. "Think about it. She killed before to take down bad people, psychopaths who'd done heinous crimes, right? So how did she know about the women these men had already killed?" She snorted. "We only just found a motive, and she took them out before we discovered their location. I mean, we had the FBI searching databanks, and yet she suddenly decided to kill them both—why?" She paced up and down trying to ignore the smell of death seeping through her mask. "Somehow, she knew what they were doing. I'd bet my last dime she was involved with the victims. There has to be a link. This was a vengeance hit for O'Connor and Gilbert."

"That makes sense." Kane's eyes crinkled as he smiled behind his mask. "I love the way you think." He bent to take shots of the floor under the table. "The Tarot Killer is an open FBI case. We'll have to bring in Carter and Jo." He cleared his throat. "It's like a second chapter. If these guys are the killers, then our part of the case is closed."

Jenna stared at him and shook her head. "Whoa, I'm not giving up just yet. If the Tarot Killer is murdering in my town, then she is my business." She waved a hand toward the body of Stevens. "She murdered one man at least. I'll hunt her down and stop her."

"Good luck with that." Kane shook his head. "After a decade of murders, she knows how to vanish without a trace. We'll be wasting our time."

Incredulous, Jenna met his gaze over her mask. "What are you—chicken?"

"Never." Kane chuckled. "If you want to hunt her down, then we'll hunt her down—but protocol mandates we inform Carter and Jo."

On the counter sat an open bottle of white wine with two glasses, and a phone. Jenna sighed. "Sure, I don't have a problem with them." She pointed to the wine, reluctant to sniff it. "I wonder if the wine is poisoned?"

"I guess Wolfe will be able to tell us. This scene was well planned like all of the Tarot Killer's murders and I figure they'll try to make us believe they've left town." Kane was recording the scene in images and video. "As soon as Wolfe gives me the go-ahead, I'll search the laptop and his phone." He pushed his phone inside his pocket and walked back to the victim. "I'll see if there's any ID on the body."

Jenna stared all around, checking the floor for scuff marks, any sign of a struggle, and found nothing. "How did she make him drink poison and then run down the man outside? Who just stands there and allows someone to run them down?"

"We'll take a closer look but from the way the body is lying, I figure he was getting something out the back and someone reversed over him." Kane shrugged. "It's easy enough to explain how she killed him but how come she was behind the wheel at the time? It seems unusual. What was the dead guy getting out of the back of his truck? I didn't see anything on the ground or in his hands."

Jenna nodded. "I figure she took it with her or left in in the Yukon and dropped it at the airport. The carwash guys would throw it in the trash."

"Oh, this is interesting. He's carrying another phone, business cards in the name of Julian Darnley, and a wallet. The driver's license belongs to Stevens." Kane, dropped the wallet, phone, and cards on the table. "This is all the proof we need."

Finding no other evidence, Jenna waved him to the door. "Leave him for now. We need to ID the man under the truck." She led the way outside and found Rio, Rowley, and Anderson. She peered under the truck at the body. A bulge in the front pocket of his jeans had the outline of a wallet. She looked at her deputies over and then at Kane. "None of you are small enough to slide under the truck to get the victim's wallet. I'll have to try."

"Your arms aren't long enough." Kane looked at Anderson. "Get under the truck and pull that man's wallet. You'll be able to reach it easier than any of us." He stared at her. "Wear gloves."

"Me?" Poppy's eyes popped wide open and her mouth turned down in disgust. "I'm not touching a dead body, no freaking way." She gaped at Kane. "Are you insane?"

"That's what deputies do, Poppy. They handle dead bodies all the time." Rio handed her a pair of gloves. "They follow orders. You wanted to work the crime scenes and this one is tame to what we usually encounter. Get at it."

Waiting for the outburst, Jenna stepped closer to give her support. "We need to discover his ID and his face is a mess, so this is the only way." She shrugged. "You're the best person for the job. That's how we roll around here. I'll be right beside you, there's nothing to fear. The guy's dead."

"No!" Poppy stepped up to face her. "Do your own dirty work."

Annoyed by her lack of respect, Jenna shook her head. "That's enough. Refusing a direct order in the field tells me you're not cut out to be a deputy. You're fired."

"I'll go and work with Mayor Petersham. He told me there's always a place for me in his office. At least he'll appreciate me and not treat me like I'm a kid." Poppy removed her badge and tossed it at Jenna's feet. "He'll put me up for sheriff in the next election and I'll have your job."

Shaking her head, Jenna stared at her. "I've already filed sexual harassment complaints with the mayor's office against you and so has Kane. If you go for sheriff, they'll become part of the public record and even Mayor Petersham won't be able to give you a job."

"Go to hell." Poppy spun around and looked at Rio. "Zack, give me a ride into town."

"I can't leave right now." Rio shrugged.

"You'll have to wait." Kane glared at her. "In case it slipped your mind, we're processing a crime scene. Go and wait in Rio's truck. He'll give you a ride to town when we're done here."

Jenna stared after her. The sexual harassment aside, if Poppy had really wanted to become a member of the team, dealing with dead bodies came with the job. She turned to Kane. "I should have fired her months ago. Now with my luck she'll walk away from here and become a victim of a thrill killer passing by."

"Lightning doesn't strike in the same place twice." Kane waved a hand toward the driveway as Wolfe's van came into view. "Maybe we won't have to crawl under the truck after all."

Relieved to see Wolfe on scene, Jenna brought his team up to speed. "I'll need the name of this victim. We've identified the other guy but figure this guy is the killer's accomplice. Unless he was some poor soul wandering by."

"You'll have to move the truck." Emily bent to look at the body. "The body will clear it okay."

"The Tarot Killer, huh?" Wolfe looked at Kane and raised both brows. "Why a catfisher? I'd figure they'd have bigger game in their sights." He gave a little shudder. "The last one attributed to them was a group of men, not one. All hunted down, all murdered with horrific injuries, left to bleed out, but if anyone had found them, they'd have died anyway." He bent to look at the body and then at Kane. "Em's right. He'll slip right out of there. Drive the truck forward. Try not to hit him again—not that it will make any difference."

"I won't hit him." Kane walked over to the truck.

Curious why Wolfe hadn't elaborated about the Tarot Killer's last murder, she cleared her throat. "You can't just leave me hanging. Why did she kill them and how? It has to be a woman. This guy Stevens and his accomplice just picked the wrong person to mess with this time."

"A woman, huh? She must be smart. Well, I guess most psychopaths are, but she's a vigilante and I kinda understand her in a freaky kinda way. Last time, she killed a group of men who traded little girls for sex." Wolfe pulled on gloves and his gray eyes went as cold as ice. "The Tarot Killer hunted them down, one by one. She went in under the cover of darkness, tied them to the bed, and removed parts of them. From what I've read, they figure the killer watched them die and left the Tarot card behind. The kids were all found, one by one, sound asleep in the local church or somewhere safe. Although, the girls were likely damaged for life by their ordeal, some had been missing for over two years. Ten men died and ten kids were found but none of them remembered anything about the person who'd rescued them. The murders were spread all over different counties."

Trying to take in the enormity of one person able to hunt down so many men, and have the desire to mutilate and kill yet show empathy for the kids, made Jenna's mind spin. "I've never known a serial killer to care about anyone. That sounds like a vendetta. Maybe she was abused as a child?"

"Not necessarily, no. Jo explained it during the conference last year. As she is the top FBI behavioral analyst, the Tarot Killer is one of her open cases, although Jo refers to these murders in public as the Midnight Stalker—the name given by the media. She figures this person has a particular hatred for people who wear a mask—not literally, but as in people who are not who they seem." Wolfe shrugged. "Tarot cards have been found all over and it's one fact that has been withheld from the press, even the details have been suppressed to avoid copycats. All I can say is this woman—if you're correct—has ways of killing people and making them suffer that most killers haven't come close to imagining yet."

Swallowing the bile creeping up her throat, she stared at him. "And she's in our town. Right now?"

"Maybe, maybe not." Kane handed her the wallet. "I figure she's through here. These were the only players in town. The dead man is Jack Sutherland, out of 22 Miles Street, East Meadow. He's on our suspects list and Rio and Rowley were planning on interviewing him today. He is a member of the same gamer clan, and his online persona is Keats. It fits for an English literature teacher at middle school."

"They knew each other." Rio stepped to Jenna's side. "They all play online together almost nightly. It will be easy enough to check if they messaged. I figure it's obvious Sutherland is the accomplice."

"That's easy enough to determine." Wolfe crouched to examine the body. "We'll run his DNA and see if it's a match to the traces we found on Shelby O'Connor's arms."

Jenna nodded. "Okay. Rio head back to the office. We'll need to examine Jack Sutherland's home, phone, vehicle, and any computers he'd been using. We'll need to see how this murder spree was organized. It's a possibility they worked together online. Sutherland would believe he was safe, not being involved online with the women. He'll have made a mistake." She sighed. "Find that mistake, for me."

"I'm on it." Rio hurried back to his truck.

It seemed they'd found the killers of Shelby O'Conner and Dianne Gilbert, but now Jenna had another mystery to solve. She chewed on her bottom lip, thinking, and then turned to Wolfe. "We need the laptop and phones belonging to Stevens ASAP. Whoever he met here tonight is the Tarot Killer. She must have planned this down to the escape in the Yukon."

"If you've recorded the scene, go right ahead." Wolfe turned to Colt Webber and Emily. "Bag and tag. I'll go and see the other scene."

"I hope I can hunt down a name or a phone number we can trace." Kane walked beside her back inside the house. "You might have solved a decade of murders, Jenna, but I don't figure anyone could plan this scenario. There are too many variables. The Tarot Killer couldn't know the private goings-on of O'Connor and Gilbert or the fact they were involved with the man known as Julian Darnley. How did she discover he was the killer?" He shook his head. "There's no way she was able to track them down. We had the FBI's whiz kid on it and he couldn't find a link." He shrugged. "Like you said, Stevens picked the wrong woman to mess with this time and, most likely, she took a flight out of town last night."

THIRTY-SEVEN

Back at the office, Kane took the evidence to the conference room and went through the little black book found at the scene. Stevens, aka Julian Darnley, kept all his information in his book, including everything belonging to Sutherland. It seemed he ran the whole show. He found the password to his laptop and it opened up on a dark web page. The last page Stevens had viewed was well-hidden cryptocurrency accounts. He found three of them buried deep in the web and all empty. Transactions, if any, had been wiped and the accounts had been set up to bounce information around the world but it had worked against him this time. It appeared that someone had drained them, including both men's regular bank accounts as well. He found no trace of any money whatsoever. Kane scratched his head. The Tarot Killer's expertise just gained a new dimension —she moved through the dark web, which made her even more dangerous, if that was possible.

Stevens had saved the passwords to social media platforms, as Julian Darnley, and his fake company webpage in the book. After logging on Kane discovered the messages on social media to the murdered women, plus another three women Stevens had on his hook ready to reel in. The burner phone wasn't locked and he found only one phone number and a number of messages. Stevens must have used a different burner for each woman. It didn't take Kane long to trace the phone number and he was surprised to discover it was someone he knew—well, he knew she owned Antlers, the steakhouse in town. He'd seen her photograph on the billboard outside. Kristina Bennett was an attractive divorcée who lived out of Cherry Street on the newer end of town. There'd been an article about Antlers in the local newspaper saying she'd recently moved and had turned over the running of the place to the manager, but she'd planned to keep her luxury apartment over the restaurant as she liked to be visible during functions.

Kane pushed to his feet, secured the laptop and phone back into evidence bags, and headed to the evidence room. He stored them safely away and, pulling off his gloves, hurried to Jenna's office. She looked up expectantly as he walked in. He smiled at her and brought her up to date. "I found the woman Stevens planned to meet was Kristina Bennett. He has messages to her on his burner. His other phone has messages talking about meeting Sutherland at the murder scene. There's no doubt they were working together."

"That's good to know." Jenna smiled. "I called Carter and they're on their way." She glanced at her watch. "They'd just wrapped up a case at Blackwater, so will be here soon. Jo said if you come up with a name, go easy. Find her location and we'll all go in loaded for bear. She made it quite clear, if this was the Tarot Killer, unless we made a solid plan to apprehend her, she'd slip through our fingers like smoke." She glanced up as Rio walked into the room. "What have you got for me?"

"Gold." Rio waved an evidence bag. "We have a ton of assignments from the kids Sutherland teaches. They're all about vacations and where they're going this break." He placed the bag on Jenna's desk. "This is how they selected the houses to murder the women. We know the O'Connor murder house is owned by a family currently overseas on vacation and so was this one. There's another not one hundred yards from the waterfall above Spring Falls Lake. What's the chance Dianne Gilbert was poisoned in that house and ran away, or the perpetrators tossed her over the falls?"

"That's tied up a few loose ends. What about his phone?" Jenna nodded at Rio.

"I haven't been able to get into it. It's fingerprint-protected, but his gaming computer was easy. I typed in 'Keats,' his player ID, and it opened. There's a ton of messages back and forth from Stevens, or Bloodlust. He even mentions the women as 'targets.' There's no doubt both the men at the house were involved."

Footsteps pounding up the stairs had everyone staring at the door. Kane turned as Wolfe led Carter and Jo inside. Suddenly glad Jenna had enlarged her office, he stood and moved around the desk to stand beside her.

"I thought, y'all would like to know, the DNA I took from the nail marks on O'Connor's arms are a match to Sutherland. The house and truck were wiped clean of prints and the wine was poisoned with a concoction of opiates. I figured you'd need these guys here ASAP." Wolfe was armed and wearing a Kevlar vest. "If this woman is the Tarot Killer, I'm here for backup. I figure y'all need all the help you can get."

Kane looked at the eager faces. "Thanks. I haven't a location yet. I only discovered her name was Kristina Bennett five minutes ago." He gave them a fast rundown of what he'd discovered and then looked at Jenna. "She owns Antlers and has two places of residence in town. She owns an apartment above the steakhouse and a house on Cherry."

"That's unusual." Jo sat in a chair opposite Jenna's desk. "We've never found a trace of her before—and from what Jenna told us, Kristina Bennett planned to meet Stevens—but did she kill both men? Why did she leave his phone behind when she'd know it would implicate her? If the Tarot Killer is using Black Rock Falls as a base, taking out people so close to home seems out of character. This killer doesn't have the usual comfort zone we usually see with other psychopaths. This person is a hunter and has the means to move around undetected."

"Oh, she has the means." Jenna waved a hand at Kane. "Dave figures she uses the dark web to move her money, which gives her universal access. The men's accounts were drained dry, and we know Stevens took millions from the two women he murdered." She raised an eyebrow. "Someone took the cash. It has to be her."

Rubbing the back of his neck, Kane cleared his throat. "All we have is evidence Stevens and Sutherland killed the women. Problem is we have a gaping hole. If this is the Tarot Killer, she killed to avenge the deaths of O'Connor and Gilbert."

"That's the general consensus and fits her MO." Jenna frowned at him. "So why the hesitancy to bring her in?"

Kane leaned his back against the counter. "How did she know about Julian Darnley, and that he killed these women? Without the jack of hearts card left on the bodies, we had no idea the cases were linked. The Tarot Killer doesn't usually go after someone who has killed one woman. My question is: how did she know?"

"Maybe Kristina Bennett knew O'Connor and Gilbert." Jenna raised both eyebrows. "They all moved in the same circles. Girl talk, maybe, and then when they turned up dead, it triggered her into action."

"The only problem with this theory, is that I don't figure the Tarot Killer risks making friends." Jo stood and buttoned her jacket over her vest and sighed. "Are we going to talk all day or go and bring this psychopath in for questioning? I for one would love to speak to her and get inside her head."

Kane checked his weapon and looked at Jenna. "How do

you want to play this? If we go charging into Antlers and she's not there, someone will tip her off and she'll get away."

"We'll send Rio and Rowley to Cherry Street to stake out the place. If they take Maggie's sedan, they'll be able to slip by unnoticed and park somewhere." Jenna stood. "We'll go into Antlers on the pretense of planning a function there to raise money for the Her Broken Wings Foundation. We'll have Wolfe, Jo, and Carter waiting in Wolfe's white truck as backup. No one will take a second glance at a white truck in town."

Stomach cramping into knots, Kane bit his tongue. It was a good move but putting Jenna up front and center with a serial killer who would stop at nothing was dangerous. He squeezed her shoulder. "Vest up. This killer will slash or shoot. She won't be taken down. I'm not taking any chances with this one, Jenna. Not this time."

"He's right, Jenna." Carter narrowed his gaze. "We found one cop with six shurikens—those Japanese throwing stars—stuck in his face and head. It happened in seconds."

"Okay, okay." Jenna stood and looked from one to the other. "I know she's dangerous, but you know my policy. I don't allow my deputies to kill people. Everyone here, particularly Dave, is capable of disabling someone." She looked at Wolfe. "Why should I be the executioner, Shane?"

"Really, Jenna? You're the sheriff and you give the orders." Wolfe rolled his eyes. "Not one of this team would kill without a darn good reason."

"Okay." Jenna lifted her chin. "I'll leave it to your own discretion. If she becomes an unstoppable threat, take her down." She waved them from the room. "Get geared up. Use the wireless coms. I'll go and speak to the others."

THIRTY-EIGHT

To validate her reason for wanting to see Kristina Bennett, Jenna grabbed some handouts about The Broken Wings Foundation, a place for abused and battered women and children she'd established with Kane. She didn't know Bennett and if this woman was a serial killer living among them, she wasn't the only person in town living a lie in plain sight. Along with herself and Kane, how many more people lived in town or in the forest under assumed names? It could be hundreds. There was no way of telling. She headed outside into the sunshine. The wind had picked up and blown the few residual clouds from the rain depression far away. Jenna stared into brilliant blue and took a deep breath of the clean crisp mountain air. Known as Big Sky Country, the clear expanse went on forever. She'd always welcomed the rain, enjoyed the smell and seeing the fresh growth across the land, but whoever had first turned the phrase *rain depression* had got it right. It had been more than a weather event. The floods, bad smells, loss of property, livestock, and trade had been depressing enough without the addition of serial killers arriving in droves. She shook her head as she climbed into the Beast. When she figured it couldn't get any worse, fate threw up another batch of nasty for her to deal with. Life, someone once said, wasn't meant to be easy. They'd sure gotten that right, that was for darn sure.

Going into a potential deadly situation held different reactions for her. She relied on her team and they worked well together, but seeing Carter's and Wolfe's grim expressions placed a new brand of concern on the Tarot Killer. When men like Kane and Carter were prepared to kill on sight, facing this adversary had become a frightening reality. The idea of any of them being slaughtered by her was a sobering thought. She glanced over at Kane and smiled. "I love you."

"Uh-huh." Kane gave her a long look. "You're not figuring on doing anything stupid are you?"

Frowning, Jenna shook her head. "No, it's just if anything happens, I might regret not telling you because I don't say it enough. I know you'll use your body to protect me. Nothing I can say will change that and this woman is dangerous."

"Nothing's going to happen." Kane squeezed her hand. "Unless you get in my way. I need a little room to move... And Jenna, I love you too."

They arrived at Antlers and Kane parked in the slot reserved for the sheriff's department. Inside a few people had dropped by for cake and coffee, but Antlers came to life at night, with live bands and great meals. Jenna walked up to the front desk and waited for the manager. He appeared in seconds and waved them inside. "Ah, we're not stopping by for a meal. I need to speak to Ms. Bennett about a function for my charity. Is she in today?"

"She's upstairs in her apartment." The man waved toward an inside staircase with a sign saying NO ADMITTANCE. "There's a door to her apartment at the top of the landing."

"Have you seen her today?" Kane smiled at the man. "We don't want to disturb her."

"She's been staying here for a few days." The manager

lowered his voice. "She usually eats down here or we send a meal up to her apartment, but last night she mentioned she had plans for dinner. No one was to disturb her because she'd wanted to take a nap. She went upstairs and didn't come back down, and I was here until late. She'd have walked straight past me. I asked the cleaners this morning if they'd seen her, and they hadn't. I was concerned and called her. She asked for breakfast to be sent up. That was about nine and she still hasn't come downstairs." He leaned a little closer. "She's been happy, like really happy. Maybe she split with the guy she was seeing?"

Jenna flicked a glance at Kane, raising her eyes to the CCTV camera and then smiled at the manager. "Okay, thanks. We'll go and speak to her. If she's eating, it can't be that bad."

She headed for the staircase and pressed her com. "She's here. Entrance is by a set of stairs back of the restaurant, and we'll have limited space to act if there's a problem."

"I have eyes on the top floor windows." Carter came through her earpiece. *"Just give me the word and I'll blow a window and toss in a flash-bang."*

Taking the stairs, Jenna nodded. "Copy. I'll leave my com open so you can hear everything."

The landing at the top of the stairs was wider than anticipated, carpet ran the entire length, and a potted plant sat under a full-length window beside the front door. She stepped to one side with Kane opposite and pressed the doorbell. Footsteps came from inside and the door opened to reveal a woman in her mid-thirties wearing workout clothes. She had dark hair and eyes and matched her media image. "Kristina Bennett?"

"Yeah, the one and only." Kristina smiled. "What can I do for you, Sheriff Alton?"

As it was obvious Kristina was not armed, Jenna looked past her and into a luxurious apartment. The fragrance from a dozen long-stemmed pink roses drifted toward her. "We'd like to ask you a few questions about Julian Darnley. I believe you were acquainted with him?"

"*Was* being the operative word." Kristina let out a long sigh and stood to one side of the door. "Come in. What do you want to know?"

"You said you were friends but not now?" Kane moved to one side a little in front of Jenna. "Did something happen?"

"Well, yeah. I missed a date with him and now he won't return my calls." Kristina raised both hands and dropped them to her sides. "Men, huh? He sent me flowers too. I took a nap and slept right through until after eight this morning. I was supposed to meet him at the library and he was going to take me to dinner at a friend's house."

If this woman was the Tarot Killer, she was good, darn good. She almost had Jenna convinced. "Did you mention your plans to anyone?"

"Yeah, to Tom the manager here." Kristina shrugged. "Well, I told him I'd be out for dinner. Not the specifics, no."

"Are you sure you've never mentioned the name Julian Darnley or your plans to meet him with anyone, even in passing?" Kane was wearing his combat face.

"Yeah, one person, the fortune teller Siofra." Kristina's cheeks pinked. "She's become quite a friend, especially after Shelby died. Shelby didn't make friends easy, but we both visited her for readings."

"Where does she practice." Kane frowned and pulled out his notebook. "In town?"

"Yeah, she has a room in the back of the Wellness Center. She's only there after closing." Kristina smiled. "We have to call if we want a reading."

Needing more information, Jenna nodded. "Thanks, that will be great. How did you find her?"

"She had a flier in the window of Aunt Betty's Café." Kristina looked into the distance. "It said: 'Forget the bad things in your past. I will help you.' I called and made an appointment. I told her my problems and my expectations about meeting Julian. She was very helpful and all I had to do was cross her palm with silver. No huge amounts of money. She asked for nothing really."

Jenna wanted more on Julian Darnley, aka Simons. "Did Julian ever mention being a financial advisor?"

"Yeah, this is what's so annoying." Kristina rolled her eyes. "I had the chance to get into cryptocurrency. I dabbled a couple of weeks ago and he made me ten grand."

"Did you tell Siofra?" Kane stood pen raised over his notebook. "Did she know where you were meeting him and the time?"

"Yeah, we discussed it and she was worried about me going with him to his friend's house." Kristina shrugged. "I gave her the details in case anything happened to me. She asked me to call her this morning, but her number has vanished from my contacts. I figure the potion she gave me was too strong and it made me sleep through."

Intrigued, Jenna stared at her. "Potion? What potion?"

"She gave me a love potion. She said to drink it one hour before I planned to leave and then lie down and imagine what I wanted in life. I fell asleep and missed meeting Julian and now he's ghosting me. So I guess that didn't work." Kristina shrugged.

"Ask her if she'll submit to a blood test." Wolfe came over the com. *"If she was drugged, it could still be in her system."*

Taking a deep breath, Jenna cleared her throat. "I'm sorry to inform you that Julian was found dead this morning. We've discovered his real name is Nathan Stevens. He was running a scheme to extort money, and we figure he had help. I think Siofra might have drugged you. Do you mind giving blood so we can run a few tests?"

"Dead?" Kristina sat down heavily on the sofa. "Oh, no."

She looked up at them blinking away tears. "Was he working with Siofra to steal from me?"

Not wanting to give too much away, Jenna kept her expression neutral. "We're looking into the possibility. You mentioned her number has vanished from your contacts. Can you check your bank accounts online?"

"Yes." Kristina grabbed up her phone and using her thumbs scanned the screen. "Nothing has been taken." She frowned. "Come to think of it, I dozed off for a moment during our session. Do you figure it was long enough for Siofra to remove her number from my contacts?" Her face drained of color and she stood and ran across the room to grab her purse. "Oh, it's still here." She held up a small book. "All my account numbers are in here." Her hands balled into fists. "She must have drugged me twice. Yes, I'll give blood. I want answers too."

"When we leave, you should change your passwords just in case." Kane gave her a level look. "It's easy to make a copy of a notebook with a phone. She might be waiting until the smoke clears before she makes her move."

Jenna heard footsteps on the stairs and the bell rang. "That will be Dr. Wolfe. He'll take a sample of your blood for analysis." She took out her notebook. "Can you give me a description of Siofra?"

"Yeah, five-six, long dark hair and dark eyes, maybe in her thirties, and quite striking." Kristina shrugged. "She wears long flowing clothes, but she's medium build, not fat or thin. She has long red nails and really good teeth."

Jenna took notes. "Thanks."

"We'd better go and check out Siofra." Kane pulled Jenna to one side. "If Kristina has been drugged and not left the building since last night, it can't be her. We can check the CCTV footage if you like, but we're wasting time." He shook his head. "Siofra means 'fairy' or 'changeling.' Think about it. What better way to discover people's secrets? She'd gotten to know these women, heard about Julian, and then they turned up dead. She wanted revenge."

Everything was falling into place. Jenna blew out a long breath. "Siofra took Kristina's place and killed them, didn't she? She took their money and played them at their own game." She shook her head slowly. "Oh boy, did they pick on the wrong person." She glanced over at Wolfe. "Shane has finished. Let's go and hunt down Siofra."

They met Carter and Jo at the bottom of the stairs. "It's not her. It's a fortune teller by the name of Siofra. She hangs out at the Wellness Center at night after closing. She has a flier in Aunt Betty's. We'll go and take a look. We'll be able to trace her by her phone number."

They drove in a convoy to Aunt Betty's Café and Jenna went inside with Kane. They searched the windows for a flier and found nothing. She went to the counter to speak to Susie Hartwig. "There was a flier in the window about a fortune teller. Did you take it down?"

"Nope." Susie balanced meals on a tray. "I recall seeing a flier but I can't recall when, sorry."

Jenna asked Wendy, another of the staff, and a few of the servers and no one recalled seeing a flier. She shrugged and turned to Kane. "I guess we speak to Steven Croxley at the Wellness Center. He must know Siofra to give her his keys."

"We can live in hope." Kane walked beside her to the Beast.

Jenna brought the others up to date and then called Rowley and Rio. She told them to abandon their watch of Kristina's house and head over to check the CCTV footage at Antlers, just in case they'd made a mistake about Kristina. She climbed inside the truck and turned to Kane, leaving her com open. "We'll go and speak to Croxley. He might have an address. You guys search the place. He has one back room for consultations and a storeroom."

They parked outside the Wellness Center and walked in

together, to the surprise of Croxley and a few of his customers. As Jo, Carter, and Wolfe melted into the store, doing a covert search. She went to the counter. "I'm looking for Siofra, the palm reader. Do you have an address or phone number for her?"

"Who?" Croxley's eyebrows shot up almost to his hairline.

"The palm reader who works here in your back room after closing." Kane leaned on the counter. "We're not interested in who you have here after hours. We just want to speak to Siofra, is all."

"I can assure you that I don't allow anyone to use my premises after hours." Croxley drew himself up, his eyes blazing. "I would never allow my store to be associated with the occult. Natural remedies, yes, even pagan remedies, but not spells or witchcraft, and I've never heard of anyone by the name of Siofra." He frowned. "Someone would see her if she tried to break in. I leave my lights on at night to prevent break-ins. When we first opened I found a window broken and a few things missing, but since then nothing has been touched."

Letting out a long sigh, Jenna nodded. "Very well. Thanks for your time."

Outside the store, Jenna looked at the others. She had absolutely nowhere to go with the case. No evidence, nothing—and now the prime suspect no longer seemed to exist. Like Kane had said, Siofra was little more than hearsay—a myth. "Now what?"

"Nothing." Jo shrugged. "This is her typical MO. She kills and vanishes like smoke. It's as if she never existed." She stared at Jenna. "You'll go crazy trying to find her, and she's long gone by now. Be thankful you've solved the murders and the killers are no longer on the streets. You have to pull the pin on it, Jenna —for now anyway. If anything comes up, I'll loop you in, I promise."

Jenna nodded reluctantly. "I guess we deal with her when she rears her ugly head again." She glanced at Kane. "Letting her get away with murder sure leaves a bad taste in my mouth."

"You solved the crime." Kane walked beside her. "The Tarot Killer killed Sutherland and Stevens. They killed O'Connor and Gilbert. We'll hunt her down the moment more leads become evident. There's nothing else we can do."

"Just be glad she's gone." Carter unzipped his jacket. "Like Kane said, there's no leads to follow and, trust me, you'll never find any. You can turn the case over to us to add to the long list of her crimes. Although, you made more progress than the rest of us. Now we know she's female and have a description. I'll add all the information to our files and hope the FBI can track her down." He smiled at her. "I'm famished. How about leaving this for a time and we go and eat?"

Jenna sighed. "Sure."

The feeling of being watched never left Jenna as she walked to the Beast. She didn't take defeat too easily. This vigilante, no matter how many monsters she'd rid the world of, had gotten away with murder and it didn't sit easy with her. Somewhere out there, the Tarot Killer would strike again and if she came back to her town, she'd be waiting.

THIRTY-NINE

I watch the sheriff walk toward her ride with her shoulders drooping and eyes set on the sidewalk, like a child denied candy. I know her reputation for catching serial killers is unique in law enforcement, but this time, unfortunately, she didn't stand a chance. My inside information led me to Julian Darnley, aka Stevens. His presence on the dark web was easy for me to find. For someone like me, who exists in data streams, it stood out like the Appalachian Trail. Darnley was the lowest type of scammer. As if extorting women by pretending to be their dream lover wasn't bad enough, he took their lives with an excitement close to mine when I watched him die.

Psychopathic killers fear me, and they should. You see, I think like them, and unlike law enforcement who follow ambiguous clues, it only takes one or maybe two murders for me to anticipate their next move. You may ask why I have the need to kill serial killers? My story goes back a long way to the time when I discovered my father and his father before him carried the Reaper on their shoulders. He found me watching him slice into a young woman, but I didn't run screaming into the night. I waited for his passion to ebb and then inhaled the smell of fresh blood. It was the first time I'd enjoyed warm blood on my flesh and the last gasp of a victim. My father recognized himself in me. It was my destiny to become like him, in the blood passed on from one generation to another, but with such a good teacher I excelled. He instructed me how to perform the perfect crime. The first kills were exhilarating but soon I found myself out of control. At the time, no one would believe a child capable of such carnage. Inside, the need to kill burned and the Reaper needed to be fed. I had skills, knowledge more powerful than any psychopathic killer before me... and yes, I know what I am. Only a fool lives in a delusion believing they kill because a person deserves to die and can't recognize they kill because holding a life in your hands is the most powerful drug on earth.

Some, like me, can control their habit, but others live a soulless existence moving from one thrill kill to the next. They are fun to watch but they usually die in a hail of bullets or sit on death row until their time is up. I use psychopathic killers to my advantage. You see, I watch them kill and if I find them interesting enough, I give them a taste of their own medicine. There is nothing better than watching a killer who believes they are superior in mind discover I've tricked them. The advantage to this ingenious plan is that, once a case of murder is solved, the cops usually push the killer's mysterious demise to the back burner and their "good riddance" attitude works to my advantage every time. You see, I get to feed my Reaper and walk away. I kind of like the name Midnight Stalker, although I don't always work in the shadows. You might turn around one day and I'll be right behind you.

I watch as Sheriff Jenna Alton climbs into the black truck. She looks over at me and sees what I want her to see. A young blonde woman with blue eyes, in jeans, a T-shirt, and wearing a white cowboy hat. I give her a wave, like most folks in town, and smile. She waves back and nods as if she knows me. The illusion is in place and I turn away. "One day, we'll cross paths again, Sheriff. You see, the thing with the Reaper is that her work is never done."

EPILOGUE

FRIDAY

Unable to let the case go, Jenna had spent the entire day going over evidence and scouring the Wellness Center and the crime scenes for fingerprints and trace evidence. She'd found nothing. Not convinced Kristina Bennett wasn't involved, she'd viewed the CCTV footage again herself and finally had to admit she hadn't left the building. The identikit picture Kristina had worked on for some hours with an FBI agent had been generic. Nothing about the Tarot Killer made her stand out apart from her eyes. The large dark brown almond eyes, perfectly surrounded by a thick liner, made her look as if of Asian descent. She finished updating her files and sent copies to Carter.

The DA had called with good news. She wouldn't need to show in court for the kidnapping trial. With six men all facing different charges, it would have been a lengthy procedure, but the accused had agreed to a plea bargain. All of them had entered a guilty plea and were awaiting sentencing. The man who'd abducted her and three of the others would face substantial jail time but not the twenty years she'd expected.

All morning she'd paced up and down waiting for Kane to

return from a brain scan. After suffering a severe headache overnight, Wolfe had dragged him into the morgue. The scan was clear. The jolt from the lightning strike wasn't to blame, he just had a headache. Kane had called the moment the results came back but then had given her more good news from Wolfe. The results of the blood samples she'd given following the kidnapping were negative for cooties. Taking a deep breath of sheer relief, she leaned back in her chair. Soon Kane would drop by the office to give her a ride home. He'd ordered a ton of steaks and all the trimmings for a cookout at the ranch the following day.

Relaxed at last, Jenna smiled at the image sitting on her desk of Rowley and Sandy's twins. They were growing like weeds and it would be good to spend some time with them. Her mind went to Poppy Anderson. She'd discovered that Poppy had contacted Mayor Petersham about a job, but he'd refused and Poppy was on a bus heading to places unknown. No doubt to cause problems in another small town. Jenna had always been a person to give second chances but during her time in Black Rock Falls, she'd discovered many people couldn't change and that was a fact of life.

Jenna stood and cleaned the whiteboard, shaking her head. The case was closed and for now she had to be content that she'd solved the murders of O'Connor and Gilbert, but their fortunes would be lost forever. Not even FBI whiz kid Bobby Kalo had found a single money trail. She heard footsteps on the stairs and looked up as Kane walked into the room. "Ready to go home?"

"Yeah, the Beast is packed with meat and Duke is in the back seat." Kane grinned. "We'd better hurry along before he decides it's dinner time." He slipped one arm around her shoulder. "Don't worry too much about the Tarot Killer." He gave her a squeeze. "Knowing our luck, she'll be back. I figure this woman likes a challenge."

Jenna laughed. "That's all I need."

Exhausted, they'd eaten and fallen into bed early, but something woke Jenna like a touch on her flesh. She lay in the darkness listening. A strange buzzing sound was coming through the wall. Not loud but as if a small motor had suddenly sprung to life. Heart pounding, she poked Kane. "Dave, I hear something weird."

"What?" Kane sat up and reached for his weapon. "Where? Outside?"

The house had a military-style alarm system and no one could take a step inside without them knowing, but something small, like a drone, could navigate around the security. "Listen, can you hear that buzzing? It's like a motor running. Maybe a drone?"

"I hear it." Kane slid out of bed. "Keep away from the windows." He eased his way along the wall. "It's coming from the bathroom."

Peering into the darkness, Jenna followed him and they went inside, but the room was empty. "It's coming from between the walls, I'm sure of it." She pressed her ear to the tile. "I can hear it." She moved closer to the vanity. "It's coming from the drains as well."

"That's impossible." Kane shook his head. "There's no way anything could get between the walls or into the drain." He pressed his ear against the tile. "This is getting freaky."

Looking all around, uncertainty gripped Jenna. She sucked in a few deep breaths. "It can't be a person or Duke would be going crazy. What if it's someone planning on gassing us?"

"Gas doesn't make a noise. It does sound as if a motor is running. Something isn't right, that's for darn sure." He pounded on the wall and the noise stopped for a few seconds and them started up again. "That's interesting."

Jenna gripped his arm. "What if it's a ghost?"

"Nah, nobody has died here, and even if I believed in ghosts, not many carry motors." He motioned her out of the bathroom and went to the closet. "We'll soon get to the bottom of this, even if I have to pull down the walls. I'll grab something that detects devices." He pulled out a box containing equipment and went through it. "Stay in here, and I'll see if I can chase down the source of the noise." He attached earbuds and turned on a device with a wand.

Jenna glared at him. "No way. I'm backup."

"I'll need someone to help me if it's gas, Jenna." He shook his head. "Please wait here."

Panic gripped her for Kane's safety, but she bit back the need to follow him. They'd disturbed Duke and Pumpkin and the dog and cat crawled out from under the bed and sat blinking at her as if she'd suddenly grown two heads. A snort came from the bathroom and she dashed over to the door, peering into the darkness. "What is it? Have you found something?"

"Well, this is something to tell the grandkids." Kane burst into peals of laughter, turned on the light, and beckoned her closer. He wiped at his eyes. "You gotta see this."

Frowning, Jenna followed him into the bathroom. "What's so funny?"

"Here." Kane bent over to peer under the vanity. It was one she'd chosen for their bathroom, with beautifully carved legs. "You must have been exhausted and forgotten to shut down your electric toothbrush. It fell down and somehow landed between the pipes and the wall." He grinned and fished out the toothbrush and handed it to her. "The ghost was this vibrating against the wall and plumbing. I figure it will need new batteries come morning." He pulled her into his arms. "You're trembling. It's just a toothbrush, Jenna. It's all good."

Grinning Jenna hugged him. "I'm not scared of a tooth-brush, Dave. It's your fault. You always make me tremble and give me goosebumps when you kiss my neck like that, but that weirdo noise did scare me. I'm not sure I'd cope with a ghost in the house. I've got enough problems with the living." She sighed. "It's been such a strange week and if murder wasn't bad enough, now we have a mythical fortune teller." She sighed. "I wonder what the future will bring for us? It's always madness and mayhem in Black Rock Falls. Do you ever regret marrying me?"

"Never." Kane scooped her into his arms and walked back into the bedroom. "One thing's for darn sure. Life with you is never boring."

A LETTER FROM D.K. HOOD

Dear Reader,

Thank you so much for choosing my novel and coming with me on another of Kane and Alton's thrilling cases in *Her Bleeding Heart*.

If you'd like to keep up to date with all my latest releases, just sign up at the website link below. You can unsubscribe at any time and your details will never be shared.

www.bookouture.com/dk-hood

I find as I'm planning the next story, we are approaching Halloween again, so book seventeen will have an extra pinch of spooky. As Jenna is faced with solving a heartbreaking case, memories of the past will turn Kane's and Carter's lives upside down. Shivers down your spine will be the added bonus as Serial Killer Central celebrates another Halloween.

If you enjoyed *Her Bleeding Heart,* I would be very grateful if you could leave a review and recommend my book to your friends and family. I really enjoy hearing from readers, so feel free to ask me questions at any time. You can get in touch on my Facebook page or Twitter or through my website.

Thank you so much for your support.

D.K. Hood

KEEP IN TOUCH WITH D.K. HOOD

www.dkhood.com
dkhood-author.blogspot.com.au

 facebook.com/dkhoodauthor
twitter.com/DKHood_Author

ACKNOWLEDGEMENTS

Unknown to many, I've battled problems with my sight for the last year or so, particularly the last three months when this book was written. After cataract surgery on both eyes, I had complications and underwent two further serious surgeries, from which I'm still recovering. My editor, Helen Jenner, and the amazing team at Bookouture, who are the backbone to my series, worked around me, shifting schedules and making my life easier. In all my life, I've never met such caring, wonderful people. Writing has been an uphill battle but also my sanctuary. Visiting Black Rock Falls and keeping busy, writing most times with one eye covered, was difficult but the support from Bookouture and my readers has been overwhelming. Over this time, it was like trying to climb up an impossible ice-covered mountain and sliding back down again. You the readers and the wonderful team at Bookouture pushed me up that mountain with your love and support. I'm so glad you did. Thank you.

Made in the USA
Middletown, DE
03 July 2023

34488804R00165